etd. rav

Gene Fowler

TRUMPET IN THE DUST

TRUMPET IN THE DUST

BY *Gene Fowler*

NEW YORK

HORACE LIVERIGHT · INC.

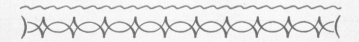

TO AGNES

THE *trumpet lies in the dust.*
The wind is weary, the light is dead.

TAGORE

PART ONE

Chapter One

I

GORDON DOLE believed he was a lucky boy to have a Granner and a feather-bed on March nights. It would be wonderful, of course, to be with his mother. But when a boy's mother lives up the street and sleeps with a man who doesn't like little boys in the bedroom, then it's a fine thing to have a Granner.

A boy and his Granner can have good times together after the day of toil is done. Then the oil lamp casts mystic shadows on the walls. One shadow in particular is mighty in its somber spread, occupying almost the entire side of the yellow-papered wall and interrupted only by a black walnut bureau and a picture of the Rock of Ages. This shadow depicts clearly enough a sable horse, with mane and tail flowing and hooves uplifted in gallant charge. Astride this great horse is a Black Crusader in helmet and cuirass, his lance leveled at the bureau. Peculiarly enough —one must look closely to see all these things—the Crusader wears the Rock of Ages' picture as a buckler to parry the swords of Saracens.

There are many secrets shared by a Granner and a boy. For example, how many fellows know that the moan of the March wind beneath the eaves is in truth the lamentation of Colonel Robert Ingersoll? Old Granner very shrewdly recognized the sound. It warmed her heart to hear the ghost of the wicked Colonel recanting his atheistic doctrines. And that knocking at the windowpane —it wasn't the dry branch of a tree at all. It was the skinny hand of Voltaire! But he needn't signal to Granner, begging Granner to pray for his lost soul, for she wouldn't. What self-respecting Christian would?

Blow down from the mountain, mad western wind! You can't crawl into our safe, warm bed. Wail across the plain in threnody of repentance! You shall not invade the piety of our dreams.

Martha Dole, whom Gordon called Granner, was mother of his mother. Gordon's mother was named Grace, but he called her "Racy." He would have liked to have called her "Mother," but somehow he never did. Perhaps he did not call her Mother because he seemed to be Granner's personal property. Racy acted as though she were his big sister and as the years went by Gordon grew too timid to come right out and call Racy "Mother."

Granner in her fifties was strong. She was dominatingly potent and could hoist a washtub as handily as a clerk lifts an inkwell. Her keen gray eyes drooped at the corners in the Irish manner and they looked intrepidly into the eyes of man and of God. In man's eyes Granner saw passion, brutality, animalism. What did Granner see in the flaming eyes of God the Father Almighty? She said she saw "grace" in God's eyes. Gordon thought she meant she saw his mother, Grace, then. He believed it with all his heart. . . . Grace, my mother, is in God's eyes—Granner said so.

Granner often talked to Gordon of Death and he early began fearing that Racy would die. He dreamed of Death as a robber on a high hill; watching, forever watching, to snatch Racy away. When this made Gordon morose, Granner said it was his stomach; that it was a touch of St. Vitus' Dance. She took him to the clinic of Dr. Eskridge, the nerve specialist, who said it undoubtedly was Gordon's stomach. Dr. Eskridge ordered Granner to put Gordon on a diet of skimmed milk. The learned physician had so much charitable work that he could not stop to ask many questions. If he had, he might have learned that it was fear that Racy would die that made Gordon thin and pale and gave him the nightmare.

Whenever Gordon asked Granner about his father, she tried to discourage the questions. When the child persisted, she revealed certain facts, chief among which was that his father was a no-good dreamer; that he wasted his time making figures from clay instead of looking for a job. The father's name was Leon Warner, Granner said. She had turned him out of her home and now no one knew exactly where he was, although it was said of him that he was a hermit in the mountains and that he already had defied Providence by blaspheming and by carving a figure of the Virgin Mary on a big rock.

"I'd love to see him and the figure on the rock."

"Hush, Gordie! You must never think of a sinner or of his sin. He was low and vile."

Granner loved Gordon's mother with a strict religiousness. Racy was dark and slim and was intended for laughter. Her lips were red and molded in a way that seemed to welcome kisses and smiles. But she was destined to live in tears. Cry and sing—in crying she eased her rebellions and in singing she found a voice for her grief. It was through his mother's singing that Gordon was able to learn the difference between hymns and anthems. When sour-throated sisters of the Methodist congregation hurled their creaking hosannas to the aged ceiling beams, it was a hymn. When Racy's voice rose above the discord and the young men of the choir looked on her as though they might faint, it was an anthem.

Granner had a son named Hiram Dole, who lived with Granner and Gordon. Hiram was built like a bullock and wanted to be a pugilist, but Granner decreed that he study for the ministry. Hiram was twenty years old, two years older than Racy. He loved his mother, Martha Dole, earnestly, but he thought her unswervingly strict. He wished to God she would keep her John Wesley and her Bible and permit him to keep his John L. Sullivan and his punching bag.

Granner conducted a boarding house. She did laundry for the boarders. The clothing of the boarders got very dirty in the glassworks up the street; in the coal yards down the street; in the blood of the butcher shop. When Granner

finished the hard day she was tired, but never too tired to
read to Gordon in the billowing sanctity of the feather-bed.
Sometimes she read other things than Bible stories; occasionally she read from histories, but never from novels.
Novels were taboo with Granner; the devil inspired those
who wrote them.

Granner often told stories to Gordon; anecdotes from
her own life, and always in these anecdotes there was to be
discerned the hand of God, protecting a child that feared
Him. Otherwise, how could Granner have escaped that
mad dog on the Pennsylvania farm? And how could her
sainted father have been rescued from strong drink to
become a circuit rider for the church, and her goodly
mother have borne fifteen children to grow up in devotion
and to die in shouting ecstasy?

All these accounts stirred wonderment in Gordon's
mind and it was easily inferred that a young chap should
about the business of life with a tremendous fear of
d. To be saved, one had to make sure that one was
ughly scared; for fear and dread formed the begin-
f wisdom. Without wisdom, how could one appre-
workings of the Divine Plan? An imprudent
Uncle Hiram was taking grave chances.

t now Uncle Hiram was taking a chance, not only
God but with Granner. Above the strident wail of
e March wind there sounded a methodical and surly
hudding downstairs. Granner had been reading her Bible
that was propped on her great bosom: "And the world
passeth away, and the lust thereof. . . ." Her voice stopped

and her knees began to churn the blankets and the "crazy-quilt." Gordon trembled. The old woman got out of bed and the springs complained as she left. She stood at the bedroom door with all the majesty that is possible when one wears a canton flannel nightgown.

"Hiram!"

"Yes, mother." The thudding ceased.

"Hiram, haven't I told you I will not countenance you having a punching bag under my roof? Put it away instantly. I'll burn it in the morning. This is the third time I've had this happen."

"Aw, mother, I...."

"Hiram!"

"All right, mother."

II

MARTHA's husband was named William Dole and he the father of Hiram and Grace. He was a Pennsyl Dutchman. Gordon called him Gramper and s adored this man who had been born near the clos rugged Jacksonian epoch. William and Martha ha as children across the plains in 1849, riding i wagons with their families. These folk went a Leavenworth, Kansas, where William strayed from wagon train and was lost two days. When searchers foun him his tongue was protruding with thirst, but it was said of him that he never cried or complained about it and that he was not particularly frightened. Gordon knew his

Gramper as a bearded, silent and stoical man of spare but sinewy frame. Gordon noticed that William softened when Racy placed her arms about him. Then his beard would wobble as though a smile were hiding beneath the gray tangle.

When Gordon pointed out that Gramper was a man of few words, Granner explained it, not forgetting to emphasize that the Hand of God also figured in this situation. She averred that old William had been so free with his profanity that Heaven saw fit to put a blight on his tongue. One night a ball of lightning darted down the chimney of their Kansas home, the celestial bolt grazing Gramper's tongue at the very instant he was snoring out curses. From then on William Dole didn't have much to say, blasphemous or otherwise. The electric visitation had cured him of the tobacco chewing vice, which was another evidence that God moves in a mysterious way, His wonders to perform.

It was darkly intimated that Gramper had had a habit of ministering to the baser wants of pioneer ladies along the Kansas frontier. He had been accused—unjustly of course—of having had a penchant for a young squaw named "Lonely Moon Cloud" on the Pottawatomie Reservation. This gross libel led to fist fights and caused a hegira of the Doles from Kansas to Colorado. William sent his outraged wife and two babies by train and gathered together his two hundred head of cattle and began to dri
them before him across the prairie. He had hoped to
the onrush of winter, but a blizzard set in shortly before
William reached the growing city of Fairmount. The hard-

pressed cattle perished and William was compelled to dig
into a drift, where he lay grimly, chewing a ration of salt
pork for days and wishing there would be an Indian war
so that he could enlist. This was the year 1883 and when
William rejoined his wife and children, Martha wondered
why God should have rescued him and why Heaven was
so patient with a sinner who was without gratitude.

Granner established a boarding house in Fairmount,
then a city of 120,000 population, but William said he would
go to Cripple Creek to drill rocks for gold. For six years
he drilled. He was tenacious and bold, unafraid of dark
pits and damp drifts and awesome shafts. He was undis-
mayed by great walls of rock and was sustained by an
optimism unthinkable to softer generations. He beat the
sides of the Rocky Mountains like a Moses flagellating for
life-giving waters, drilling and blasting, blasting and
hoping. Always hoping. William faced To-morrow with
confidence. He ate beans and salt pork and biscuits made
from a sour-dough formula that he held second to none,
and to look at him as he sat in his cabin, one would not
think that he missed "Lonely Moon Cloud." To look at
him as he blasted with yellow-papered half sticks of dynamite, one would believe that he thought the veined flanks
of the hills more yielding to him than had been the body
of his praying Martha.

Sometimes William wondered what he would do if he
were to leave this solitude that had become a sort of mistress to him. He was so well mated with the silences, so
congenial with the peace of the hills. There was no one

here to yell Squaw-lover or Tom-Tom-Romeo at him and there was no one here to cringe if he said God damn it when a timber proved faulty or he mashed a finger.... And when snow settled, he fancied his own hill was a bride, dressed in white, waiting for him; and he went to her eagerly, knowing there would be no suspicions, no resentment, no holding back ... no regret.

In 1889, and after six years of absence from his family, William Dole struck gold-flecked quartz. Soon thereafter he sold his claim to an English concern and wrote home about his luck. He packed his tools, all but his anvil and the forge at which he had sharpened his implements every morning, and shipped them to Fairmount. He left the anvil and the forge standing there before his log cabin as a sort of memorial altar. He found it hard to leave the hill that had been mistress to him, but he was not a man to grow maudlin. He untied his three pack burros at the shed he had made for them and gave each one a rather friendly kick. Then he watched them trot along the trail to disappear in the wilderness.

When William Dole came home from the hills, he wondered how Grace looked. She was twelve years old when he had struck off to rummage the bowels of the Great Divide, so she would be eighteen now. Indeed, William wondered if Grace wasn't the only reason he had come home at all. As old William reached Martha Dole's boarding house, he paused on the veranda for a few minutes and fought an impulse to go right back where he had been for the last six years. Perhaps this impulse was

sharpened by the sight of some boys playing Indian near
the iron gate of the boarding house. The war whoops of
the children aroused in him the nausea that is said to be
entertained by a man who wanders listlessly through old
documents and comes across his divorce papers. Finally he
knocked. Why in hell should he knock? Only strangers
were supposed to knock. Well, hadn't he been a stranger
to Martha ever since that Indian squaw canard?

Martha Dole rose from her sitting-room chair, where
she had been reading the Gospel of St. John, and reached
fumblingly for her other pair of spectacles, the far-sighted
ones. Then she went to the door and stared hard at
William. There were no kisses and no hugs, to be sure, but
just a "Come on in, Paw; you sure need a haircut and
your boots are muddy."

"Where's Gracie?" William made a feint at the mud
scraper on the drab porch step. Yes, he would be mighty
glad to see his daughter, for she was sweet and clean like
the air of the hills. She would smile on him like the dawn
smiled as he had stood at the forge, hammering red hot
drill edges. His knapsack felt heavy and it was good to be
home again—that is, it would be good to be in a home
where Gracie would laugh and sing and sit on his lap. He
wanted to thank her for the condensed milk and the warm
underwear she had sent him last Christmas.

"Where's Gracie? Why don't you answer me? Is something wrong?" William came into the house and let his
knapsack plop leadenly to the hall floor. "For Christ's sake,
Maw, she ain't dead!"

Martha shook her head. "No, Paw. She's run off with a loafer named Leon Warner."

"But they're married, ain't they?"

"Yes."

"Then what the hell difference does it make, if she loves him? Where's she now?"

"They'll be back soon. I got a letter yesterday."

"I'll be God damned tickled to see her."

"You'll lose your immortal soul for taking the name of the Lord in vain.... Did you bring the money?"

William reached into his flannel shirt bosom and brought out a frayed wallet and untied the greasy leather thongs. He showed Martha an order on a Fairmount bank for $12,000 and then handed the draft to her. Martha was shaken by the sight. "Now, William, we can send Hiram to the seminary in Kansas."

"I don't give a God damn what you do! Which is to be my room here?"

Martha showed her husband to a chamber she had prepared off the kitchen, but after supper the old man grew homesick for solitude. Without Gracie it wasn't home, this rambling house where hungry people trooped in and out and yelled for second helpings of pie. He kept out of the way as much as possible but finally took his blankets to the dirt-floor cellar, where his mining tools lay in a scramble.

The cellar became a place of constant refuge for this glum rock-jabber.

III

HIRAM maintained that he had had no call from God to go into the ministry, but Martha entered correspondence with a Kansas seminary and Hiram was enrolled there almost before he knew it. A little later Grace came home with her husband. Martha forgave Grace perfunctorily, but old William smothered his daughter with whiskers and pumped his son-in-law's hand.

"What's good enough for Gracie is good enough for her old Paw," he said.

Grace had such frequent attacks of stomach sickness and melancholia that Martha put intimate questions to her. The old lady was thoroughly disgusted with Leon, saying to Grace: "I might have known it, because it's the only thing men want with women."

Martha made it plain to Leon Warner that he was an unwelcome guest and finally told him to get out and stay out; and she prevailed on Grace to let Leon go. When Martha repeated the circumstances to her pastor, Dr. Merritt, he held that she had followed the procedure of gentle Jesus in casting out devils.

In March, 1890, Hiram came home in disgrace from the seminary where he had engaged in a brawl and had been stabbed. After the stabbing, he had endeavored to hide his guilt by stitching his belly-wound with a needle and thread, but the Chancellor himself discovered the miscreant. Hiram refused to name his assailant, swore horribly and was expelled.

Soon after Hiram's inglorious return, a baby boy was born to Grace. She suffered greatly. Old William moved aimlessly up and down the cellar steps, wishing he could take the labor on himself. Martha supervised everything, including the activities of a student physician, and received the child in an ancient woolen shawl. From that time on, Martha took complete charge of the baby. She decided its name would be Gordon, after her own father, and furthermore, that it would not be Gordon Warner, but Gordon Dole.

Fearful of becoming blasphemous, Martha checked herself in the middle of a wish that the child had been the result of immaculate conception. Well, if her own son had been weighed in the balance and found wanting, her grandson would grow up to be a minister. Martha dedicated Gordon to God, kneeling beside the cradle and looking at the red, puckered face of Gordon Dole—certainly not at Gordon Warner.

Old William sat beside his daughter's bed and held her hand in his own twisted hands.

Chapter Two

I

GORDON DOLE'S first definite memory emerged
from the nimbus of his infancy at the age of four. Perhaps
this dawn of a knowable past was so thunderously certain
because it concerned his status as Racy's son. Memory comes
to a boy as a pioneer to a far wilderness. There is a name-
less floundering in the marshes where slime sleeps on the
reeds; there is directionless stirring of underbrush. Then
there is heard a plashing of unseen oars on hidden waters
and muffled blows of an ax on pines that have held their
virginity for a thousand years.... Then Memory, the
Pioneer, breaks through like a Daniel Boone, and stands
in a clearing. Then again into the forest, hacking trees,
blazing a trail, making pathways through the vagueness
...and Innocence begins to die as Recollection's children
come as settlers to build cities along the frontiers of the
soul. The thin, winding pathways become wide roads, along
which the pilgrim goes, stopping now and then to learn
the meanings of unspoken, unwritten languages ... home,
human contacts, behavior, pose, the wetness of kisses, the

irony of embraces, the virtues of hatred and the sins of love.
... The first memory is the dawn of the soul's civilization.

Racy, in white, stood in a room decorated by palms
and heavy-smelling blossoms. Her eyes were lusterful but
sad and there was a wanly sweet smile on her lips as she
moved beside a strange, self-assured and athletic man in
black. Gordon sat at a small table with the two Remson
boys, eating cake and ice cream, as much as he wanted, and
watching his mother and the strange man in black, who
laughed and shook hands with everybody. Then, as the
guests began to depart, Gordon was told that he was going
to live with Racy in her own house ... but with that strange
man in black, who was to be his new father. His new
father! Why, he never had known an old father. It would
be great to have a father—the father of the Remson boys
was so jolly and handy at making whistles from spring
willow twigs.

The new father's name was Christensen, Blair Christensen, and Racy's name was Mrs. Blair Christensen and
Mrs. Grace Christensen ... but Gordon's name was not
Christensen. It was still Gordon Dole, like Granner's name
was Dole. Somehow the fact that Racy could change her
name and Gordon couldn't seemed to remove his mother
yet another step away from him. It was the first discrepancy
in life that Gordon discovered and he never became
reconciled to discrepancies. They hurt his soul.

When the last guest had gone, Gordon felt sleepy and
someone lifted him into a bed that he vaguely sensed was
strange and chill. He awakened with a stomach-ache—it

seemed years had gone by since Racy had taken a new name, and Gordon was face to face with the darkness, and he didn't like being alone. Alone where it was dark and uncertain.

He got up, terribly afraid, touching unfriendly objects in the darkness, but he did not cry out, for was he not a descendant of strong Granner and of silent old Gramper? Then he remembered—always he remembered this with torturing sorrow—wandering into another room and running against a bed in which people were whispering, and then the awful voice of a man:

"Get the hell out of here and go back to your bed!"

The voice out of the darkness; from a bed; his new father's voice. Then a short altercation between the man and a woman...the woman was Racy. She got up and took Gordon back to his bed, but when he begged her to stay with him, she said she could not...now. Some other time, perhaps some other night, but not now. He distinctly remembered that tears fell on his cheeks.

How dark it was then. How dark it always would be without Racy.

When morning came, Racy asked Gordon to take the little white sugar bowl, the one with dogs' heads for handles, down to Granner's house. "Borrow some sugar, Gordie. Be careful and don't break the bowl."

Granner clasped Gordon and kissed him. She cried and asked if he had been lonesome for her and then he told her about being alone in the dark and how a man, his new father, had sworn at him. He never wanted to go back; no, not even for Racy, so long as she slept with that new father. Granner told Gordon to wait; that she would be back soon. She went to see Racy. When she returned, she told Gordon that he never need leave her; that she had arranged to give him a home with her as long as she lived, and he was happy. Still, he worried about it and thought it all very strange and unfair that your mother could be stolen from you and that no one was sent to jail for the crime.

Granner tried to explain to him why his name was Gordon Dole and not Gordon Christensen, and why Racy's name was Mrs. Christensen and not Mrs. Warner, and why Mrs. Warner's name had not been Mrs. Dole. Names made no difference, Granner said; but they made a great difference to Gordon. He said nothing further about it and felt very safe when he went to sleep with Granner in the feather-bed.

II

Old William and Hiram retrieved from Granner—who was very Irish and open-fisted—four thousand dollars, with which they opened a grocery and meat store. Dole & Son, the new sign read, with blue lettering against a white field. The sign was Gordon's first spelling lesson. He marveled at the many good things there were to be eaten in this bazaar.

Granner did not permit Gordon to go to school until he was seven, maintaining that he was too delicate. If Granner said he was delicate, Gordon knew it must be so;

but he wondered how it was he could lick neighborhood boys when he was so delicate.

When Granner learned that Gordon had fights under Uncle Hiram's sly tutelage, she upbraided her son and kept Gordon away from the store. To shield Gordie further from physical ills, Granner made him a straw-sided sunbonnet and kept him penned up in the front yard like a pet puppy. She would not let him participate in street games or go swimming and on Sundays he had to sit in sacred torpor while those who should have been his playmates passed his door. They called him sissy and little girl.

Granner made Gordon's clothes, fitting him out on Sundays with velvet breeches, ruffled cambric waist and a large bow tie of red that puffed out from his neck and ears. When his hair was sleeked back, he looked like a bantam rooster with great wattles. Of a Sunday Granner conducted him through a day of devotions long enough to sap the patience of St. Francis of Assisi himself. After the day and night of evangelical labor, Gordon's feet were so heavy as to seem half-soled with big Bibles. Only one light shone through the dirgeful stupidity of the Sabbath. Racy was soloist in the choir and her voice stirred wide rhythms in the child's heart.

Old William didn't go to church at all, but sat in his cellar and read the Sunday newspaper. Granner refused to permit a Sunday newspaper in her home, holding it a sin to read anything but the Holy Writ on that day, but Hiram smuggled *The Fairmount Clarion* to his sinful father. Miner's candles burned in wrought iron sconces, the spikes of which were thrust in the dirt walls. Gordon sometimes slipped into William's burrow to peek at the contraband comic section.

Gordon's longing for playmates and for play left a lasting psychic wound that never ceased to torment him. When he grew up he would play and play hard; he was certain of that, bitterly certain.

III

BLAIR CHRISTENSEN was a hustler, but his feet were not on the ground in a commercial way. He tried to be a professional photographer and on Sundays played baseball, receiving two dollars a game for pitching. After a family conference it was decided that Racy and Blair come to Granner's; it would be more economical all 'round. Gordon hoped that Racy would become more affectionate toward him, for he was starved for her love. He almost gave up hoping for her caresses, for Blair wanted Racy for himself, so Gordon began to look elsewhere in his seventh year, his first at school.

Virginia Hartman sat across the aisle from Gordon and he suffered a boiling of emotions when he looked at her. He became feverishly fond of her, but in the absence of a like feeling on Virginia's part, he grew thin and pale. One day during recess he put a note on her desk, asking her if she would be his girl. The disdainful look he received when Virginia found the note caused him such pain that Granner took him again to Dr. Eskridge. That eminent sage once more diagnosed the condition as nervous dyspepsia and Gordon had to undergo another course of skimmed milk for a week. Then, one morning, during opening exercises, Gordon saw Virginia picking her nose. He immediately lost interest in her and in a few days made strides in health and weight. Dr. Eskridge pointed out that his skimmed milk diet never failed.

Toward his eighth birthday, Gordon felt a mysterious yearning, akin to curiosity, for the opposite sex. He wondered why mankind was divided into two abrupt classes and determined to find out about it. He talked the matter over with little Carrie Hoyt and induced her to reveal herself in an outhouse, where the question was admirably solved.

IV

IN September of his eighth year Gordon asked Blair what he was going to get him for Christmas.

"What do you want, Gordie?"

"A bugle." Gordon had heard the brave and challenging blasts of a trumpet during a parade of soldiers going to the war with Spain. There was something so defiantly independent and stirring in the trumpet sound.

"Oh," Blair said, "a horn!"

"Not a horn, Blair. A bugle!"

"You just wait, Gordie, and when Christmas comes you'll be surprised."

Every night Gordon thought of his bugle and he wondered if prayer, after all, wouldn't help. Not the long-winded ones such as Dr. Merritt shouted up to the throne of God, but just a modest, well-meant prayer; a prayer that Blair would not change his mind—a bugle prayer. He would have written to Santa Claus, but eight-year-old boys didn't do that and anyway he never had subscribed to the Santa Claus myth. Granner had told him at the beginning that there was no such person; that it was a sin to lie to children and that she wasn't going to lie to him. So he took the bugle matter directly to God.

Gordon rose early Christmas morning, trembling with eagerness to grasp the shiny barrel of the bugle; aching to blow into the brass tube and to sound the brave challenge. He went to the baseburner stove, beside which were stacked packages for all the household. His gray eyes opened widely and he looked expectantly...but what he saw was a clarinet!

He could not speak, for something choked him and he tried hard to keep the tears back. If only Jesus, who could perform miracles, were here. Jesus had changed water into wine at the feast—unfermented grape juice it was, Granner claimed—and he certainly could change a clarinet into a bugle.... Then, like a true descendant of stoical Gramper, Gordon walked up to Blair and shook hands with him; but what he really wanted to do was to open the cast iron doors of the baseburner and toss the clarinet into the fire that was licking the isinglass windows of the stove.

Chapter Three

I

OLD WILLIAM perpetrated a desperate deed in the autumn of 1900. Instead of meeting the bills due wholesale dealers that served the firm of Dole & Son, Gramper wagered the money on William Jennings Bryan to win the presidential election. When the two Williams—Dole and Bryan—lost out, Granner described the act as downright embezzlement.

Uncle Hiram was a bit upset by Gramper's gambling technique, but he was mindful that in his own seminary escapades Gramper never had condemned him. Rather, Gramper had held that it was better to be a good bartender than a rotten parson. Uncle Hiram flexed his powerful arms and postponed a plan he had for getting married. It could wait.

Gramper's political and financial reverses had little effect on his doughty spirit. He was erect and strong at sixty, although he had a touch of pleurisy, an asthmatic wheeze that startled his whiskers and recurrent cramps in the right calf. After the Bryan debacle, he kept to his cellar retreat as much as possible and quit taking meals at Martha's table. He did very well in the day, regarding victuals, eating cheese, crackers and bologna at the store. He found a rusty stove on a dump and installed it in his basement, where he cooked beans and salt pork and brewed tea as strong as fish brine.

When Gramper had a cramp, Gordon would hear him stamping heavily and would run down the cellar steps to beat Gramper's leg with a stick of kindling wood until the knot left the muscles. Gordon never heard the old man groan or complain, but he noticed that saliva dripped down his beard as Gramper patted the child's head.

As payment for Gordon's work on the cramps, Gramper taught him the secrets of mining, insofar as the cellar would permit of laboratory work. One Sunday Gramper was demonstrating the proper manner for using a sledge and drill. He had chosen the west wall of the cellar for the experiment, above and beyond which was the front porch. Gramper had just settled down to some serious and deft drilling when there was a cave-in which half-buried professor and pupil. It was a God-forsaken moment, for as they shook free from the moldy clods, they beheld Granner as she stood halfway down the steps.

"You lost everything we had on Bryan! Now you want to wreck the very house over our heads!"

Gramper was in the clutches of a cramp and couldn't very well reply in kind.

II

STILL other untoward happenings emphasized the distress-
ing position in which the household of Martha was placed.
Hiram, thwarted as a pugilist and delayed as a bridegroom,
had begun to drink heavily. Martha had lost her sense of
smell through years of catarrh and she did not realize at
once what was wrong with her son. Finally she learned the
truth after Hiram had gone on a spree and had been
brought home with a broken leg and a touch of alcoholism.
Granner sent for Dr. Eskridge and Gordon shocked the
boarders by saying: "Doc Eskridge will put Uncle Hiram
on skimmed milk for a week, because it surely is his
stomach that ails him."

Without Hiram's presence at the store, the firm of
Dole & Son was in a bad way; so bad that it passed into
the hands of a receiver. William continued to hold his head
high, Martha maintaining that this fool who had bet on
Bryan didn't know enough to feel humiliated in the eyes
of his fellow man.

Blair Christensen wasn't doing so well, either, and
gave up his photography to start a laundry. That didn't
go, and he began the manufacture of candied popcorn,
which Gordon helped him peddle from door to door.
There was some talk of taking Gordon out of school for
a year, but Granner had hopes that he would become a
minister. She exerted all her strength in keeping her boarders half satisfied and in doing extra washing for other
boarding houses. Racy helped her wash and Gordon didn't

like to see his mother at a steaming tub, her calico sleeves uprolled and her face flushed. Some day he would make enough money to let Racy rest and sing and then she would know who really loved her. Then she would know what it meant to have a son.

III

GORDON had two major ambitions when he was growing up. One was to take a watch apart and the other was to see Gramper in the nude. Whereas the first ambition was realized, the second never was attained.

Blair left his watch on the sideboard one day as he hurried off to answer an ad for real estate salesmen. Real estate, Blair told Racy, was more profitable than popcorn confecting. Gordon went to work at once on the watch, prying open the back lid of the case and manipulating tiny screws with Granner's buttonhole scissors. The operation was a decided success and so was the storm that Blair raised when he came home.

The visualization of Gramper in the nude was one of those dreams that never come true. Gramper slept in his clothes—a fashion heartily endorsed by gentlemen who belabored rocks for gold. Finally Gordon compromised and planned to see a part of Gramper, but that wasn't practicable either, for Gramper was ruggedly modest.

IV

TOWARD the Fall of 1901, Blair Christensen, a man of action and ideas, had a magnificent plan for saving Martha's house from complete ruin. He had made several hundred dollars in real estate commissions and explained to the family council that this would provide capital for his scheme. He pointed out that the Pan American Exposition was on at Buffalo, New York, and said he was in contact with an inventor and together they had evolved something conducive to the welfare of mankind. He took a sample of the invention from his overcoat pocket. It was a pants hanger, a rather small device, about as long as a man's trousers are wide at the cuff.

The pants hanger was black-enameled and springy; just press one end of the contraption and it flipped open with the force of a wolf trap. Put the pants cuffs in, flat, between the top spring and the lower one and bear down hard. There you are! Then hang it up.... In his enthusiasm, Blair removed his pants—to Granner's consternation—and demonstrated. The pants hanger didn't work quite as readily as it might have done and it tore a jagged hole in Blair's trousers which Racy sat down to mend while Blair talked. He said he'd sell a million pants hangers on the Exposition grounds.

Granner beamed and observed that Blair was a hustler, so unlike her first son-in-law. Hiram, who had a hangover, hiccoughed that Blair would land in jail if one of the hangers flipped open and put out a customer's eye. Racy told Blair to do as he thought best and Gramper said what in hell was the difference what happened?

Blair came home next day laden with cartons of pants hangers. He brought pads and stamps and gilt powder and the whole family helped label the hangers: "The Eureka Pants Holder. Patent Pending." Then Blair went to Buffalo to teach a nation the importance of caring for its trousers.

It was agreed that while Blair was away, the now unprofitable boarding house would be shut down and that the family would move to the mountains for a time. Gramper said he knew he could strike it rich again for he had a promising claim in Clear Creek County and a dirt-floor cabin. Hiram stayed in Fairmount, going to work for a Mr. Cousins, who had a mercantile house that served the segregated harlots of the city with groceries and meats. Mr. Cousins offered Gramper a job, but old William said No, explaining that he was pretty well fed up with city life and that he felt best in the hills. William asked Mr. Cousins what the hell difference did it make where a man was, so long as he was let alone? Mr. Cousins said it made no difference at all.

Chapter Four

I

WILLIAM DOLE was a changed man in the mountains, moving with authority in and out of the shaft while Gordon watched him with pride. There was no sullen timidity here, such as there had been in the cellar that day when the west wall crumbled like sponge cake. Gramper walked up boldly to the rock door and knocked with mighty hammer blows. Open up, Mother Earth, and give Gordie some gold. If you don't open up, I'll break into you!

Granner had been a Catherine the Great in her boarding house, but in the cabin she was throneless and when she objected to Gramper warming dynamite sticks in the oven of the sheet-iron camp stove he ignored her. Martha often ran outdoors, praying desperately to a just God to stay Gramper's hand; imploring Heaven to spare the family a scattering, untimely death. When Gordon heard Granner's anti-dynamite supplications, he wondered if an explosion would rip off Gramper's clothing as had happened to the two Berg brothers up the Mormon Road. If so, Gordon would get to see Gramper in the nude.

Perhaps this visit to the hills was the happiest time of Gordon's entire life, for Racy hugged him and kissed him on the lips and he thought her beautiful and fragrant. Gordon and Racy took walks in the valley groves where pine needles formed deep rugs and squirrels ran out on old branches to scold them. Gordon had a burro for his own, which he rode valiantly, thinking of many things but principally counting the moments until it would be time for him to lie beside his mother for a while, his arms about her and his head on her firm breast. I used to be held in Racy's arms to be fed at her bosom, he would say inside himself. I really am a part of her.

Once, after Gramper had gone to town for supplies and had returned with a show of mystery, the old man whispered to Gordon to go with him a piece up the trail. Gramper opened a stoutly wrapped box and in it was a gleaming bugle of brass! In presenting the bugle to Gordon, Gramper said he would confide in him the secret of real happiness:

"Stay single, mind your own business and keep away from towns."

The trumpet became a mighty symbol to Gordon, never to be forgotten, for with its brave voice he could defy Time itself and through it he could speak the language of the Eternity that Granner so often talked about. It was Gabriel's trumpet. Without it he was just Gordon, but with it and astride his burro, moving gallantly along the Mormon Road, he was Gabriel. What big ears you have, Granner! The better to hear your trumpet, my dear.

II

ONE evening while Gramper was swearing because someone—he looked accusingly at Granner—had thrown away a
pan of his sour dough, Racy took ill. Next day old William
and Gordon didn't trudge up the trail, but sat beside Racy's
bunk, watching her anxiously, while Granner made tea
from mountain sage for Racy. Gordon again was afraid
and when his bedtime came, he lay there holding his trumpet close to him and wondering if Racy were safe from
Robber Death. William went to Neighbor Blake's to borrow
some money and they left the hills next day for Fairmount.

Dr. Eskridge said that Racy had appendicitis and that
he would have to operate and that Racy was very sick.

III

A DAY of waiting. Gordon, approaching his twelfth year of
life, waiting in a strange boarding house with Gramper.
Granner had left them there, Gramper in agony with
pleurisy, cramps and heartache—waiting.

Late in the afternoon old William said he could stand
the suspense no longer, so he drew on his boots with difficulty and got up from his bed while Gordon clung to him.
When they got to the street, Gordon saw Granner and
Hiram getting off a trolley car. Gramper looked at the
woman and at the man, peering at them until he could
see their faces distinctly. Then Gordon saw his Gramper,
who always had been so straight and so strong, so defiant

of years and of hardship, grow suddenly aged, withered, futile.

Granner seemed unable to speak and Hiram's face was drawn and his heavy jaws sagged as he tried to tell briefly that Racy had gone away ... for always. Gordon felt that the world was opening and letting him fall into a pit of blind nothingness and his terror and his grief were accentuated by the unforgettable sight of Gramper, who now sank to his hands and knees and crawled along the sidewalk like a wounded goat. Hiram lifted the old man as though he were straw and carried him into the house, Hiram holding himself against Granner so that she, too, would not fall. Gordon walked alone behind them, wondering how anyone could end a prayer with the words "God's will be done."

From then on, Gordon walked alone in Life.

IV

CLODS of earth on a pine lid and then a filled grave and a mound of newly-stirred earth on which old Pauper Death might crouch, all hollow-eyed and haunting. Someone at the graveside whispered that the beloved President, William McKinley, was dead from an assassin's bullet; that he died singing "Nearer, My God, to Thee!" That was terrible, too, Gordon thought; still what was the loss of even a President compared to the loss of a Racy?

One year goes and yet another year goes—where do they go? They never seem to grow old and feeble. Blair

Christensen is married again and William and Martha, Hiram and Gordon establish a small home on Edgeworth Street. Gordon is almost fourteen now and he begins to feel something that possibly may be manhood crawling into his skin and crowding out the being that was a boy. It is a stranger that creeps into his skin, draping itself about large bones and becoming himself instead of the old himself and it is all very mystifying.

Gramper told Gordon that if he ever took indecent liberties with himself, he surely would die of softening of the brain; and Gramper recited real and imaginary cases to prove his words. Gordon was dreadfully upset to learn of this and he would shake his head rather violently when he was alone to ascertain if his brain wobbled softly about in his skull.

A timid furze began to shadow his lips and chin and he was ashamed of his voice, which was high, then harsh, and then uncertain—all in one short sentence, when he asked if Granner would please pass the jam.

Chapter Five

I

GORDON was glad when his voice settled down
like a squirrel that has made up its mind where to hiber-
nate. He had his first shave with Uncle Hiram's razor;
his hair began to darken and he could say Damn it in
Gramper's presence without reprimand. He had dreams
that puzzled him and he would awaken from them with
a feeling of languor and emptiness. Uncle Hiram, in inter-
preting these dreams and with masculine clumsiness, counseled Gordon not to go about girls in the wrong way. See?

Granner, the Minerva of the feather-bed, thought it
time to lecture Gordon and told him that women were
sacred vessels and that men should revere women and protect them. It was a sin for men and women to give in to
their natures; yes, and it was a sin even for a man to look
on a woman with evil thought.

When Granner asked William to talk to Gordon, to
emphasize to him the existence of pitfalls of sex, the old
man said what the hell difference did it make if he talked
until he was blue in the face? You couldn't talk down

something that had lasted since the beginning of time. Granner then said something sarcastic regarding a squaw named "Lonely Moon Cloud" and Gramper hastened to a new cellar burrow he had established in the Edgeworth Street home. There he peeled an apple with a bowie knife and munched it noisily.

After certain misgivings, Granner consented to Gordon's taking a job at Mr. Cousins' grocery store. Granner said she had heard that loose ladies patronized that establishment, but Hiram pointed out that he and Gramper worked there and that they would look out for Gordon. Hiram also observed that if loose ladies were barred from public places the cities of America soon would become deserted villages.

The talk about loose women fascinated Gordon. What were they like? What made them loose? If there were loose women, it was to be implied that there were tight women, too; just when did a woman leave off being tight and begin to get loose? and was there a balancing mark, where a woman was neither loose nor tight? He would find out about it.

Mr. Cousins sold wine in his grocery store and permitted Gordon to bottle the wine and to paste handsome labels on the bottles. He showed Gordon how to use a rubber siphon for drawing the wine from casks and sometimes Gordon swallowed several mouthfuls. It gave him a pleasing sensation, particularly if he had been working at the bottling before lunch time and while his stomach was idle. He got to liking the wine, because it injected some sort of feeling into him that he could meet the world and shake hands with it. For a time it dulled the awareness of brutalities that seemed to leer at a sensitive nature.

Gordon drove the Cousins' delivery wagon through alleys that abutted cribs and parlor houses of the loose ladies, and he could see women sitting in short dresses and could hear them howling blunt invitations to men who passed by their doors. Sometimes the men didn't pass by, but stopped in. When Gordon shouldered his basket and went into kitchens, he sometimes saw at close range the women who worked at this puzzling business and he thought they looked haggard and defeated beneath their face paint.

One morning he went into a kitchen with a heavy load of groceries on his shoulder and was about to put the basket on a table when he heard a woman saying: "Keep your head turned, fellow, and don't look this way."

Gordon peeked through a cleft formed by a sack of crackers and a package of cereal that lay on top of the basket. He saw Trixie, a plump blonde, who was quite naked. This was the first time he had seen a woman in the nude. He once had seen a picture of a nude woman when Carl Gard had shown it to the boys at school; but a picture was nothing compared to this breathing, smoothly bare woman. Gordon dropped the basket, not waiting to empty it, and hurried back to his wagon. He didn't bother to latch the back gate, for the laughter of Trixie followed him like a tin can tied to the tail of a dog, clatteringly and shameless.

He made several mistakes that day, delivering a duck to Madam Rosalie's place, whereas it should have gone to Number 2112 Market Street; short-changing a pimp named Diamond Duffy after the sale of a jar of caviar, and drawing a criticism from Uncle Hiram for upsetting a crock of dill pickles. Gordon was glad toward the close of the day when Mr. Cousins asked him to bottle a special order of Port wine. Gordon pulled hard at the siphon tube, so hard that his head became a drum on a merry-go-round and his feet as clumsy as butter tubs.

When Gordon got home, Granner thought he was ill, but he said he wasn't and went to bed supperless. He had two catastrophic visions that night but felt better next day.

II

Gordon expressed a desire to be a physician when he went to high school, but Granner said the ministry was to be his objective. Gordon did not ask Granner how a man could be a minister if he kept remembering Trixie, a nude woman?

There were many freshly radiant girls in East Fairmount High School, but Nada Halpin was accounted the most beautiful as well as the most talented. She didn't seem to study much, but her marks were high and she was popular with all but the women instructors. Nada was splendid, aloof, and Gordon pictured her as unattainable. She had extremely light hair, sometimes offering the illusion that it was white as the afternoon sun came through

the study hall windows. Her eyes were green but large
and widely set and her long lashes were not as light as her
hair but more of an auburn shade. If Gordon had known
at this time what the word meant, he would have described
her rather tall and slender body as seductive.

Gordon thought Nada looked at him occasionally with
interest but denied to himself that she could be attracted
to him under any circumstance. Still there were three more
or less minor incidents that seemed significant to him of
something—he did not know what. Once he had a small
part in a school play in which Nada was a principal. During
a rehearsal she tripped on a rug and Gordon caught her
about the waist and felt the soft warmth of her flesh beneath
silk. He knew he was turning red when she looked her
thanks and he half hated her for her almost diffident dis-
missal of the incident; her easy resumption of her lines in
the play and her failure to put her thanks into words.

Another time Nada was coming down the broad stair
in the hall leading to the assembly room and Gordon was
standing there looking absently at the stairway. Suddenly
he was aware of Nada pausing on the stair and he was
embarrassed to feel that she certainly thought he had been
looking at her legs, which, as a matter of truth, he was.
For weeks after this incident Nada turned her head swiftly
whenever he looked her way.

Gordon decided he must quit thinking of Nada or of
other girls for they were sacred vessels, and when he
drew too near to them, he almost forgot they were sacred.
They were apt to become just vessels. Uncle Hiram had

said he must not get gay with girls, so he plunged into study and athletics, although he had to carry newspapers after school and his spare time was limited.

It was while he was on the track team as a sprinter that the third incident occurred which he regarded as possibly indicative of Nada noticing he was in the world at all. Ralph Masters was captain of the team and was the school's fastest dash man. Gordon usually ran second to Ralph, but this day Ralph had been compelled to withdraw from the lists in a dual meet with South Fairmount High School on account of a pulled tendon. Much to his own surprise, for he had neglected regular training, Gordon won the one-hundred-yard dash and Masters congratulated him.

"I want you to bring a girl to a party at Nada's house to-night," Ralph said.

"I have no girl."

"Shall I get you one?"

Gordon wavered. He never had been to a party in his life and he wouldn't know how to act with a girl. Anyway he couldn't dance and he didn't know if his clothes would pass in a group of well dressed young people. Masters decided for Gordon, telling him to go to Nada's at 8 o'clock and that the girl would be there.

Gordon was confused when Nada met him in her home and directed him where to sit among others of his school who looked so gay and so different than they always had seemed in the classrooms. They talked easily, laughed, gathered about the piano and sang. Elizabeth Wells, daughter of a wealthy real estate man, came over to Gordon and sat down beside him. They knew each other only through schoolroom contacts.

"I'm your girl," Elizabeth said.

That sounded very funny. His girl. Well, if she was his girl, that was fine. He thought her very pretty with her black hair and dark eyes and she seemed very graceful and full-blooded; but he much preferred light hair and green eyes. Gordon tried hard to seem sophisticated, but he wished he had not come, particularly when it came time to play games and a kissing game was begun. Gordon dreaded his turn, but it came and he was supposed to kiss Elizabeth Wells. He made an awful botch of it, kissing her on the neck, entirely missing her lips and hearing his schoolmates laugh. They had cheered him this afternoon when he had breasted the tape ahead of a fast field. Now they laughed.

Gordon looked scornfully at the group of gamesters and there was something in his expression that caused the laughter to fall abruptly. He looked at Nada and saw she wasn't laughing but that her eyes held a peculiar light. Gordon felt hurt and thought every one believed him to be stupid. He walked out of the room, found his hat and went home without saying good-by to Elizabeth Wells—his girl— or to anyone, but bit his lips and looked questioningly at the rim of the moon that was wearing Earth's shadow like a hangman's blindfold.

III

ELIZABETH WELLS became very much interested in Gordon and during his first two years in high school taught him to

dance and took him to her home, where her father had a
fine library. Due to Granner's opposition to Gordon playing
football, Elizabeth proposed that he keep his gridiron togs
in her home, dressing there for the games, returning there
to change back to his regular clothes and making himself
one of the family. Elizabeth's father liked Gordon and even
went so far as to visit Mr. Cousins, gaining from the store-
keeper permission for Gordon to absent himself from work
on Saturdays when there were football games.

One Saturday in his third high school year, Gordon
went to the Wells home after a football game. He had made
two costly fumbles and was disconsolate. Elizabeth walked
with Gordon from the football park and when they reached
her home her parents were not there. Gordon climbed
through a parlor window, pulling Elizabeth in after him.

After his tub, Gordon looked for a towel but couldn't
find one; but he knew where the linen closet was; outside
the bathroom and at the head of a stair. He opened the
door and started toward the closet, and then he saw Elizabeth standing there. She was shaking and her arms were
held out to him.

Gordon was amazed and seemed unable to move as
Elizabeth came to him and put her arms about him. Water
from his body was blotted by her shirtwaist and skirt.
Gordon said they mustn't, but Elizabeth told him it didn't
matter; that she loved him.

That was Gordon's first transgression of Granner's
code.

Chapter Six

I

TOWARD the end of summer Blair Christensen and his new wife called at Granner's and had Sunday dinner with the family. Gramper came up from the cellar and reported to Blair that his cramps were misbehaving; that his asthma made him breathe like a locomotive on up-grade, but that pain couldn't keep a good man down.

When Granner inferred that she wanted Gordon to go to State College at Martinsberg, Blair said he would pay the entrance fee. Gordon could work his way through the first year and perhaps Blair would then be in a position to finance him the rest of the way; particularly if he realized a fortune on a grouse whistle that he had been perfecting.

When Gordon started for college, Elizabeth Wells was at the station. She threw her arms about him and Gordon was gravely polite and self-conscious. He didn't relish the scene and mumbled something about writing often to her, but somehow he never got around to doing it. Elizabeth, it is true, had helped him discover the meaning of kisses and through her he had become sex mad, but he wished it were Nada here to see him away to school.

Gordon had fifteen cents when he arrived in Martinsberg, which was a town of some two thousand persons with an additional fifteen hundred enrolled students. He found himself among strangers and without a definite plan for upkeep, but he recalled reading how many great men had begun their careers penniless. He thought it an unfair edge that he had fifteen cents, for he intended to be a great man, too, one that Nada would be glad to welcome to her fine home. To achieve the penniless condition so necessary to great beginnings, Gordon purchased five cents' worth of cherry lozenges and spent the remaining dime on a street car ride out and back on the only trolley in town. It took him up a long, sinuous hill to a Chautauqua at the end of the line, in the auditorium of which the immortal Bryan once had lectured on "The Bible, and How True Its Prophecies Are." Gramper had lost his shirt on Bryan; how many men and women would come to hear Gramper preach on the text: "Bryan, What a Bust You Turned Out to Be!"

While knocking at doors and asking for work, Gordon came on Ralph Masters, who was rooming at a house conducted by a Mrs. Noble. Masters thought Gordon looked worried and offered to lend him half his first month's allowance; but Gordon said he had plenty of money. Gordon would lie if his pride were involved—perhaps his pride was his outstanding passion.

Ralph introduced Gordon to Mrs. Noble, who said she had a tent in the back yard that leaked and that if Gordon would fix the leak, he could sleep in the tent rent-free for two weeks. She would give him an oil lamp to study by. Gordon was not an Omar Khayyam with tents, but he repaired it as best he knew how and moved in, settling down to his first night of study as a cloudburst descended. The tent couldn't bear the brunt of the storm, water pouring through, putting out the light and cracking the chimney. The rain drenched Gordon and soaked the bed while he said God damn it to hell in perfect, immoral security.

Next day Gordon had a bad cold but he had to look for work and for food. Mrs. Noble's daughter said that the Alpha Tau Epsilon sorority needed a dishwasher, but they wanted to see the candidate before hiring him. When the girls saw Gordon, they knew he was the very man for the job, but some of them tittered.

Titter, you petticoated vestals! If you knew that I was born during a mad March wind, you wouldn't simper and giggle, for you would be terribly afraid to have such aching youth as mine in your virginal household ... or, now, would you?

II

GORDON spent one year at State College and led a retired life, but occasionally he broke out in madcap fashion, drinking to excess, singing Rabelaisian ditties and composing off-color verses. After these sporadic storms, he would suffer a moral sweat, during which repressions would ooze from every pore. He would again enter his shell, becoming rather grave and introspective and thinking of Nada and her supple, elusive body. Gordon's professors held that he had a facile brain but that he refused to concentrate and more than likely would be sentenced to be hanged.

Portia Mann was the bright spot of Gordon's year at college and whenever he went to the neighboring mining camp of Horton to get drunk, she understood him. Portia was not beautiful, according to collegiate judges of pulchritude, but she was handsomely and strongly fashioned. Her brow was full beneath dark bangs and she was thought to be a bit cool toward men because she seldom smiled at campus strollers.

Why he had selected Portia was a mystery to Gordon, but he thought she looked unattainable and he was going to quit shrinking from unattainable things. After several months, Gordon and Portia found each other's company highly gratifying, and they both felt that it would not be long before they were to reach a boundary line which they either must cross or must not cross. Finally Gordon decided that he could forget that Portia was a sacred vessel if she could and she said she could. Their plan to attain the ultimate resulted in a rather peculiar anti-climax.

They would steal away on this March night, Gordon said, and go to the foothills. They would sleep there together, even though the early spring still held frost in its breast.

"Bring blankets, Portia, for it's cold. I'll bring some blankets, too, and sweaters."

"Yes, Gordon." Was her voice trembling?

"Slip out the basement door of your house, for we don't want the Dean of Women to get wise. . . . Are you game, Portia?"

"Yes, Gordon. I'm game and I long to sleep in your arms. I love you, Gordon. Nothing else matters, does it?"

"No. But be sure to bring blankets. It's cold."

"I shan't be cold in your arms, Gordon."

"Well, anyway, don't forget blankets. . . . Ten o'clock."

March winds, so disturbing, so terrifying, howled down from the hills; Jeremiah winds that preached of woe; melancholy winds that chanted like the voices of warning priests. Up the trail in the steel moonlight the two love-seekers climbed, with the wind whipping down and the wind seeping through woolen sweaters; through Portia's Tam-o'-Shanter of white wool. But Portia will not play with you, O March gale, for to-night she plays with me. We shall be lovers.

When they came to a level place on the trail, where the students often built fires to broil steaks, Gordon was uneasy. They lay on a blanket, their arms locked, but when he kissed Portia he felt cowardly and upset, and he wanted to leave her and go down the trail again. He didn't know what excuse to give, for it was he who had urged this thing; it was he who had engineered this almost fanatical plan for dream accomplishment. Portia, breathing swiftly against his cheek, seemed so fine and lithe and hungry. Gordon had waited frettingly during an afternoon of anticipation, but now, with Portia in his arms, he didn't dare go through with it. He rose abruptly and stood before Portia, looking like a mad friar with the blanket draped about him and the March wind blowing his dark hair as he stood against the steel of the moonlight.

"We're going back to the valley." He seemed so cross; his tone implying that Portia had done something offensive.

"Why?"

"I'll explain on the way down. Come ahead."

They went down the mountainside, but Gordon didn't explain and Portia didn't ask him questions. He kept thinking of Nada, asking himself how he would feel if anyone had taken Nada to a hillside and made love to her in that way. Or to Racy? Racy had been pure and good and trusting.

At first Portia seemed hurt and very much concerned, but as they said good night, she became cool and distantly disappointed and she did not hold her face up to him for a kiss. When Gordon returned to a fraternity house where he now was a member, he tossed in his narrow bed and asked the darkness:

"I wonder if I didn't make a mistake? Perhaps I should have gone through with it. . . . Oh, well. . . ."

Gordon and Portia avoided one another, but the day Gordon started for home, his year of college done, Portia was at the station. He was surprised to see her and could hardly believe she had come to say good-by to him. Her frankness, too, puzzled him as she said: "I'm glad we didn't lose our heads. Still ..."

"We'll meet again some day. So long, and good luck to you, Portia."

Gordon knew it was his last year of schooling, although he couldn't tell how he knew it. He just felt it and he didn't care particularly one way or another.

Chapter Seven

I

GORDON, arriving home with one-fourth of a college education, was sensitive about his failure to go through to a degree, but Uncle Hiram said not to mind it at all. Gramper said what the hell difference did it make anyway, just so long as a man learned a little something without becoming effeminate or a consumptive.

"I'm going to work," Gordon told Granner, "but I don't want to go back to Cousins' store. If I can't be a doctor, I'll try my hand at writing. Not now, but later."

To save street car fare, Gordon assembled a bicycle. Uncle Hiram got a second-hand frame and Gordon re-painted it a robin's-egg blue while waiting a week for rims, which Gramper contributed. Granner, who had gone in for chicken and rabbit raising, managed to purchase handlebars without grips and a chain. A lucky call by Blair Christensen, who by this time was selling concrete tombstones under his own slogan: "Every Grave Can Afford One," resulted in enough capital for tires and a seat.

Aboard this synthetic bicycle, Gordon cruised the city, looking for work.

He found time, however, to call on several of his high school classmates, visiting certain girls he used to know when he was an athlete at East Fairmount. The girls seemed delighted by the polish Gordon had acquired at college, remarking that he had a manner that could—and sometimes did—lead to romantic intimacies.

After much meditation on the subject, Gordon called on Nada Halpin who was attracting considerable attention by her dancing and her acting. The Fairmount Stock Company gave her occasional parts in their productions. Gordon had followed her career through newspaper notices and by making guarded inquiries of Ralph Masters. He now wanted to show off a bit before Nada, striking a few poses to indicate to her that he, too, was a person of affairs.

He rode gallantly to Nada's home, rising on one pedal as a Cossack might do, if bicycle-minded. He dismounted with a sweeping leg flourish and placed his synthetic bicycle against a mounting block, where the sun could accentuate the glimmer of robin's-egg blue.

Nada answered his knock and as he caught the perfume of her and as he felt, rather than saw, the growing beauty of her, his well prepared words became meat in a sausage grinder. If in school she had stirred within him the beginning of love, now she possessed him wholly. He definitely, fearfully sensed that from now on he could not be complete without her. He looked hungrily at her eyes, which seemed a shade deeper in the gloom of the doorway, half hoping to find in them a welcome that was more than friendly. He found no such welcome there nor in the mystic, almost conventional smile on her lips. Those lips were a paradox, for they seemed to be placidly and classically formed yet capable of passion and storm. And he felt blasted and withered when he recalled that Ralph Masters had told him that Nada soon would be Mrs. Masters.

"Ralph and I were speaking of you yesterday," she said. He loved her voice, which was rather low and of rich timbre. "Ralph is going to run in awhile this afternoon. Can you wait?"

"Why, yes, of course."

"He's awfully sorry you're not going back to college this Fall."

"Sure be glad to see Ralph." Gordon thought Nada's hands expressive and whitely dazzling. I must hold those hands before Ralph comes, no matter what happens; no matter how mad she gets; no matter how wrong it is to attempt to cut in on a friend. I like Ralph, but you can't help it if you love Nada, can you? Decidedly not. Anyway, it won't kill Ralph. She has me insane over her. Doesn't love meet love in this world? Isn't there ever a double love, a man loving a woman and a woman loving a man? Will Nada show me the door? Damn it! Ralph has money and can go through school. "Ralph's a swell fellow, Nada."

"I like him."

Oh! The hell you say! You like him and I suppose you

let him hold your hand and perhaps he kisses. . . . Gordon suddenly kissed Nada's cheek and it made him sick with longing. She seemed astonished, but she kept calm and looked at him wonderingly. Then she rose to answer a knock at the front door and Ralph Masters came into the parlor.

"Why, Gordie! You're the last one I expected to see. . . ." Masters paused uneasily and added lamely: "Here."

"I just dropped in on Nada." Well, why not? Do you own her? Are you a monopolist of this girl? The words haven't been said yet that are to consign her to you, ready to be unwrapped by you, the ribbons to be untied by your damned fingers. . . . He felt upset and guilty and wished he were on the bicycle with his thighs pumping furiously up and down, the frame of robin's-egg blue between them.

Masters told Gordon that he had heard of an opening, a job in the signal department of the Telephone Company. Gordon said he would look into it, and as he spoke he saw Nada gazing at him with a restrained but intense expression. He wondered if she was offended with him or if she was pitying him. He wanted to get out as soon as possible, so he said good-by.

As he leaned over his handlebars, he fancied that Nada's slender self was in the shadow that chased him, and the breeze he stirred seemed to caress him as he wished to be caressed by her corn silk hair. He pumped at the pedals until his calves were taut.

Gordon found Granner among the rabbit hutches,

where the smell of alfalfa was sweet and soothing. He watched Granner put a Belgian hare buck into a pen with a doe and then he saw her hang a gunny sack hastily over the door of the pen. She placed a brick on the top edge of the burlap curtain and she had a pained look as she turned from the sack-shielded honeymoon of the hares. What big eyes you have, Granner! The better to see that rabbits are mated, my dear.

"I think I've got a job," Gordon said.

Granner, still chagrined by contact with the facts of animal life, said she was glad. Then he went to the cellar to ask Gramper's advice about signal catching and rummaged in a trunk to find a photograph. It was a group picture of the class in which he and Nada had been graduated from East Fairmount. He put the picture beneath his coat and took it to his room.

II

It was night work in the signal department. Whenever watchmen wound red boxes in dark lofts and silent corridors of city buildings, bells would tap in the signal room. All night long the bells beat down on Gordon, from six in the evening until six the next morning and there were no nights off. The smashing little anvils with their round, clapping hammers, played an endless mad medley that poured into Gordon's brain. Through the funnels of his ears the discord was spilled until his skull ached with the bells.

How could anyone tell which bell was which and what numbers each bell spat out? Yet the five other men at the high table snatched the numbers like monkeys pick out fleas and there was a rickety ticker before each man, disgorging paper ribbon jerkily. There were perforations on the ribbons corresponding to the bell numbers in case a recorder needed to check up.

Gordon finally got used to the bells and learned how to sleep in daylight and in time he stopped dreaming of monks that castigated him with whips, each thong of which was tipped with a white-hot, deafening bell. He stopped dreaming of brass apes that spat out paper ribbons on which were written hieroglyphs. He began dreaming of Nada. He would awaken breathless, with a throaty fullness. He often pursued her through acres of black clouds, her white body gleaming between sable folds of mist.

On his way to work he would think up stories he wanted to write, but the moment he got within clacking distance, the bedlam of the bells descended on him like man-eating geese. They plucked from his brain his dreams; they bit his buttocks with their hissing cacophony.

During his lunch period, Gordon sometimes scurried away from the basement of the bells and, mounting his robin's-egg blue bicycle, he would breathe deeply of the night air. He would look at the stars. Once, in gazing so intently at the sky, he ran into a patrolman, who said: "Why don't you look where you're going?" To which Gordon, looking again at the stars, replied: "I am!"

III

GORDON wondered if he always would be a lonely soul. He had grown up among persons much older than himself and had been denied the comradeship of laughing playmates; so much so that he hardly knew how to act when among those of his own age. Now that he was free to take a drink and to knock about, he thought he might go to an extreme, taking too much freedom and going too far with life.

He sometimes visited with Granner in the rabbit pens as he started off to work. She was getting wrinkled and she moved her nose in a manner that suggested to Gordon that she might turn into a big, stoop-shouldered rabbit if she didn't watch out. He also dropped in on Gramper at the cellar on Sunday afternoons and felt that something had gone out of the old man, never to return, since Racy had been taken. He asked Gramper to get out of the cellar and move about in the open air to ease his asthma, but Gramper answered that the ground had been good to him and that he would stick to the ground for his companionship.

Chapter Eight

I

*W*ILLIAM was of little use at the Cousins' store. He was seventy-one and Mr. Cousins finally gave him a week's pay and told him not to come back. The old man now sat in his cellar, staring at the wall, and sometimes he wished he were in Heaven with Racy.

Gordon tried to rouse the old man from his mood. You'll live to be a hundred, Gramper. O God! How I hate to see him crumble and waste away. A strong, firm man once lived in that shell; a man who knew passion and caresses and who hammered heroically at the rock ramparts of the world; but now he lives feebly and stares at a cellar wall. Racy, oh, Racy! When the trumpet sounds and God sends for Gramper, come to him, my mother, and lead him through the Gate. His feet are tired and he might stumble and fall. Granner's angels, Granner's seraphim and cherubim, must not laugh if he stumbles and falls. Poor old feet and dim eyes.

"Never mind losing your job, Gramper. I've had a two-dollar raise and pretty soon I'll begin writing."

Pretty soon, hell! What I'll have to do is to cut out so much drinking. How can I drink, spending money for booze, when Gramper sits and stares at a wall? At a wall and at memory. O Grave, where is thy victory? I'll tell you, Grave, you cowardly man-eater! I'll tell you where your victory is. Right where Racy lies and right where Gramper sits. O Death, where is thy sting? I'll tell you, Death, you stinking wasp! Here's your sting. Here! Right in my heart.

II

Gordon had had nine months of the bells, and sorrow stagnated like bilge water in the hull of his heart. Sorrow for Gramper, sorrow for Racy, sorrow because of his longing for Nada. . . . Nada, what did your eyes say? What was the dead language they tried to speak as I went through your door?

Nine months of bells. If I had been a woman, I should have conceived and have become pregnant with bells. Nine months—by this time I should have delivered a bell-child, a cow-bell, one to be hung about the throat and flapping against the brisket of a cow that feeds on mountain grass beneath the dancing aspens. . . .

Gordon hadn't seen Nada in nine months. He would have attended a matinée of the stock company in which she had been playing, and once he had started thither; but at the box office he lost heart. He was frustrated by a belief that he could not sit in the theater with Nada there on the stage before him. The time he hesitated at the box office, he saw her picture in the lobby; Nada in the arms of an actor who bent above her. He walked away, hand-in-hand with timidity and frustration, twin brothers that crowded close to him, one on either side, Timidity pressing him flat on the left and Frustration pressing him flat on the right, like slices of bread clinging to the meat of a sandwich.

That night Gordon asked Scotty, foreman of the signal ring, for two hours off and went across the street to a saloon where he bought drink after drink of whisky. Through the small bottom of each glass, he saw as in a telescope the evasive, taunting figure of Nada. He went to a telephone at 1 o'clock in the morning and called her number. A butler didn't want to disturb Miss Halpin. But damn it, this is important! This is Gordon Dole.... Thank you, sir, I'll see.

Whisky in Gordon's veins and Nada in his ears. Her voice.... It's late, Gordon. Is something wrong? ... Plenty wrong. The world's wrong and I'm wrong. I must see you.... But not to-night, Gordon. Surely it can wait.... It can wait until to-morrow night, Nada, but I must see you, for I.... Mother is having some people in for bridge to-morrow night.... I don't give a damn, I've got to see you or die! ... You talk so strange, Gordon. Something is the matter with you.... Are you mad at me, Nada? ... No, I'm not mad; just a little confused.... Then why aren't you mad, Nada? ... Come to-morrow night to the theater, after the show and I'll see you.... Where shall I meet you, Nada? ... Come to Mrs. Mathers' dressing room, Gordon. ... Well, Nada, I'll ... Damn it! She's hung up. Tried to stall me off with her mother's bridge, didn't she? She can't stall me off.

"Here, bartender, give me another drink. Rye."

Back to the basement of the bells—drunk. I wish I could see that clock. Which is the minute hand and which is the hour hand? Hands! Hands! Go to hell, hands. I'll sleep it off here in the battery room until my time comes.

Gordon lay on the floor beside a motor, removing a tarpaulin from the motor and putting the covering about himself. Go on and catch your death of cold, motor. Gordon takes your blanket for himself. I won't share the blanket with you, motor, but if you'd turn into a woman, motor, I'd share it with you.... Dizzy, drunken sleep and then a call from Scotty, the foreman.

"Pull yourself together, Dole.... Say, you're drunk! What you been drinking, hey?"

"Sarsprilla, you God damned old pussyfoot! What'd you think I'd drink? Carbolic acid?"

"You go on home. I ought to fire you. Don't stop by the way or I will fire you!"

Gordon reached home and went noisily upstairs at three o'clock in the morning but Martha did not awaken. Hiram did and he caught Gordon who was sinking under the closeness of the indoors and undressed him tenderly.

"I'm glad Racy didn't live to see her kid like this."

III

GORDON didn't know the procedure in calling on an actress and felt awkward at the stage door. He was shaky from

his drunkenness of last night and his eyes were blinky
and shot with red filaments. As the doorman went to
Nada's dressing room, Gordon studied the flimsy realities
of backstage. He thought of his views of harlot-houses from
the kitchen side when he was a grocer boy. Was the stage
a courtesan, too? Paint and make-believe and simulation
for those who paid for a night of illusion? He looked at the
bare, stark mechanisms, with their ropes and rolls and drops
and sets. Here the real theater was opened to him, just as a
beautiful body is opened on an operating table, revealing
beneath the skin the organic engines of life, throbbing in
homeliness and weeping with blood.

The doorman showed Gordon the dressing room. What
would she say or do? There she was now, sitting with her
back to a mirror, beneath which was a shelf on which were
pots and puffs and grease sticks and a rabbit's foot. Granner
held rabbits' feet while she clubbed them to death for
market. A beautiful actress held a rabbit's foot against her
oval face. Gordon wished his lips were rabbits' feet to be
dabbed against skin of pale velvet. Nada rose and smiled.

"I'm glad to see you, Gordon." She held her hand to
him and he sat facing her, madly wondering why he was
thinking of his bicycle. Should I have brought it through
the stage door? Well, perhaps it will be safe in the alley
against the wall. Am I losing my reason? Certainly you
are.

"And I'm glad to see you, Nada." I should have taken
a drink, two drinks before I came, but I didn't want her
to smell a whisky breath. I'll have a couple of shots after

I've left her. I'm getting to be a secret drinker. . . . Gordon felt as wooden as a hobby-horse. . . . Rock, rock, rockety rock, hobby-horse Gordon. Rock and squeak out something, even though it's only an oaken whinny. Say something, dumb hobby-horse, for Nada is looking at you. Nada is a sacred vessel.

"Sorry I bothered you, Nada." You're a damned liar, Gordon, you know you are. Why do you tell lies? "I had something on my mind."

"Yes?"

"I waited as long as I could." I hope nobody steals my bicycle. Shouldn't have left it against the wall. My bicycle. . . .

"Aren't you well, Gordon?"

He ignored the question, standing up and then beginning to pace the small dressing room. Then he faced her, his lips twitching and his hands clenched. If only someone with a stick could beat the cramp out of his heart as he beat the cramp out of Gramper's leg.

"It's about that kiss, Nada. It wasn't fair of me to do that, because I knew that Ralph loved you; that Ralph wanted to marry you. . . . It was a sneaking thing to do."

"Forget it, Gordon."

"But I can't forget and I don't want to forget, ever." He was speaking burningly. "I kissed you because I loved you. I loved you then and I love you now, Nada. I love you. My God, Nada, I am empty without you. . . . That makes me twice as rotten as the kiss did, doesn't it?"

There! I've done it. Now for the big turndown. Out

the window you must go. . . . You must go. James, my hat and coat! How critical and how calm her eyes are; eyes of jade green that hold a tremendous mystery in them. Here, have I told her after all that I love her, or was I just thinking it and not saying it?

"I said I love you, Nada."

"That's what you said, Gordon, but I'm just wondering."

"What?"

"If it isn't yourself you love when you make love."

This is a pretty situation! She is going to read me some lines from a play. "That's hardly fair. I've been sick about you since that night nine months ago. You asked me if I had been well. I haven't. Inside the heart, I mean. Bells pound through my head all night and your face is in my heart, hiding from the clamor of the bells. I love you and only you, Nada. I can love no one else. I must have your love or die."

Nada motioned to a chair. "Here, sit down and I'll tell you something, for I may as well. I shan't be demonstrative about it and I don't want you to be demonstrative, either. I am leaving here the day after to-morrow for New York."

"You . . . going? . . . Why? . . ."

"Yes, going. I'm not going to marry Ralph, if that's any consolation to you." She paused. "I'm not going to marry anyone, ever . . . if I can help it, and I think I can."

"You would if you loved someone."

"No, I wouldn't. I have ambition, Gordon, that takes the place of love."

"Nothing can take the place of love."

"Then let's say I'm the exception, for I'm ambitious. I've signed up with a New York production. It's a small part, but I'll be heard from."

"I hate to see you go, Nada. Maybe it won't bring you the happiness you think."

"Who said I was looking for happiness? I am looking for success." Gordon didn't say anything but sat there with his head lowered and his hands clasped. "I'll tell you frankly that when I was in High School I loved you secretly; yes, almost madly."

"I wish I had known."

"Never mind that. I used to see you in the football games and at the track meets and I used to watch your body flash along the lane and I used to breathe heavily as you breathed after the dashes. All that is gone. You were so strange, so indifferent . . . well, maybe you weren't to Elizabeth Wells."

"I loved you then, Nada, I swear I did."

"You didn't seem to, but let's not drag in the past."

"If we could have those years back again. . . ."

"Don't whine. Every old beggar in the street goes about speaking with his lips for money but calling with his heart for yesterday. . . . Let's be different. I'm merely telling you this. . . . Oh, I don't know why. Maybe for an instant I, too, wished for yesterday. . . ."

"Nada! Nada! I love . . ." he was rising as though to place his arms about her.

"It cannot be. I tell you it cannot be, Gordon. When

you came back that day and kissed me, I was rather startled. I was amazed at the change in you but more amazed by the fact that I was able to feel no temptation in your direction. I had suddenly grown up and I had learned to keep my feelings where they should have been and where they always will be."

"Won't you wait for me?"

"Good-by, Gordon. I wait for no one. Love isn't going to mock me and make me put out the eyes of ambition. Homer and Milton could sing in the dark, but I can't. I haven't stature enough."

"Is this good-by for always?"

"In all probability. I hope you succeed. . . . I know you will."

Well, anyway she had loved him. Yes, and he might have found a sack of diamonds in the alley; but he hadn't found either love or diamonds. What in hell was the matter with Fate? Fate has butter fingers. Fate can't catch hold of the right threads, and the wrong puppets dance on snarled strings. Fate is the Queen of the Might-Have-Beens.

"No matter how many years go by, Nada, I'll always love you, dream of you. You won't wait, but I shall. Even if it breaks my body and my soul, I'll wait and long for you."

"Gordon, you have one of the brightest minds I've ever known. You can do things if you will. Why don't you do them instead of thinking about doing them? You'll turn into sentimental putty if you don't."

"Maybe you'll hear from me, too, some day. I love you, but I'm too proud to crawl at your feet."

"I'd despise you if you did crawl."

"Well, I'll not crawl. Good-by, Nada."

If he had turned.... He reached the exit and looked for his bicycle and found it on the cobblestones, lying flat; the rims smashed and the handlebars twisted. Apparently a wagon had run over it and he surveyed the once valiant frame of robin's-egg blue and then he lifted his chin, turned his back on his beloved wheel and walked to the basement of the bells. He stopped at a saloon for three straight rye whiskies and didn't bother with water chasers. He'd turn to putty, eh? Yes, putty flavored with rye!

IV

GRAMPER in bed, sick, and in Granner's bed, too! His first visit there in decades—and his last, the doctor feared.

The old man was glad that Gordon stayed beside him. You'd better go to work, Granner said, but Gordon declared he wouldn't leave Gramper, job or no job. He went to a corner store and called old Scotty, the foreman. Scotty thought Gordon was drunk again, but Gordon told him to go to hell and to take the job and to put it where he couldn't. Fade out, bells! Bleat and bang against other men's ear-drums and scurry into their brains like rats to gnaw away their sanity. Try to be a pied piper, Scotty, and see if you can get those rats out of their brains. But you can't. No. I'm never coming back, for I'm firing myself, see?

Old William wanted to go to his cellar, but the doctor

said he wouldn't think of permitting it and then went on
to another patient. Hiram and Gordon took turns sitting
beside Gramper while Granner stayed in the dining room,
reading the Gospel of St. John. "There is a lad here which
hath five barley loaves and two small fishes: but what are
they among so many?"

"Gordie." Old William's voice was faint.

"Yes, Gramper."

"Will you take me to the cellar? That's where I feel
most comfortable."

"The doctor said not to."

"What the hell difference does it make where a man
dies if he's a goner anyway? You ain't turned against me,
too?"

Gordon wrapped the old man in blankets and a quilt
and carried him downstairs. How wispy and frail he was!
Just a few shanks of bone with a furred knob for a head;
the bones covered by parchment. Gordon laid Gramper
tenderly on the cellar bunk and lighted a miner's candle.

"I feel better already, Gordie."

Granner, who had viewed this scene skeptically, didn't
attempt to interfere, but she hastened to Hiram's room and
told him about it. When Hiram went to the cellar, Gordon
had a finger to his lips. "Gramper's asleep now."

"That was a hell of a fool trick," Hiram whispered.
"But I guess he oughtn't to be disturbed now. . . . Gordon,
you got to cut out booze because it's making you dippy."

When Gramper awakened an hour later he took some
water and grew brighter than he had been. The cramps

were gone and the pain in his chest was dull; only a heavy feeling was there, he said, like an anvil pressing his lungs.

"If I see Racy," he said, "I'm going to tell her what a fine son she has."

He went to sleep again, and he never awakened.

V

GRANNER moaned and explained to Dr. Merritt, her pastor, that she and William had been happily married for fifty years. He consoled Martha, pointing out that all shall rise again as in life to shout praises before the Mercy Seat.

Two days after the funeral, Gordon stopped Granner in the act of selling the array of mining implements to a junk dealer. She said she couldn't see for the life of her why Gordie wanted to keep those rusty old tools.

Chapter Nine

I

THE Woodmen of the World paid one thousand dollars to Granner for the death of William Dole. With it she was able to meet the interest on the mortgage of their home; pay the feed bills for her rabbits and chickens; install a white enameled bathtub; buy a new Axminster carpet for the parlor, and make a contribution to the church. Granner bought Gordon a blue serge suit, double-breasted, some shoes and a gray felt hat which he turned down on the right side to appear rakish.

Hiram laid the new carpet in the parlor, grunting with the knob of a stretcher against his middle and crawling about, his mouth teeming with tacks. The old Wilton parlor carpet was taken to the clothes line to be beaten with wire loops and was then placed in the dining room. The old dining room carpet, worn down to its jute backing by a decade of boarding house stampede, was cut and laid in Gordon's room. He felt a close comradeship with this carpet, for he believed it still held the imprint of Racy's feet. Gordon's attitude toward things that he liked, no matter how inanimate they were, was personal. He gave such objects names. For example, he called his bed "Cleopatra," but to be sure, he let no one know of this idiosyncrasy; he didn't want to be accounted a freak.

As the thousand-dollar windfall slipped from the aging fingers of Martha, she wished Gordon would hurry up and get a job. It was a mystery to her why he had quit such a good one as the signal ring position. She loved Gordie, but he was beginning to get under her feet. Hiram loved him, too, but Gordon was getting over Hiram's head, what with his far-away look, his mooning about and his talking to himself in his room. Granner had called Hiram's attention to Gordon's self-talks. Together they listened one Sunday morning.

"I wonder what Nada is doing in New York? I wonder what anybody does there? It must be a tremendous thing to go there and be a part of Life. I shall go there some day and I shall become a part of Life."

Granner looked at Hiram blankly. "Hurry up, Gordie, and get ready for church."

Hiram was amazed to hear Gordon say: "Hurry up, Gordie, and get ready for Life."

II

GRANNER, who reduced everything except God to terms of herself, was—as a good woman—the world's great common denominator. What appeared to her to be virtue, she knew was virtue for everyone, and her conception of vice was what vice surely must be. There could be no compromise, no elasticity of interpretation. Granner was a moral bureau of standards.

Gordon, who subscribed to a theory of rhythms, thought of pleasure as harmony and of pain as discord, and he rebelled against frigidity and rigidity. Granner's world was frost-bitten and passionless. Gordon's world—even though he was compelled to create it himself, for himself—was warm, tolerant and resilient. His world looked to him like a bubble stuffed with rainbows, but it was too brave a bubble to be ruptured. His world was a woman's life-sustaining breast, as smooth as softly heated white wax—a breast with dual powers, capable of passion or of peace. Passion in Gordon's world was rhythm at full gallop, while peace was rhythm of starlight sleeping on the trees.

Where will I find completion? Gordon asked himself. It cannot be in a mother, for I have lost her, and still I want the mother love. Will my pathway take me to a wife, to a mistress or to a hermitage? Nada, you could tell me, if only you would—not with your words, but, God forgive me! with your glamorous, lovely body. Yes, Nada would be fruition, completion, the perfect rhythm; but to reach her I must forge mighty imaginings on the anvil of my soul. Yet if I do forge them, who will understand unless I am paid for them? In Heaven you are given a golden harp, free; but on earth you must sweat and groan and be lashed to a wheel to earn a tin whistle. Even then it may be taken from you—the tin whistle—for of such is the Kingdom of Man. Yet I must enter Life, going into the Kingdom of

Man, meeting the gods of greed, envy and malice and I must not cry out. Secretly I shall create within myself my own world and creep thither to hide until my wounds heal. Nada, what a wound you made upon my heart. . . .

"I'm going to get a job on a newspaper," Gordon said to Granner.

"Does it pay well?"

"It does if you have the right stuff in you."

Granner was dubious. Hadn't Gordon better go back to the signal-catching business? No, he would rather be a dog-catcher. He was going to be a newspaper writer, and that was that.

"I don't know much about this newspaper business," Uncle Hiram said. He thought newspapers were something you found on your doorstep when you came home from the butcher shop. How they were made, he didn't know, and what's more, he didn't give a damn, so long as they published sports results copiously and accurately. "But I hope you get busy soon, because Maw's getting old and we got to save our home."

Blair Christensen was enthusiastic about Gordon's plan. "A fellow like you can't miss. Maybe you can put something in the paper about a new invention I got."

"Not pants hangers?"

"No, it's something for the women this time; a hollow rolling pin that holds a cooking knife, a fork, a can opener, a grater and book of recipes. I call this utensil 'Woman's Best Friend.' " Blair shook hands with Gordon and when

Gordon took away his hand there was a ten-dollar gold piece in it.

Gordon in his new clothes and with the ten-dollar gold piece in his pocket began an offensive on the journalistic entrenchments of the town. He had carried papers years ago for *The Fairmount Clarion* and he believed he had more than ordinary insight into the profession. He called on his old circulation manager, who couldn't for the life of him remember Gordon, but who told him to go to the third floor and ask for the City Editor. Gordon started out of the mail room as the press began to turn and as he reached the steps leading to the editorial section, he thought the printing monster was hissing at him.

III

GORDON had felt large and strong-corded when he entered the slovenly City Room of *The Clarion;* but as he sat, seemingly through a clockful of afternoons, waiting for a chance to get to the pale, fidgety man at the city desk, he felt as if he had been punctured. He felt as though he were shrinking. The arm of an ancient and scarred oak bench on which he waited began to grow beneath his elbow until it was a high wall. Then, after men had hurried to and from the desk with important though worried expressions, the city editor himself came to the bench and stood there. His eyes were metal. Swiftly-incising razors that cut slits through Gordon's clothing, through Gordon's chest and into Gordon's vitals, exploring him inside. The city editor had a strong tobacco breath on which inquisitive phrases sailed like fretful kites.

"Can you use a typewriter?"

Gordon hesitated. All he knew about typewriters was that they usually were black and that they made rapid, knocking noises with the zing of a bell every so often; a bell sound that would mean Number One in the basement of the bells. Go ahead and lie, Gordon. If it's a big enough lie, they'll publish it on the front page.

"I do fairly well on a typewriter."

"College man?"

"Yes. I went to State College."

The editor, whose name was Dave Morgan, hemmed and hummed and played with a wrinkle in his vest. "Well, you can start in to-morrow afternoon. One o'clock. This is a morning paper."

"Thank you." Gordon walked past a copy desk where men were bent over enough paper to feed a valley full of goats for a month. Nobody paid the least attention to him, but he believed they would pay attention to him some day. He'd show them and he'd show Nada, too. Just wait!

IV

WHEN Gordon reached his home he found Granner setting a rat-trap in the rabbit house. Hiram was in the kitchen, washing up after the day's work. Come into the house, Granner, and hear the big news. Turn off the hot water faucet, Uncle Hiram, and hear the wonderful news. Now they'll know that dreams pay. Speak up, dreams, and make a noise like nickels in a blind man's cup.

"Well, I got a job on *The Clarion* and I'm to start to-morrow."

"A printer, dearie?"

"No, Granner; a writer."

Hiram couldn't understand it, but he guessed it was better than sitting under the mulberry tree in the back yard, reading funny kinds of books. "What's the pay?"

"I guess I don't get any pay for a while." Gordon's tongue groped. "You see you have to start in for nothing when you haven't had experience."

Uncle Hiram didn't say a thing. He tucked in his lips until his mouth became a cynical crevice, shook his head and walked back to the sink and turned on the hot water faucet.

"There isn't much sense to that, is there?" Granner looked at Gordon disapprovingly. "Why quit a good job at twelve a week and go to work for nothing a week?"

As Gordon went to his room, he could hear Uncle Hiram grumbling beneath a facial lather and he knew that the creaking of the kitchen floor beneath Granner's feet was an echo of the doubt in her heart. He opened a drawer and took out the picture of the graduating class in which Nada stood far over to one side from where he stood and he wondered if they always would stand so far apart.

V

GORDON spread Blair's ten-dollar gift over three weeks of unrewarded toil, using it for carfare, rental of a typewriter on which he practiced dutifully at home and for an occasional glass of beer which entitled him to free lunch. Editor Morgan then gave Gordon a salary of six dollars a week and this evidence of money made his sin in quitting the basement of the bells only half as onerous to Granner as it had been at the beginning.

Joe Gates, the managing editor, was a cranky old loon, one of the reporters told Gordon. Keep away from him because he's as mean as hell and will fire you if he doesn't like the color of your tie. He never laughed in his life, the reporter added, except once and that was when his wife broke her leg. In studying Gates, Gordon wondered if the old man was such a sprig of poison ivy after all. Gordon was interested in persons who were cried down; morbidly drawn to them, just as he had been drawn to his own father when Granner got out the family pile driver.

Joe Gates drank heavily but knew how to retain, being a two-bottle man. He roared like a cyclone, blood gorging his neck and face in apoplectic blushes whenever a mistake crept into a headline or a name was misspelled in the body of a story. He had a close-cropped gray mustache and an enormous, bald head on a thick neck. When he gave written orders to subordinates, he did it by passing slips of paper held by long shears. His voice was high and squeaky, as though his larynx needed oil, but he had worked in an office with Eugene Field and came of a brilliant school of journalists.

One day when Gordon was thinking how little six dollars a week was in terms of food, clothing and beer, he saw old Joe pouring water in a pan on his window sill. Then Joe crumbled bread and birds flew down to eat and drink as Gates watched them. Gordon was deeply stirred by this act and wrote an article on birds and what it means to come out of the sky to a world of winter white. If there were no crumbs for them, birds became cynics; but if they found food and drink, the birds would maintain a stout belief in God and a profound faith in man. Gordon slipped the story casually to the city desk and then pretended to read a newspaper, but he was watching City Editor Morgan, hoping he would find merit in his first self-appointed work.

He had to wait a long time before Morgan picked up the bird story and when the editor looked at it wonderingly and appeared pained, disgusted, Gordon crumpled up inside. Then, as Morgan tossed the bird story to the high wicker wastebasket, Gordon thought his heart had been tossed there, too. He wondered how Morgan could get up so coldly, lighting a cigarette, playing with a wrinkle in his vest and then saunter out to lunch without looking his way.

Gordon would do something about this, no matter what happened to him. He went to the wastebasket and got his bird story and reread it. He wanted to quit, but what would Nada say if she thought him a quitter? He'd be turning to putty if he quit—that would be her feeling. I'll never quit, Nada. I'll die first, because I have pride.

Gordon thought it over and then took his story to Bill Deering on the copy desk and handed it to Bill as though he had been asked to do so. Bill put a head on it and sent it up to the composing room, there to be set in type. The story appeared in the paper after Morgan had gone home.

Next day old Joe Gates came from his room, his rusty larynx creaking while the whole office waited for the czar to issue a ukase. "Who wrote that story?" Old Joe pointed with his long shears to the article on birds and Dave Morgan looked as though he were ready to tender a resignation. Morgan gulped and pointed to Gordon. "Come into my office, young man." Gordon went in. "How much salary you getting, son?"

"Six dollars a week."

"No, you ain't."

"That's what I'm getting."

Gates snipped his long shears. "Don't contradict me. There's too much impudence here; the impudence is almost as bad as the ignorance in this office." Old Joe was sizing up the young man. "From now on you're getting thirty dollars a week, but don't let it go to your head."

"Thank you, Mr. Gates."

"Do you drink?"

Oh, hell! Now he's going to let me down after lifting me up. He's an old harpy after all. Well, I'm getting tired of lies; lies to Granner, lies to Nada, lies to Morgan about the typewriter. Lies! Well, I shan't lie now. "Yes, I drink when I feel like it."

Old Joe grunted. "Feel like havin' one now?"

"I'd just as soon."

"Then we'll go to Finner's and have one. Come on, son, but don't think it will get you anything, this drinking with the managing editor, because it won't!"

The staff wondered how it was that old Joe was walking through the office, chatting with a gangling cub reporter who had written a lousy, maudlin yarn about some damned birds. Joe went to the city desk and said: "Listen, you rum-head, that was a great story about the birds. This rag has been so dull and cheap of late, I can't figure how you'd let anything of beauty get into the paper. Let's have some more of it."

"Yes, Mr. Gates." Morgan played with the vest wrinkle and thought that Gordon must be Joe's illegitimate son at the very least.

VI

I'll show you yet, Nada; I'll come to you all covered with fame; muffled to the eyes with fame. You'll want me then, Nada. God knows I'll always be wanting you. I sleep with my head on my bare arm and make believe my head is on your bare arm. I go to sleep that way, laying traps for dreams of you; baiting my traps with love-thoughts that ride high against the ceiling of the sky to go to you wherever you may be; to you in the City where Life is lived. . . .

Gordon received on the first payday after his phe-
nomenal raise a twenty-dollar gold coin and a ten-dollar
gold coin. He went to Finner's saloon, bought a rye whisky
and asked the bartender to change his gold into small silver.
Then he went to a delicatessen, his pants pockets dragging
lumpily with silver cargo, and began to purchase foods
with gay generosity. He bought long rolls of French bread,
anchovies, stuffed olives, slabs of cheeses and an apple-
shaped cheese from Holland, pickled herring that Granner
liked so well but seldom afforded, German spice cakes,
Danish pastries. . . . It cost him five dollars to do this and
then he started home on a street car and when he got to his
house and entered it, he could hear Granner and Hiram in
the kitchen.

He burst upon his grandmother and his uncle with
Santa Claus gusto and spilled his bundles on the kitchen
table. Now they'd know what a fellow he was! He had said
nothing concerning his unbelievable raise in salary but had
waited for this great moment. The moment was here.

"Just unwrap those things!" he shouted. Uncle Hiram
feared for the worst now—Gordon at last had gone dippy.
Hiram caught the smell of whisky. Too bad. Granner was
working at the twine that girded the bundles and as she
undid the packages silver coins cascaded from them, small
coins that fell in profusion to the oil cloth on the table, to
the floor and some of them on Hiram's sturdy knees. She
was beside herself. A miracle! Had Gordie robbed a bank?

Hiram was glad, of course, that Gordon had made
good; still it made him feel as though he himself were

being shoved out of the picture after all these years of toil and sacrifice; wifeless years and laughless years that leave a man standing like a stag in the zoo. Gordon from now on would be the economic leader of the family, but Gordon was so generous and so hearty about this turn of affairs that Hiram loved him all the more. It was not Gordon's success, the way Gordon put it, but it was our success, our money and our job. Maybe it paid to be a little bit dippy after all.

"Your old Granner is proud of you. Maybe you can save up enough to study for the ministry."

Granner went out to see that the chicken house and rabbit hutches were locked for the night and Gordon saw her raise her starched white apron to her eyes, dabbing beneath her spectacles.

Well, old Granner had done the best she knew how for him. When two or more clocks in a house don't agree, who is to say offhand which is right and which is wrong? One has to wait until one gets the right time from someone who passes by; someone who knows what time it really is.

Ho, there, Son of Jehovah! Is my clock of life slow or fast?

Chapter Ten

I

*G*ORDON'S first year in the newspaper world was one of adventure and he felt that he was fingering the pulse of Life.

Ink smells and paper smells, sourly insinuating. Press sounds and linotype sounds, like the clashing of arms inside a Horse of Troy. Gay sights and sad sights—the newspaper is a sewing machine, running up and down the seams of the day's garments; the pressed side, the dressy side, turned to the world—the seamy side, the rough side, is seen by the men who sew endlessly on the big machine.

The worst news was the best news, Gordon found. The bigger a catastrophe, the more space it commanded on page one, for men liked to shed their little, personal sorrows in the bigger, more devastating sorrows of others. When Mr. Soretail had a fractured clavicle, he was vastly encouraged when he read that Mr. Allclod broke his neck by falling out of his mistress's bed. Infinite cheer one could find in the witch-pot of the press, where the history of twenty-four hours disclosed who shot who's wife and how skeleton babies bit the flaccid breasts of Russian peasants.

As a police reporter, Gordon rode the motor ambulance and he watched the police surgeon ram stomach pumps down the seared throats of acid drinkers. Stretchers and gongs. Hospitals and operating tables. Melancholy harlots with cotton stockings. Negroes crushed by falling scaffolds. Death in the ambulance—how loud death is and how quiet it is; how death can wail and how death can laugh.

Gordon held the hands of dying persons and sometimes their grip was hard to loosen. He would fancy himself the last link these broken souls had with a world that had used them so ill but a world which they seemed reluctant to leave. Once Gordon cried—it was night and he could hide his tears from other reporters that rode in the ambulance—when a girl who was dying from poison fancied that Gordon was her lover, for whose desertion she was paying. Then you still love me? He could not see her face as he leaned over her and whispered that he always had loved her and always would. The ambulance went to the morgue instead of to the county hospital.

Gordon was changed to the courthouse "run" and his salary was raised to thirty-five dollars a week; an unheard of amount for a reporter. When the men at the Press Club learned that he later refused to accept a position as Sunday editor and had threatened to quit before so doing, they were mystified. They asked him why he had turned down such a flattering post, to which he replied: "With few exceptions, editorial chairs are refuges for incompetent newspaper men."

Joe Gates called Gordon to his office. "You've got a sharp tongue, Gordon. Watch out for it and for your impulsiveness." He twirled his scissors. "I rather enjoyed your characterization of editors, though. It's the God's awful truth and we all ought to be in the old men's home."

"I didn't mean you, Joe."

Gates, Dillon, the cartoonist, and Gordon often ate and drank together at Finner's. Gordon hoped to be a two-bottle man like Joe, but he knew he'd have to take a lot of drinking lessons before he advanced to that state. Granner was beginning to realize that Gordon drank, but the fact that he made thirty-five dollars a week and the self-reminder that he was twenty-two, nearly twenty-three years old, led Martha to hold her peace.

There were weeks when Gordon didn't touch liquor. He underwent what he described as ascetic spells and during these spells he abstained from meat. Thoughts of Nada and the uneasy silence that cloaked her life in New York contributed more than any other cause to these ascetic spells. After a certain amount of asceticism, Gordon would declare to himself that he was merely practicing simple negation; that his rhythms had become barnacled, and that he was going about life in the wrong tempo. Then he would descend on the bottle and drink until he was as dizzy as a tumble weed.

II

GORDON tried hard to be true to Nada, although she had given him no hope of achieving her love. To gain her esteem, even, he knew he would have to become little less than the President of the United States. He endeavored to be high-minded in thinking of her, but sometimes in his dreams of Nada he wanted her body and reached for it so desperately that his mental slate was written over with chaotic symbols. He felt that he must apologize to her some day for certain of his dreams.

He had affairs with women on occasion. It was rather hard not to when they came to him with mattresses on their backs; but they didn't count much—just relief.

The society editor of *The Clarion* overwined herself one night and Gordon was assigned to cover the Country Club Ball in her stead. He found himself thoroughly out of his sphere among the fashionable young people of the town that gathered on the ballroom floor. He didn't quite know what to do in asking questions, still he knew that all these folk were publicity hounds, regardless of their indifferent poses in dealing with reporters. He saw one girl who danced splendidly and who impressed him with her fresh and vibrant personality, although he watched her at a distance. While wondering where to begin and whom to tackle for news of the occasion, Gordon kept returning his gaze to the girl. She was young—he judged she was about four years younger than himself—she had vigor, confidence and a sort of maturity about her that attracted him. Gordon recognized the man with whom this girl danced most of the time. He was a chap named Briggs, a son of wealth and prominent in the young polo set. Gordon made up his mind to introduce himself to this girl. Then to his immense relief, he saw Ralph Masters, and singled him out of a group of men going to the smoking room. Ralph looked rather down about something.

"You're quite a guy now," Masters said, shaking hands with Gordon. "Didn't know you went in for the society stuff though."

"I don't. The society editor is indisposed and I am sitting in for a night." Gordon was wondering if Ralph had heard from Nada, but he did not have the courage to ask. Perhaps Ralph sensed Gordon's wonderment, for he said: "Nada has quit writing to me. I guess I wasn't meant for her anyway, and now that she's on the road to success, we're small potatoes for her."

"I suppose so," Gordon said, wishing he could get Nada out of his mind long enough to concentrate on his job. "You mean the engagement is off?"

"There really never was an engagement. I tried hard to make Nada see that marriage would be a fine thing, but she went away talking a bit odd about love. I couldn't make out just what she was driving at. Only she seemed upset about something. She's too damned ambitious, but by God she is the most beautiful creature in the world and I'm pretty blue about the whole mess."

"Well, cheer up, Ralph, and introduce me to that girl in the blue dress. Who is she?"

"Which one? Oh, that one! That's Margery Hamilton, a hell of a swell girl but somewhat prudish. At least she doesn't let the boys get within wrestling distance of her. She's going to marry that Briggs fellow."

"There's something fine about her."

"There's a lot that's fine about her. She's not at all intellectual...."

"Women don't bear babies with their minds, do they?"

Masters looked at Gordon appraisingly. "Say, Gordie, you're not thinking of having a child by her, are you?"

They both laughed. "I've got to get busy, Ralph, so introduce me. No, I'm not thinking of becoming a father just yet, but she certainly has something about her that appeals to me to beat hell."

"You're still the same old guy, Gordie. Well, come on and I'll introduce you, but remember this girl is engaged."

Gordon studied the full-bosomed, handsome Margery as she shook hands with him. He liked her very much when she offered him a dance, saying that her program was filled but that Mr. Briggs wouldn't mind. Mr. Briggs, it seemed, wasn't at all pleased, but he retired to the lawn to smoke and to think of his polo ponies.

"You're a peach to do this," Gordon said. "I'm not gaited to write the puff that's expected of me, so the best I can do for my paper is to fill a column with names. They've got to be spelled right, though. My editor thinks the correct spelling of names is at least six of the Ten Commandments."

"Don't newspaper men ever break the command-ments?"

"Whenever possible." Gordon learned that Margery had a firm, womanly body, as he held his arm about her waist, and her hand, too, was strong and steady as though she knew how to hold life without fearing it. There was something about her that commanded his respect; perhaps the way she danced conveyed this feeling, for whenever he came too close to her, she managed without effort or significant movement to keep him properly spaced.

"We'll have another dance," she said, "and you can sit out part of it to take down names."

"Won't your partner object?"

"I'm afraid we'll have to do our journalistic work whether he objects or not." Gordon sensed she was not strongly in love with this Briggs; in fact, he believed that she did not yet know what love was. Girls like Margery, he thought, were made for motherhood rather than for romance, and he felt decent and uplifted when he talked to her. Mr. Briggs came in and in an aside with Margery objected to her going into the newspaper business to such a wide extent; but he finally agreed to take a long walk about the club grounds.

"I'd like awfully much to call you by telephone some time to thank you for your help."

"Can't you thank me now?"

"It would be much more satisfying if I could hear your voice again."

Margery seemed thoughtful and Gordon knew she was weighing the propriety of the proposed call. She was handsome, he told himself; not beautiful as Nada was beautiful and not seductive, but handsome with her deep blue eyes and her medium brown hair.

"You may call me," she said at length. "Now I guess I'll have to go back to my partner. I've enjoyed our dances very much, Mr. Dole."

"Gordon's the name. Good-by, Margery."

"Good-by, Gordon."

Mr. Briggs told Margery she should be more careful in being so kind-hearted; that this Dole was said to be a heavy drinker and that his morals were as loose as an Eskimo's trousers.

III

WHEN Gordon felt mad impulses to escape—he didn't know what it was he wanted to escape from—he would disappear from home and from his work for two to four days at a time. Not often. About every two months.

No one knew where it was he went and the office staff wondered how he got away with it; but Joe Gates permitted it. During his employment on *The Clarion,* Gordon was driven hard, sworn at and pressed from every angle by old Joe; but all the pressure was exerted during work hours. In private old Joe advised Gordon, saw his viewpoint and often spoke to the young man in a fatherly manner. Gordon understood from this that Gates was trying to mold him, to develop him, and that was why Gates stormed at him in the office, picking him to pieces and teaching him the fundamentals of the craft.

They were oiling their throats with rye at Finner's one evening. "You're too damned impulsive, Gordon. You say and do things too quickly. I know it is spirit and pride, but you've got to hold in at the right times and let out at the right times."

Gordon told the bartender that this one was on him. He tossed off his drink. "Listen, Joe, a man can't put Westinghouse brakes on his soul. You think I'm going to amount to something, don't you?"

"With proper self-restraint, there's no telling where you'll go, son."

"Then listen. Confidentially, I'll never amount to a good God damn, because I've got a world that's all my own. It suits me and I'm going to live in that world and nobody else will be in that world to applaud or to censure. Do you follow me?"

"I wish you could learn either to carry your liquor better or give up drinking entirely, for you sometimes talk like a damned fool."

"In my world the fool will be a wise man and the wise man a fool."

"You're drunk."

"I'm not any such thing. I'm sane and clear."

"Listen, Gordie, I'm awfully concerned with your future. You remind me of the greatest fellow I ever knew —Gene Field—only he was of sweeter clay, and that's why I'm trying to get you wise to yourself. Of course Field loved children...."

"Well, God damn it! Who said I don't love children? I'm crazy about them."

"Then you'd better settle down and get married. Don't

you know any nice girl? It might be the making of you. Maybe a kid or two would get random notions out of your head."

Gordon thought of Margery and determined to call her up...some day, not to-night. Then he thought of Nada and wished he could call her up. Drunk or sober, he wished he could yell into the telephone: "You'll want me yet, damn you! Go ahead and wrestle with Success, old Whoremaster Success! Wrap him 'round and 'round with thighs and kisses, and then wake up to find that your lover is pock-marked, pot-bellied and impotent."

Gordon went on a spree that lasted three days. The one person who knew where he had disappeared was Madam Francis, who operated a parlor house. She had known Gordon when he was a youngster carrying groceries for Cousins' store. She had met him again when he was a police reporter and when she had gone to the station to give bail for one of her prostitutes. Madam Francis had a great deal of mother in her for Gordon. He never touched any of the girls in her house and he didn't want to touch them. She wouldn't have let him touch them if he had wanted to do so.

She took care of him and nursed him through his drunks, and when he sobered, they had long talks and she permitted him to drink a little champagne as a pick-me-up when he left the parlor house. The Madam saw him only when he was escaping. What is it, Gordon, that you wish to escape from? From yourself, perhaps? You shouldn't leave yourself—it's unclubby.

Chapter Eleven

I

*I*N 1913, while Gordon was writing sports news and a column of sports comment, he received from *The New York Morning Star* an invitation to join its staff. Old Joe Gates said he had anticipated losing Gordon but assured him he wouldn't stand in his way.

It was a flattering offer that promised to open the gates of a great and mysterious city to a provincial young journalist, but Gordon didn't accept the call. He had dreamed of it and he had longed for it; but when the time came it found him afraid. He was afraid of the big bully whose name was Metropolis. He tried to make believe that it was because Granner was going on seventy-three; that he didn't want to run out on Uncle Hiram, who was getting gray and defeated. He wrestled with his problem, interjecting excuses for his lack of aggression. I mustn't throw Granner and Uncle Hiram down.... Yes, Yellow-belly, you are afraid and you don't want to get drowned in the Big Place! You can wade tall and handsomely in this shallow puddle of Fairmount with its two hundred and fifty thousand neighbors, but you'd sink and splutter and strangle in the big sea of millions of strangers. Quit kidding yourself, Gordon....O Nada, come look at him! Come look at old Afraid-of-the-Mob! He wished he could turn off consciousness as one does a water faucet when a tub runs over.

The men at the Press Club envied Gordon this great chance. They told him New York was the only real place in the world; that all other towns were echoes; that everything west of Broadway was just sand in the spinach. Harry McGorman, who once had worked fleetingly on *The Star,* said that paper was the most go-getting sheet in the Big Town and that its owner, John G. Ward, was easily the Lord Northcliffe of America. Gordon should jump at the chance. He said he'd rather play a game of poker than sit in the Club hearing all this rumpus; so, instead of girding for metropolitan combat, he stayed up all night at cards and had the same luck Gramper had had when he bet on Bryan to win the presidential election.

He went home in daylight, sick at the stomach and half vertigoed with rye whisky. He slumped on the bed that he called Cleopatra and felt chilled, although the January morning was unseasonably mild. The stench of a smoldering cigarette butt became offensive to him and the metallic purring of a street car's wheels on far-away rails droned through his open window. He heard Granner plopping in slippered feet along the hallway and saw her open his door and stand there, holding her spectacles in one hand. The temples of the spectacles stood up from her palm like the antennæ of a large insect. It made him think of men and women as insects. As Granner closed the door, fancying her grandson asleep, she was startled to hear him say: "We're all gnats—gnats singing to a lamp called Life."

Then Gordon stumbled into a distraught slumber and dreamed of a topsy-turvy land, where clocks moved backward; where horses were whipping their drivers—and a sphinx found a voice in this incongruous phantasy, saying: "Nada is a sacred vessel."

II

IN the sports field, Gordon found some relief from the puzzles that challenged him. There was an unconventional freedom in the movements of athletes that didn't bear down on him. Most of the muscle-benders, the professionals, were limited mentally, but they were sincere in their way and not a few of the managers of prize fighters were sharp and nimble-brained. Gordon wrote letters for some of the visiting pugilists when they needed fancy-wording to impress their women friends and in return they boxed with him in private. He thought them considerate when they did not try to knock his head loose from his neck and he wished that he was as courageous spiritually as he was physically, for one needed plenty of spirit before one could go to a menacing New York.

Gordon refereed several prize fights in Fairmount and thought himself an excellent arbiter. In later years he laughed about it and wondered how he had done it, but now he enjoyed the nearness to the clash and he liked to move about swiftly, watching well-trained bodies sway and thrust in graceful, though sometimes brutal, rhythms. The sweaty symphonies gave him a play outlet that had been denied him in Granner's sanctified shrine.

One experience in the ring left a scar on Gordon's psyche that never was wholly effaced. A young Mexican named Juarez Kid was fighting Pal Bratton, an old-timer, and Gordon was third man. The boxers were middle-weights. Much money had been wagered on the Kid, who was looked on as a coming champion. The bout was held in the Fairmount Armory, where several thousands gathered in anticipation of seeing an unusual contest between promising youth and crafty experience.

It was mid-summer and the powerful ring lights added to the heat of the battlefield as the fighters and their principal seconds came to the center of the ring for instructions. Gordon cast a sly, satisfied glance toward the press row, where he had placed Joe Gates and Uncle Hiram as his guests. Apparently they were hitting it off fine together, for they were sharing a flask of liquor as the boxers squared off.

The bell opening the first round brought the Juarez Kid gliding swiftly from his corner, his left hand darting like a copper serpent. He didn't wait to fiddle about, pecking for an opening, but set to work with slashing rapidity, springing in and out, dancing on the balls of his feet like a ballet master. The flurry of his gloved hands was amazingly graceful, and for a time there was such silence that only the crackling of small resin lumps on the canvas beneath elk-hide soles, the short breaths of the fighters and the plopping of leather was heard. Seven snaky jabs without a return on his part brought blood to Bratton's ring-worn lips. The red drops began to trickle like lazy rubies down his beard-blue chin.

The old-timer found the pace hot and heavy. A roll of fat spilling above his trunks showed that even severe training could not erase the evidences of his athletic age. But he was cool, sneeringly cool, taking the punishment like the campaigner he was, and he was dangerous. Anyone with a punch such as he owned was dangerous. Those who had wagered at short money on him consoled themselves with the recollection that Bratton never had been a fancy ringster.

The Juarez Kid slipped punches, blocked, ducked and feinted with precision and speed. Toward the close of the first round, and with the crowd now urging the young phenomenon to further effort, the Kid seemed to lose his head. He suddenly elected to step in and slug with the puffy-lipped, grim old warrior. Less than twenty seconds before the bell, Bratton, his mouth twisted like a cruller and his eyes slitted and squinting, found an opening. His left hand moved in a short, springy arc. It found the Kid's jaw, between chin and ear lobe. The Mexican dropped like a heavy book from a high shelf and with much the same sound. First he was on his side, his knees drawn almost to his chest. Then he turned on his back, his eyes staring widely. His gloves flipped against the canvas. Then he half-rolled to his knees at the count of eight. The count of nine found him coming up on sheer instinct and just as he lumbered to his feet the bell rang. The Armory was bulged by the lusting roar of the crowd.

Gordon went to the Mexican's corner and looked critically at the youngster, speaking to him and hearing him mumble that he was all right. The Kid's seconds told Gordon not to worry; that it was a lucky punch; that the Kid would come out strong after the minute's respite.

"Well, be sure he is all right," Gordon told his handlers. "Don't let him get injured. It isn't worth it."

The Mexican weathered the second round, but he clinched and stalled a lot. He started the third round a bit fresher than he had the second, but after two minutes of that round had gone Bratton got in another left that downed the Kid. He rose and was battered down again, this time with a crushing right cross to the jaw. He again rose and clinched desperately, blindly. Gordon had to go between the men to pry them apart. The crowd was calling for a knockout and Bratton weaved about, evading the Kid's groping embrace and setting himself for the pole-ax blow that would bring victory. Gordon kept peering into the Mexican's eyes. They were glazed and sightless. He was badly hurt. The bell rang and Gordon helped the boy to his corner where the seconds slapped him sharply about the back and one of them sprayed his chest with mouthfuls of water like a Chinaman wets laundry. They put a sponge on the nape of his neck and gave him a drink of whisky which drooled from his lips.

"You shouldn't let him come out," Gordon told the chief second.

"The hell we won't! You mind your own business."

"That's what I will do if I see he isn't fit to continue."

"If you stop this fight there'll be a riot."

When the Mexican shuffled out for the fourth, his legs were wobbly and he wasn't on his toes. The boy who had begun the battle like a bronze poem of rare beauty now was a ragged bit of doggerel verse. His eyes were filmed and he couldn't seem to locate his opponent. His arms dropped limply, leaving his jaw protected only by a hunched shoulder.

Gordon decided to wait no longer. He stepped between the men and raised Bratton's hand.

The crowd began to hiss and boo. There was a welter of catcalls. "Burn a rag!" someone shouted above the din. "Fake! Fake!" "You must have bet on Bratton!" The cries toppled into Gordon's brain like red hot rivets in a steel worker's bucket. He remembered looking toward his uncle and toward old Joe, as though to signal to them that he wasn't a crook; that he had done his duty. He saw Hiram rise to punch a yowling fight fan in the nose, and he saw dimly the figure of pudgy Joe Gates, who shook hands with Hiram and passed him the flask.

Police fought through the crowds that jammed the aisles and surrounded the ring. Gordon stood there, smiling defiantly, as the Mexican was carried from the ring to his dressing room. The promoter of the fight crawled clumsily through the ropes and began to argue with Gordon.

"To hell with you, too!" Gordon said. "I did what was right. To hell with this crowd; the bloodthirsty bastards!"

Gordon went to the Mexican's dressing room, refusing a police escort and walking boldly through groups of men who stood staring at him. Let them hiss; when men turn into snakes or geese, they've got to hiss or blow up.

The Juarez Kid was sitting on a rubbing board as Gordon entered. Too bad they had pushed this boy ahead so fast. He asked the Kid how he felt, but he got no reply. The boy just sat there, humped over, the bandages still on his knuckles and his hands hanging limply over his loins.

"Here, somebody!" Gordon called. "Get this boy on his back and rub him gently. Don't let him sit here like this! If he had won, you bastards would be swarming all over him, slapping his back and telling him how great he was."

He found a water bottle and a sponge and told the Kid to take it easy. Then he put his hands on the Mexican's drooped shoulders and shook him. The boy's breath was sucked in sharply and Gordon looked anxiously into his face. Suddenly the Mexican collapsed. He would have fallen to the floor had Gordon not caught him. He listened for heart action and called to an attendant to get the club doctor. The doctor finally came to the room and put a stethoscope on the bronze chest.

"He's dead."

"Good God! He had to die to prove I was right. Let the crowd hiss now and burn rags and call me a crook. I'll spit in their lousy eyes! They'd let a boy die in the ring and they yell crook and fake if you don't let them see him die."

The news of the Juarez Kid's death reached the half-emptied auditorium before Gordon got there. He saw three policemen standing beside Joe Gates, Hiram and a group that had been baiting them. These two men, at least, knew he wasn't a crook, and now the crowd seemed to know it, too. That crowd was silent. Men stood there looking at the ring as though they expected it to speak to them. They gawked morbidly at the arena where death had delivered a knockout blow. The bleary, suspicious leers had vanished now. The crowd was ashamed of itself.

Gordon, Joe and Uncle Hiram went together to an alley exit. Gordon was depressed and when men sought to reach him to apologize for the earlier mood of the throng, he shook their hands off as though he did not want to be contaminated. When he heard some of them say he had done a wise thing in stopping the fight, he longed to kick them in the groins. These unthinking, blithering clods! These chunks were his fellow townsmen, his fellow citizens, and they voted for Presidents.

"Don't let this lick you, Gordie," Hiram said as they stood in Finner's saloon.

"By God! You'll never see me licked. I may be licked some time, but I won't let anyone see it."

For several weeks Gordon withdrew to his own self-created little world. From that time on he always felt timid when in crowds.

Chapter Twelve

I

GORDON saw Margery Hamilton for a second time at a football game between State College and the Agricultural School. She called to him as he was on his way to the press section, a bench set on the ground in front of the high stand, to report the game for his newspaper. As he turned to reply to Margery's greeting, Gordon was pleased to see that she wore the Red and Yellow of State College. My alma mater, he said to himself; my alma mater, several times removed—my one-fourth alma mater. He thought her voice a bit like Racy's, only not quite as high, and it occurred to him that her voice had attracted him that night at the Country Club Ball.

"Why, hello there, Margery." Mr. Briggs, Margery's fiancé, nodded stiffly as Gordon stopped at their seats and then walked away to confer with an acquaintance. Gordon thought him a sap. She'll marry that sap. She'll marry him and they will have some little saps—little Johnny Sap, Jenny Sap and Whoozis Sap. Saps come from saps. Look, Gordon, that's where saps are to come from! He was holding Margery's firm little hand. The teams were running through their final short drills before the whistle.

"I'm going to call you soon," Gordon said. "Got to go to work now, Margery. S'long."

"I'll believe it when you call. I hope your college wins."

"My college.... Yes, my college, Margery. That's right, you've got to hope your college wins, don't you?"

Gordon picked up his telephone headpiece and adjusted it to his ears and began dictating a running story of the game to his office. He scored the game mechanically and kept thinking of Margery. He thought of Nada, too, and of Racy and of women in general, but his thoughts to-day always came back to Margery. She was so wholesome and gentle and good. Several times during the game he looked up to the stand and fancied she was watching him. She was.

In the twilight, Gordon wound up his dictation and prepared to hasten to his office to write the story for a later edition. He must not linger, for the Sunday paper was big and unwieldy and the makers of it had to get their stuff in early Saturday afternoon and evening so as not to clog up the composing room with a last-minute skelter of type. Old Joe, brandishing his shears like a cavalry officer with a saber, yelled "Early copy" and his troops rode hard in the Saturday night charge.

Gordon waved to Margery and she waved back. Well, Nada was beautiful. Nada was radiant, brilliant, compelling; slender, seductive and graceful as a reed. Nada's face was an oval of latent emotion and her lips were mobile ...

but Margery was handsome; so confidently, womanly handsome. Margery might not appear capable of impulse, but
she looked as though she could give a man something that
he needed to quiet his soul and soothe his body. Yes,
Margery was too fine to be a sap-mother.

II

JOE GATES and Gordon were sitting at a round table at
Finner's early Sunday morning, waiting for the final edition of *The Clarion* to be brought to them.

"That was a bully yarn you wrote about the game,"
Joe said. "Lots of color in it. You've got color, Gordie, and
don't let anyone grind it out of you."

"I haven't had a chance to read it over yet." Gordon
wished that Nada read his signed stories. But, oh, well!

"I read it in proof. I don't know much about sports,
but I could see and understand the game as you wrote it."

"Thanks." They had another rye and downed it as a
copy boy came in with the papers. Gordon began to read
the sports section while Old Joe got out a heavy black
pencil and performed an autopsy on Page One. He was
in thoroughly professional mood now, hawk-eyed and
irritable. Suddenly he called on all the saints and even
invited Pontius Pilate and Balaam to look at the paper.
Gordon glanced up quizzically.

"Can't anyone in all the ignorant, God-damned outfit
ever learn to spell names!" Apoplexy was knocking at
Joe's forehead. "Here's a name, a prominent name and an

easy one to spell, but they have to spell it Hampton instead of Halpin. Holy damn! Why did their fathers get married anyway?"

Gordon's fingers felt clumsy, like big clothes pins, and he could not hold his pencil steadily. "Halpin! What Halpin?"

"What Halpin, hell! The only Halpin in town."

"Let me see it."

"Look at your own paper. I'm glad you didn't do this iron-head trick, Gordon, for so help me God I'd fire you for it. I'd fire my own mother for such a boner."

As Gordon looked at Page One, his eyes were drawn to a two-column picture of a woman. A full length picture of Nada, standing, just as she had stood in Mrs. Mathers' dressing room that night when she asked him not to turn to putty. Well, he was turning to putty right now, and he was putty as he read the story that accompanied the picture, an account of how a home town girl had made good in the great City of New York. Made good! Made good!

Yes, Nada, you have made good. You've married, have you? You lied when you told me you never would marry, lied to me and lied to yourself. Married to Grosserly, the millionaire silk manufacturer. Sold down the river, Nada, that's you. Now you have success—well, then, sleep with it. Ha! Ha! Nada, go ahead and sleep with a silkworm; get into his cocoon with him; get all tangled up and lost in Mr. Grosserly's nice cocoon.

Old Joe was watching Gordon's face, where pale ghosts

seemed to be reveling. "What the hell's eating on you?"

Gordon looked up from the picture of Nada, from the blatant, bragging story about her wedding at a Fifth Avenue church. "Not a God-damned thing is the matter with me, Joe, except I want another drink."

"Let's not have any more. I'm so discouraged over the spelling in the office that I wish I was a hearse driver."

"If you take up hearse driving, let me be your first passenger."

"You simply can't carry your liquor. Here's how."

Nada's getting into bed now. Nada's getting into bed with her silkworm. Granner, hey, Granner! Get that burlap sack and hang it over Nada's bed so that we can't see Grosserly.

Gordon tossed off his rye. "And here's how to you."

Chapter Thirteen

*G*ORDON went on a week's drunk and Madam Francis took care of him. This time he had a touch of delirium tremens and the Madam put cold compresses at the back of his skull and suggested bromides. Headless violinists played at the foot of his bed and he wondered how they could perform without having chins against which to tuck their fiddles. He didn't like the ragged, unreasonable fiddling that accompanied the jerkings of his diaphragm; nor did he think highly of the gargoyles that looked down on him from the corners of the room, craning their skinny bronze necks and ogling him with scarlet eyes. Madam Francis wanted to call a physician, but Gordon said he would stick it out. He even attempted a few jokes about his condition, but his humor was forced and at night he asked the Madam to leave the lights burning in the room.

When he reached home, he found Granner upset about his latest disappearance and Uncle Hiram had a talk with Gordon, urging him to reform.

"I ain't no philosopher, but I don't have to be smart to know that you're going plumb to hell. Catch yourself by the seat of the pants and stand up to Life."

How sagging and lumpy Hiram's muscles were getting at forty-five and how laggard his step. I'm a blunderer, Racy, forever stubbing my toes on the stairway to the stars.

Gordon was seized with a remorse that was unbearable as Hiram walked away from him. He wanted to go to Uncle Hiram, put an arm about him and say he was sorry; that he would try not to do this thing again. To tell him of Nada and what she had done to him; that she had broken his heart. To tell him how his longing for Racy, when she was here on earth, never had been assuaged. To tell him how he missed Gramper from the cellar. To explain to Uncle Hiram that in all his boyhood he had been kept from play and that pals never had come to his house to dig caves, fly kites, wrestle or play ball and how the play instinct had been quelled, crushed and perverted ...and when freedom came it had brought recklessness and turmoil.

He wanted to speak these things, frankly and man-to-man with his uncle, but he didn't. He went to the drawer where he kept the picture of the graduating class and said he would tear it to fine bits, throwing the fragments like confetti...or like rice at a wedding. But he ended by taking the picture to bed and shedding tears on it in the dark, and then he withdrew into his lonely, self-made microcosm and went to sleep.

II

GORDON's spree was followed as usual by an ascetic spell, during which he abstained from drink, cards and brought most of his salary home. Granner saved enough out of it to buy a stone for the family burial plot and told Gordon he should write something sweet to be put on the tombstone. He said he'd try, but he couldn't think of anything that was sweet. All he could conjure were phrases that smacked of blasphemy or words that would astound cemetery visitors in their morbid strolls through the garden of Nevermore. A mason covered with marble dust and holding a chisel and mallet recommended a monument already labeled "At Rest" and Granner made the purchase.

Gordon worked hard and his articles improved in tone and in composition. Early in 1914 he received another invitation from *The New York Morning Star* and felt that he should accept it. Those great journalists wouldn't always be standing there beckoning him to the City where Life was lived; but without Nada as an inspiring potentiality, he felt slack and ambitionless. Then, too, Uncle Hiram really was in need of his help now, for he was losing weight and was working contrary to the advice of the doctor. When Gordon asked Uncle Hiram to take a long vacation, he told his nephew to mind his own business. Gordon said nothing of the New York offer to his grandmother or his uncle and grieved quietly and alone when he thought of Nada.

He was not bitter about her now, for after all, she had

made it clear to him in their dressing room interview that any interest she may have had in him was dead. She wasn't to blame for his anguish—yes, she was, too. . . . He hoped she would find happiness, but he couldn't help thinking of Grosserly as a silkworm.

III

On Gordon's night off, which came on Wednesday, he telephoned Margery Hamilton. That was in March of 1914 and at the close of his rather overdrawn "ascetic spell." His usual custom of descending on the bottle at the conclusion of such spells was checked with no little difficulty. Indeed, he had gone to Finner's with an intention of taking aboard a few rye whiskies, but as he passed a telephone, he thought he would call Margery.

I wonder when Margery will marry that Briggs fellow?

"Hello, that you, Margery?"

Yes, this is Margery. Oh, that you, Gordon? This is a surprise! . . . I just thought I'd say hello, Margery; kind of lonesome. Well, I certainly would like to call on you, Margery! Be up there in no time. S'long, Margery.

Well, what do you know? She said she'd have to cancel a date to see me. I hope it's with that Briggs. He has an expression like a betrayed overshoe anyway. Say, I kind of like Margery. . . . It's been so long since I called on a decent girl that I hope I don't get absent-minded and say: "Good evening, Margery. . . . Which did you say was the bedroom?"

IV

WEDNESDAY evening calls on Margery began to grow habit-
ual and sometimes she would meet him in town where
they ate dinner at a cafeteria. They had lots of fun pulling
the aluminum trays along the brass counter slides and
selecting food. Margery laughed at Gordon because he
usually took two and sometimes three desserts. Gordon explained that when he wasn't drinking he ate unstintingly
of sweet things.

"Do you drink much, Gordon?"

"Plenty." Gordon was impudently honest regarding his
moral shortcomings. "I love rum." Now she'll lecture me
and that will spoil everything. Go ahead, sweet little Margery, and give Gordon a Thou-shalt-not harangue. I like
you to beat hell, Margery, but come on and shoot the
works. Tell Gordie it is naughty-naughty to pot shot his
tummy with booze. Go on. Lips that touch liquor....
What's this? She isn't lecturing. Maybe I didn't speak
plainly. "I surely like to get a gizzard full of rye." Now
you have it, Carry Nation.

"I think I understand. With all that night work, a
chap's got to play some. You're the kind of fellow, though,
that can handle it."

O my God! She's complimenting me on my vice. Bully
for you, baby. That's a home run with the bases full. Margery, you've got something. Something great, whatever it
is. Can a man love two women? How about it, King
Solomon?

"This is swell apple pie," Gordon said.

"I'll make you a better one some time."

"You know how to cook?"

"Certainly."

Say, would Polo Pony Briggs marry her if he knew she did anything so vulgar as pie baking? She'd better conceal the fact that she's leading a double life, cooking on the sly.

"Say, Margery, will it get you in bad, my calling on you so often?"

"Don't you want to call on me?"

"Most certainly, but you're such a great girl I don't want to handicap you. You know I'm not regarded as a social lion, and...well, I'm just asking you."

Margery laughed. "You keep on calling. I've thought it out and maybe it isn't quite conventional, seeing that I'm engaged. Frankly, my mother doesn't approve of it, but I told her I was going to let you call. I'm too old-fashioned to sneak out to meet you places; that wouldn't suit me at all. Maybe I don't know just why I act as I do, but perhaps you need a certain sort of companionship and I'm going to give it to you for just this little time out of my life. It can't kill anybody."

"Then you must like me a little bit."

"A little more than a little bit. Why pretend I don't? I'm not a flirt and I'm not going to be a hypocrite, either."

"But Briggs?"

"Mr. Briggs and I have had a talk, not a very pleasant

one, about this. You see I didn't sneak about it with him, either."

"He probably didn't applaud you."

"No. He said he was entitled to dictate what my conduct should be."

"And you said?"

"That I wasn't a polo pony and that the sooner he got that out of his head the better."

"Would you let Briggs go back to his stables and his blue ribbons if I asked you to be my girl, Margery?"

"What kind of a girl?"

"Your kind of girl. I think you're the best kind of girl a fellow could have."

"You mean to break my engagement and become engaged to you?"

"I don't know. You are so honest that you make me want to be honest. I'm not very reliable; morally I mean, and I do some damned fool things. I hardly think you'd want to marry me."

"One never can tell."

"I have nothing to offer you."

Margery looked at him earnestly. "Don't get all tangled up in a proposal that you can't mean. Let's not discuss engagements or marriage." She paused for a while. "Yes, I'll be your girl, but it is not to be one of those spooning affairs. If you want me for true friendship and on a sort of girl-in-name-only basis, I'll try to see you through your loneliness."

Gordon never had come in contact with this sort of

creature before. She presumably wasn't stirred physically, yet she must have something approximating love for him to dismiss Briggs and a sound social position so calmly. There's something fascinating in the way this girl goes about life, so honestly, so unafraid, so deliberately certain. I've got to study her. She's certainly not dull and smug in the belief that her charms are a trophy to be won by the survivor of a seduction tournament.

"Do you like babies?" Now why in hell did I ask that? Well, I did ask it. For God's sake! Imagine such a ninny, eating apple pie and asking Do you like babies! Suppose someone had gone up to Savonarola during the bonfire of Vanities to ask: "Say, bo, do you like frankfurters?" I do the damnedest, queerest things!

Margery was amused: "I'm crazy about babies and when I'm married, I'll have at least three....Do you like them?"

Well, you brought this on yourself, Gordon. Come on, what's your reply? "I surely do love them." Gordon caught the deep, kindly look in her eyes and lost his feeling of embarrassment.

"That makes us both liking babies," she said. "Now I'll ask one. Do you like horses?"

Gordon laughed more heartily than he had in months. Margery understood his floundering about, his impulsiveness. She sort of fathomed him, no matter how crazy he acted or talked.

"Sure I like horses," he said, "and when I am married, I'm going to have at least three of them."

V

GORDON was obliged to work without days off as the European situation grew more complicated. With everyone getting into the war across the Atlantic, *The Clarion* was asking men of all departments to help in the handling of foreign news. Joe Gates, using his scissors as a pointer while indicating on maps the probable course of the conflict, was sure that America would be drawn into the mess. Gordon said he hoped not and told Joe he wasn't at all interested in war or in those that made war. It was a ghastly waste of time, lives and materials. He cared little for the quarrels of nations, past or present, and he declared that the work of checking up on maps and boundary lines of Europe made him dizzy and disgusted.

"Just the same," Gates said, "you'll help us with this work and you'll work like hell on it. And be God damned sure you don't misspell any of those foreign towns."

It was a relief to get to Margery's house during the few hours off he had that summer. He joked when they met, telling her that her face was a relief map to him. One night in August—she didn't complain at having had to wait for him until past midnight—they sat in the grape arbor. Margery said she didn't want to disturb her mother, who had insomnia, and who had taken a sleeping powder to-night.

"All right, Margery, it's warm and fragrant in the arbor. We'll sit here and talk. I've been lonely and blue."

"What makes you so alone in the world, Gordie?"

"Because I'm really not in the world at all." Now she'll

say she thinks me odd, as they all do.... What! She doesn't say I'm odd. I appreciate that and I appreciate a lot of things about her, for her silences are as refreshing as rain on an upturned face.

"Maybe you have a world of your own ... and I know it is a beautiful world if you live in it."

"I like to be with you, Margery."

"I'm happy that you do."

"I can relax, rest with you. I'm not on edge when I'm here with you." Margery never tries to pry into me, for if she did, I'd compound grewsome psychological pictures. That's the way I drive peepers from my soul. My soul is a virgin. My soul is not a prostitute that sleeps with anyone that tosses it a coin. "I'm wondering if I don't love you, Margery?"

"You wonder about lots of things, don't you?"

"Yes, lots. There's lots to wonder about." He took her hand and moved close to her. He felt that she was drawn to him, but she wouldn't let herself be hugged or kissed— at least she had not yet permitted it. He wanted to hug and kiss her now. He sat there thinking of the world and its meanings. What was Margery's world like? Surely each one of the millions of men and women had a separate world, in fact, a private world—just as he himself had created one into which no human being but Self could come. Or, he asked himself, was it but one world instead of many worlds, but a world with many centers, each human being existing as a center and the total of humanity representing the true circumference? He longed to enter

Margery's world; to merge their centers and to know only each other's secret world.

"How alone everyone is," he said. "How few bridges can be thrown between humans to help dispel the soul's exile."

"Friendship is a bridge. Kind thoughts...."

"No, friendship cannot destroy the isolation of self. Margery, only the mingling of man and woman, and that but for a fleeting moment, can dispel the aloneness and then there is an ecstatic interlude of understanding."

"I'm trying not to be frightened, Gordon, but you tell me things of which I can only vaguely guess. Something says to me that we must not look into secret places...yet."

"Kiss me, Margery." Yes, he must go at once into Margery's world.

"I'd rather not. It wouldn't mean anything if I did."

"We could make it mean something."

"I don't want it to mean anything. For the first time in my life I am afraid. We mustn't kiss."

"Other girls of your crowd don't seem to mind it."

"That's their business. They can do as they please. I guess I'm hopelessly old-fashioned."

"It wouldn't kill you. Just one kiss wouldn't be fatal."

"Gordon, I don't let myself ache for anybody. Physically, I mean. When the time comes, I'll give myself, for that's to be expected, I guess. I hope I shan't regret. I wish I could help you see things clearly, sanely and without the longing.... I don't know what it is you need. I wish I did."

"I want you, Margery. You know, you are Earth to

me. My mind wants the stars, and I look to them. But my body wants the Earth, something sweetly, primitively earthly. Men tell women they are angels, spiritual and divinely wrought—yet in you I see the Earth in its truest sense." Gordon spoke as though thinking aloud. He was carried away by his trend. "Often, as I toss fitfully, I think of the planet as a gigantic breast with men tugging at it for life. Mother Earth, men call it." He reached down and picked up a handful of earth-mold from the roots of a vine and in the darkness he loved the handful of earth and found solace in its texture.

"I thought you didn't like the world, that you tried to run away from it."

"I love the World as Earth, but not the Earth as World," he said.

"I wish I were able to follow you more closely, Gordon. You think and talk in a way that saddens me yet thrills me."

He spoke on, still voicing thoughts. "It is the Earth as World that I fear and ache to escape, but the Earth as Mother, I love. God created the Earth but the World is a satanic abortion. So, Margery, in one globe I find a duality of Earth and World. And the fruits of the sphere are two-fold. Flesh, impure, unchaste and doomed to decline, wither and rot, comes from the benign Earth. Spirit, changeless and sublime, is born of the hated World. We are caught in a vortex of paradoxes, jests and enigmas, and who are these human bodies that walk, talk and strut? Beggars." He whispered as though discussing something forbidden. "Beggars going to a fair, and over all of them the fear of the unknown and of the dark."

The souls of men now seemed to be fluttering through the night like bats, blunderingly, although Gordon told himself it was only the sound of leaves whirling from the grape vines. He thought of his self-enforced chastity of past weeks, of his denials and his desperate struggles to think in terms devoid of bodily contact. He was a pilgrim, he declared to himself, a pilgrim marching barefoot over a pathway strewn with broken glass. And now carnal imaginings descended on him like succubi, and the more he resisted, the keener became his physical craving. The devils of lust whistled in his ears.

"God!" he said, putting his arms about Margery, "I thought you liked me a little bit more than ..."

"Funny thing, Gordie, I do. But I'm serious minded. I can't help it, but it's true. In later years, when I'm married, I don't want to have to avoid anyone because I ever spooned with them." She disengaged his arms.

Margery has a high, full bosom, but there is no lust in her bright, honest eyes. Margery is health and youth. She hasn't been awakened yet, although there is a vague stirring that I can feel as she fights free from my arms. How would you like to awaken her, Gordon? Shut up, lecher! Hey, get Gordon a chastity belt! Margery would make a fine mother and she wouldn't let step-fathers chase babies away from her bed. Margery would let her babies play. Even on Sundays, she would let her children whistle and play. I know she would. But would she let a husband play ... ?

"Didn't anyone ever try to get fresh with you, Margery?"

"Certainly. Boys are pretty much the same."

"How did you meet the problem?"

She didn't reply at once. The moonlight was so faint that Gordon couldn't catch her expression. "How did I just meet it with you, Gordon?"

"I don't think I tried to get fresh with you." This body business doesn't seem to disturb her. What will be the end of this?

"You were getting ready to." Margery was laughing. How in hell can a woman laugh when a man sits pantingly beside her, aching and trembling and his blood unbearably hot? "Gordon, when men get fresh, I make out that I don't know what they are leading up to. I just play dumb. That's the way I meet the problem. Now you know my secret."

Gordon's desperate mood began to subside a little. The frankness of this woman encased her in armor that seemed invulnerable to passionate pleas. Still he fancied she trembled a little. Well, Nada, I don't know what you and Grosserly are doing at this precise moment, but he's probably neglecting the silk business. . . . Nada, I'm at sea, rudderless, and although I am at this minute, this second, mad about you, still I feel funny about this Margery person. She has taught me not to feel jumpy and upset and I have quit getting up from one chair to change to another and then get up from that one to scamper about like a passionate goat. Margery threatens to make me forget that I must keep running; running but never escaping from tin cans that are tied to my tail.

"Margery, I hope I don't offend you ... you are so good and fine, but I'd like to have you. I'm just honestly wanting you, that's all."

"I'm dreadfully sorry." Margery didn't act pleased nor did she act angry, but seemed impersonal and detached. She wore no mask of innocence and Gordon knew that she knew exactly what he meant.

"Why sorry?"

"Because it's wrong and because I want so much to give you whatever you want. I don't want you ... that way, I mean. But stronger even than passion, I would like to bring peace and understanding to you. If only I could...."

"You could."

"By doing that, you mean?"

"You could bring me peace if you would give me you. Here! Now!" There was a strange tightness at the base of his brain. Out of all the girls in this town, hotly receptive, must you come to this clean, fine character, Gordon? Take care.... Take care.... "But, of course, if you don't love me, that's different."

"I do love you. I'm not demonstrative, Gordon. I simply don't know how to give. I have nothing to use for a comparison, and there's a lot I don't know, but I do know I love you. I couldn't love anyone else ... ever."

"Well then ..."

"I see." Margery breathed deeply. "It's the only way I

can show my love for you, is that it? You couldn't understand any other language than bodily love?"

"I could understand all languages through it."

"If that is so, I must give to you, Gordon, but it makes me sad. I'm not terrified by it now. I thought I should be, but instead I'm merely sad."

"Why sad? I don't want you to be sad. Can't you give joyously, madly?"

"No, I can't. Although it is a mad thing to do, I am decidedly not mad. Your love makes you mad, and to take that madness from you—all right...I'm yours, Gordon. Tell me what to do. It sounds silly. I don't know those things. I only hope it will bring you happiness."

Margery went into the house to see if her mother was asleep. Is she never coming back? She returned with pillows. Undisturbed and unexcited. Prepared to give as though her gift were utterly unimportant compared to his desire.

The moon's sickle dropped below the horizon and the empty altars of the east were ready to receive the dawn's first fires. The grasses made obeisance while the wind hastened like a glad herald from the birth-bed of the morn. A throbbing chorus of awakening birds pulsed in rising, falling sequence like the systolic rhythm of a great heart. The crumpled grape leaves that were beginning to twist into autumnal dryness shook like the bells of temple dancers....

As day came upon them, Gordon kissed Margery goodby. He went toward home, passing a house where a still-lighted bulb burned against a porch ceiling. From the house came a muffled groaning, and as the gladness of the sun struck that door, Gordon shivered and for a while was unable to take his eyes from black crêpe that fluttered grotesquely on the rusty knob.

Only the innocent wind dared play with Death.

Chapter Fourteen

I

GORDON wished he could strangle his conscience and hide it in a pit. He had heard that girls sometimes were ashamed to meet fellows after such initiations as Margery had had in the grape arbor, but he felt that it was he, not she, who should be shame-faced. They had traded something after the moon had slipped away.... What had they traded? I know what, Gordon thought. I gave her indecency for decency. I short-changed Margery. Horse traders laugh and brag when they give spavined horses for sound horses, but I cannot laugh over my trade.... Maybe I'm getting effeminate.

The manager of the Fairmount Baseball Club telephoned Gordon, inviting him to take the final trip of the season with the team. Gordon didn't see how he could get away. Football time was approaching and anyway he had to double his days and rewrite war cables.

He sat at his desk, trying to write an advance column of sports comment, but he couldn't concentrate. Battling Krug looks like the next welterweight champion.... Mar-

gery was so detached when she gave herself to me.... Kid
Platzo is about through; his legs are gone.... What an unusual experience it was. Margery gave herself out of generosity; not from passion or longing for me. She said it was
because I wanted her and not because she wanted me that
way.... It looks as though the Phillies feel comfortable
only in the league cellar.... I am so in debt to Margery
for it wasn't a fair trade. I gave her a note, a sexual note,
and it was not indorsed. How can I pay? She didn't ask
me to marry her and I don't want to marry. Imagine being
married for a lifetime just because there was an hour or
two in a grape arbor! O hell! I can't write this column.
I'm going stale.... Just imagine an hour costing you a
whole lifetime of obligation; saying over and over, day
after day: "Thank you for the Grape Arbor, Margery.
Thanks for the Grape Arbor...." I wish I could take that
trip.

Joe Gates told Gordon he was sorry, but he simply
could not be spared for the baseball trip.... I wish Margery
was a trip and I'd forget her, too. I wish Nada was a trip,
and I'd forget her. I wish every woman that ever lived was
a trip and then we wouldn't have to forget, for we
wouldn't be here.... Go to hell, Gates! Go to hell, you
damned old slave driver.

When Gates started home that night, he was astounded
as he looked through the half-opened door of the sports
room and saw Gordon standing there. Rather, Gordon was
bowing and genuflecting to his desk, saying solemnly:
"Thank you for the Grape Arbor, my dear. Thanks and

thanks and thanks until Time shall be no more. I'll rise early to-morrow, darling, for my matins of thanks. I shall have a rosary of grapes."

Joe Gates went back to his own office and called Gordon on the telephone. "Come in to see me ... right away."

"Be there as soon as I can put on my roller skates."

"Good news," Joe said. "It's about that trip. Been thinking it over and believe you ought to go, but for Christ's sake keep reasonably sober!"

What had made this old crab change his mind? Maybe it was second childhood creeping on him. No, it couldn't be second childhood; that was too conservative. It must be third childhood.

"Thanks, Joe." Gordon checked himself just in time, for he almost had said Thanks for the Grape Arbor. Whew! Now I can get away from the scene of the crime. Call Margery, Gordon. Tell her you're sneaking away.... Shut up, Whatever-you-are-inside-me! I'll do as I damned please.

II

GORDON was gone nearly a month and he didn't telephone Margery before he left and he did not write to her from Nebraska, Iowa and Kansas towns where the team played. He even denied to himself that there was such a person as Margery. There really couldn't be a Margery when there was a Nada, could there? One heart can't be in two places at the same time.... How are you getting on with Mr. Grosserly, Nada? ... As fine as silk, Gordon. How are you getting on with Margery? . . . Sour grapes! I am a fox and the grapes.

On his return to Fairmount, Gordon doped out football camps in the day and war camps in the night. To hell with war! Hurry up with those statistics, Mr. Dole. . . . O.K., Mr. Gates. Coming, Mr. Gates. I'm coming. I'm coming. And my head is bending low. I hear your squeaky voice a-calling, Cracked-Pot-Joe.

Three weeks after his return from the baseball tour, Gordon received a note from Margery. It said simply that she wondered why he had not called her; that she was hoping to see him soon. He looked at the handwriting. It was firm and even like her character. He didn't call her or reply to the note, but tore it up and flipped the pieces in a basket and settled down to work.

All day long and into the night the fragments called to him. When he discarded telegraph flimsy into the basket, he fancied the note cried out that it was being buried alive, and when the basket became full and he had to press down the waste paper to get other scraps into the receptacle, he felt that he was pressing the life from her note.

Another week passed and he tried to drink his mind free of Margery. Two months now had gone and he had not got in touch with her. . . . Then she called him. He couldn't very well say he wasn't in, for she had recognized his voice as he answered the telephone. Why did Bell invent this thing, anyway? Only the wrong people call you on it and it's never anyone that wants to give you something.

"I hate to bother you, Gordon, but I must see you. I believe that it's important that I see you."

"I've been awfully busy. No time off and a lot of night work."

"I realize that.... Perhaps I should come to your office?"

I'll tell the world she won't come here! I don't think she would make a scene, but you can't tell. Nobody should gamble on a dame. "We'll meet somewhere else, Margery. How about a restaurant? The Clarke House?"

"Anywhere you say."

"Clarke House then, at noon to-morrow."

"I'll be there.... I've thought of you often...."

He hung up. The hell you thought of me! One turn of a silly key in a silly lock and they begin to think of you. One opening of a door and they never want the door to close again. What good's a door if it won't close again?

Margery was already at the restaurant when Gordon arrived fifteen minutes late. She was sitting in a corner settle, where semi-privacy could be had and he thought she looked concerned. She smiled, however, when he sat beside her.

"I wouldn't have troubled you, but if ever I needed advice, it's now."

Gordon believed she had undergone some scene relative to Briggs. Perhaps the old lady, parading in her night shirt, had seen them leave the grape arbor in the growing dawn.

"I'm not much of an advice dispenser."

"Don't think me a whining, ignorant fool, Gordon, but I don't know where to take my problem. You'll forgive me, won't you?"

"Problem? Forgive? What is this, Margery?"

"Lean close to me, Gordie, so we won't be overheard.... Something's the matter with me. I don't know. ...I don't want to act excited or to bother you, but I think something's happened from that night we were together."

Get out your rosary of grapes, brother! ...Let us kneel and pray.

"You mean that you want me to marry you then?"

Margery didn't become emotional nor did she employ frantic words. She simply sat there looking at him wonderingly. "I didn't say that. I only want to ask you what shall I do?"

Well, Gordon, are you a welsher? Do you pay your gambling debts? In all your blundering, selfish life have you done any particularly honorable things? Shut up, will you? Shut up, Whatever-is-inside-of-me! Let me pull myself together.

"Are you sure something is wrong?" Gordon was pale. "You don't mind if I order a drink, do you? I am a bit upset." He was served with a whisky and drank it and when the waiter had gone, he repeated: "Maybe you'll be O.K."

"I have missed two times."

"Let's leave here and get the air. I don't feel like eating. If you do, we'll go somewhere else. I've got to keep moving."

"Whatever you say."

They walked through the noon-hour crowds without speaking for a while; then they left the main business street and went into a side street, where not so many folk were walking. Gordon thought of his early experience, the night he had awakened alone in the dark and in a strange house and had groped, so afraid, into a room where there was a bed and two persons were whispering in the bed. Poor Margery! She is groping in the dark, too. She is too fine to be humiliated like this. What are my fool-made dreams compared to a heart break such as hers? Perhaps one decent deed out of a life of indecency may shrive me. Perhaps through one fair and square payment of a debt I may find clarification of soul.

"I'll bet you don't know where we are going, Margery?"

"I don't know ... to a doctor's, I suppose."

"Yes, to a doctor's, but it will be a doctor of divinity. You and I are going to be married."

She stopped walking and caught his arm. Well, why does she act so astonished? Did she think I'd have to be flanked by shotguns to make the altar? Uncle Willie with a breech-loader; cousin Jake with a Colt's; Grandma with a trench mortar; mother with a blunderbuss—all pointed at Gordie's trembling buttocks until the conclusion of the Smith & Wesson wedding march.

"I wouldn't want you to do this, Gordie, unless you loved me.... I'd rather go away and ..."

"You're the finest, gamest person I know," he said and

meant it. "Instead of a preacher, we'll have the Clerk at City Hall marry us to-day, now."

"You won't feel forced into this?"

"Hell no."

"It would be terrible if you were to regret it. I'd almost rather ..."

"My mind is made up. We'll keep our marriage a secret until I can get on my feet. You're a great girl, Margery."

"I love you so. I couldn't love anyone else.... I couldn't let anyone else ever touch me."

Gordon felt easier, less selfish. Maybe he had a glimmer of manhood in him after all. Perhaps he had made a mistake in creating a personal world in which to hide away. It was possible that the only true escape lay in doing something for others, something outside self. True, he was only doing his duty now. Still he was doing more than certain others had done in similar circumstances. He had given too much of himself to himself and now he must begin to give of himself to others. Margery had given of herself freely just to make the man she loved happy—or at least less miserable and alone.

They were married by the clerk on November 12, 1914. The clerk pasted the page, on which their application for a license was written, to the page that preceded it. Reporters turning the pages probably would skip this record.

Gordon kissed Margery, his wife, good-by and then went to work. He wondered how it would be to have a baby on his lap. He thought so much about babies that he sat down and wrote a poem on baby kisses. He absent-mindedly sent the verse upstairs to the composing room. When it appeared in the sports section of *The Clarion,* old Joe Gates was puzzled. He stopped Gordon in the hall and asked:

"What's wrong with you to-day, son? Drunk again or pregnant?"

II

In keeping Briggs away from the house, Margery finally had to admit to her mother that she was married. Mrs. Hamilton suffered a joint attack of insomnia and hysteria and said she would never contribute a cent to the upkeep of her daughter. Margery called Gordon at his office at midnight two days after the wedding and he agreed to go to Margery's home to begin married life on a formal basis.

In asking permission to leave early, Gordon told Gates he was married. "It is a fine thing," Gates said. "Be true to her."

I'm going home, to my lifetime home. The marriage vow says it will last forever. Male vitality may fade and romance may fade. Love may sicken and desire will die, and hatred may sit at a dressing table, dabbing rouge on its cheeks. Indifference may sit there, too, drawing silk stockings on limbs that have grown meaningless...but marriage is there, never budging. You have two homes now, Gordie, and you haven't any home at all.

Chapter Fifteen

I

THE first night of wedlock in the home of her mother brought uneasiness to Margery. At twenty—she was nearly four years younger than Gordon—Margery was old enough to appreciate the civilized safety she had achieved in marriage, but she was young enough to feel cheated of true romance. She told herself that she loved Gordon deeply and that love would make up for everything, but the brutal fact was that it didn't make up for everything.

Margery tried hard to dismiss her mood as she waited for Gordon to come to her from the midnight shadows. She wondered if he, too, were not sullenly conscious of the situation. Still, he was a man, and this really wouldn't be a first night for them.

It would take a lot of trying and striving to weather the conditions attendant on their marriage. Mrs. Hamilton, groaning and ranting in the next room, was a reminder that the start of this married life would be bitter enough. Margery wanted Gordon beyond any other man or any other thing, but she was feminine enough to want him with an aura of romantic splendor.

Then what had she been given up to now? Other girls of her station, girls of the comfortably wealthy set, would not be sitting here alone on such a night. Other girls would be whirling away on honeymoons, carried by trains or by ships to new and inspiring places. Yes, Margery, but other girls wouldn't have two months of forbidden life in them on such a night. Other girls would have had weeks, perhaps months, of courtship and open avowal of love and anticipation. There would be a delightful buzzing about while hope-chests were filled and the trousseau was mobilized. There would be plans and maps and railroad tickets and a compartment. Yes, Margery, but you gave all those rights away in the grape arbor. Other girls had the privilege of naming the marriage day and of selecting bridesmaids for a solemn, prideful assemblage before an altar. I know all that, Margery, but you should not be thinking of a trousseau when you should be thinking of a layette. Other girls...

Across the street from Margery sounded the quavering voice of a fife and the roll of a snare drum. Old man Chilvers was entertaining comrades of his Grand Army Post on his eighty-third birthday. The fife and the drum were playing "Listen to the Mocking Bird."

Gordon was at the door and Margery checked her mother from going downstairs. "Please stay in your room, Mother. I'll go." When Margery stood before Gordon, she forgot that she had been mourning the romance that had been denied her. She put her arms about him and he held her thoughtfully.

"Well, I'm here, Margery."

"Did I do wrong in calling you?"

"Of course not. It doesn't matter.... Why, you haven't even been to bed. I thought you'd be undressed by this time."

Margery didn't know what to do about her mother. Should she call to her, telling her that Gordon, her husband, was home? Home! There had been no throwing of rice; there had been no engagement ring, no wedding ring and no clergyman. No bantering by envious wedding guests. Home! There wasn't even a home of their own and there couldn't be while Gordon had to share his salary with an old woman he called Granner.... But there was to be a baby and there was a fife and drum that played "Listen to the Mocking Bird."

The first night at the Hamilton house was a bitter one and Gordon's brain-processes creaked like the wheels of an over-loaded dray. When they were in their room, Margery tried to welcome him as best she could, but she had been reared in a Never-let-yourself-go School. Marry if you must, but submit without semblance of emotion, and submit as seldom as possible. Margery tried.

For a while they lay listening to the breaking up of the G.A.R. party at the Chilvers' house. Some senile tenor was singing "Tenting To-night." What a charivari! Unsteady drum beats and the trilling fife and the thin, bleating voice..."on the old camp ground."...Octogenarians raised night-cap liquor rheumatically and then went home. Muffled groans came from Mrs. Hamilton's room and then the sound of feet prowling the hall.

Gordon was restless and dismayed. Lady Macbeth is putting on her somnambulistic act. His eyes were weary and sore-lidded. He thought he would dab some cold water on his eyes and went to the bathroom. He had brought no night clothes and he didn't have anything to drape about him. He feared bumping into Lady Macbeth, and that is what he did do. Mrs. Hamilton seemed ready to swoon, but she managed to jerk the electric light chain as a conductor pulls an emergency cord. Gordon said he was sorry and then he heard Mrs. Hamilton snorting and retreating in the dark. Now, he thought, Mrs. Hamilton will mortify the flesh.

In the morning Gordon left early to stop at Granner's on the way to his office. Mrs. Hamilton waited until he was out of the house then she told Margery that Gordon was shameless. He'd have to wear something if he got up and roamed about. She wasn't going to turn the home where her God-fearing husband had lived and died into a bawdy house.

Gordon came on Granner in the rabbit yard. She was killing a rabbit and it made Gordon sick at the stomach to see her strike the creature at the base of the skull with an old hammer handle. She looked like Fate, standing there and holding the animal by the hind feet.

She was instrumental in giving these rabbits to the world. She introduced nose-twittering males into hutches with nose-twittering females and then she hung gunny sacks over the cages. Then she was a meticulous mid-wife when the baby rabbits came, snuggling them and confusing their scents so that she could safely mix families of does that had large litters with does that had small ones.... She fed them generously, cared for them assiduously and suddenly one day she would throw aside her mask to become Fate, the executioner.... From honeymoon to hammer handle is a jest. We are God's bunnies, Gordon said.

"You're neglecting your old Granner. I think you've got a girl."

He didn't like to shock the old woman but he decided not to dissemble with her. He put his arms about her. "Listen, Granner, I want to tell you something. Don't be mad, will you?"

She looked at him vacantly for a moment and then said: "You're married! I can tell that you are." He nodded.

"I had hoped you wouldn't desert me."

"Fat chance of my deserting you, Granner. I'll give you half my pay the same as always and I'll bring my wife to see you. I think you'll like her. She's a fine girl."

"Is her name Nada?" Gordon felt as though he had been struck by the hammer handle. Why had she said that? Why had she hit him at the base of the skull that way?

"No, her name is Margery." He was dizzy. "What made you think her name was Nada?"

"I've heard you say the name in your sleep."

What if I should say Nada in my sleep at Margery's?

Well, her name is written on my soul and I suppose there's a carbon copy of it on my face. "I'm going to spend at least one night with you each week, Granner. I think you'll like my wife."

"I hope you'll like her, too."

"Hey, there, you shouldn't say a thing like that! What made you say that?"

"Nothing, only I think you love somebody called Nada. That's all."

"Well, forget it."

"God bless you and keep you, Gordie. You're lost to me now."

"And you forget that, too."

II

DURING the fourth month of Margery's pregnancy Gordon was dreadfully upset by Mrs. Hamilton's insistence that Margery was going to die; that she never could survive the ordeal of childbirth. He tried to hold his temper and avoided his mother-in-law as much as possible.

One day he asked Margery to go with him to call on Granner, but Mrs. Hamilton begged him not to walk her girl so much.

"The exercise is good for her," Gordon said. "Don't you know it is?"

"It's her back I'm afraid of," Mrs. Hamilton said. "It will kill her sure, your walking her so much. Weak backs are the family inheritance."

"I don't want to contradict you, Mrs. Hamilton, but your weakness is not in the back." He pointed to his head.

As they started to Granner's, Margery remarked that he should not have said that. "After all, she's my mother."

"I'm sorry."

Blair Christensen was at Granner's and it was the first time Margery had met his step-father. Blair called her by her first name and kissed her. She was shocked by Blair's appearance, for his brows, lashes and most of his hair had been singed off; the rims of his eyes were red, and there were bluish-black specks in his cheeks. He said he had been in an accident.

"It happened in the interest of science," Blair explained. "I just got back from New York and started to work on an invention of mine—when, blooey!" Blair slapped Gordon's back and exclaimed: "What a town New York is, boy!"

"I suppose it is," Gordon said.

Uncle Hiram came in and Gordon thought him more defeated, more futile in manner than ever. Hiram liked Margery and thought she would be Gordon's salvation.

"What in hell happened to your mug, Blair?" Hiram asked. "Did you get it caught in a pants hanger?"

"No, not a pants hanger. I was experimenting with some powder over a gas jet."

These people spoke a language that Margery couldn't quite understand. She wished Gordon had taken her to a movie instead of to this place. Gordon was listening to Blair, who was talking full tilt about his trip to New York.

He said he had introduced a saving device to chain restaurants there.

"I sold them an idea for the ribbed sugar spoon," he said. "It is a shallow spoon that has ribs sticking up in it." He turned to Margery. "It is all based on psychology. People take one or two spoons of sugar, regardless of size, and when they use two of my spoons they don't get as much sugar, but they never know the difference. I got five hundred dollars for the idea."

"What are you going to do with all that money?" Hiram asked.

"I'm starting in the undertaking business."

Granner was startled. "An undertaker! You an undertaker, Blair?"

"Surest thing you know," Blair said. "You know I got wise to the profits there are in that business when I was peddling those concrete tombstones."

Blair said that his undertaking venture would not prevent him experimenting with many other things. He described at length his powder experiments, saying he had all but perfected gunpowder that was colored when it flashed from rifles. The idea was that each regiment would have a particular color and that a general, sitting back of the fray, could tell by the color of the gunfire what each respective outfit was doing.

"Great idea, hey?" Blair looked about the room for approval. "It will be of enormous value to the side that accepts my invention. Which side should I sell it to, Gordie?"

Gordon didn't give a damn; perhaps he should sell it to both sides.

"I kind of lean to the Allies," Blair said, "so I may sell it to France; especially because my wife likes French perfumes."

"According to the shape your face is in," Hiram said, "the side that takes it will lose the war."

"Did you like New York, Mr. Christensen?" Margery asked.

"Did I! A bunch of inventors showed me around. Talk about fun!" He looked at Gordon. "They took me to see an old friend of yours, an actress. You know...Nada Halpin!"

Gordon felt giddy and confused and he knew Granner was watching him. Of all the actresses in New York, why had Blair gone to see her? and why did he have to prate about it here, calling her an "old friend"?

"Nada Halpin and Gordon were schoolmates," Granner said.

Blair winked at Margery. "You better watch Gordie, daughter. He's a gay one if there ever was. You know these newspaper fellows. Wasn't Nada your girl in school, Gordie?"

"No, she wasn't my girl." Gordon wished Blair's powder experiment had given him lockjaw. He tried to reason with himself, telling himself he shouldn't be mad at a chance remark, but he did think it was unfair of Granner to sit there watching him that way. She was making a rabbit out of him, looking at him with disapproval as though he were a buck Belgian hare that chased does. He fancied Margery was watching him, too. Everybody was watching him. How the devil is it that when you try to bury love deep in your heart somebody keeps digging it up again? Why can't the secret of love be a real secret? Gordon got up to go.

"He's a great joker," Blair said to Margery as he went with them to the door, "and when he denies he ever had girls, don't you believe him."

"I don't care if he had girls," she said. "All boys have had them."

"You two ought to go to New York. If you do, be sure to go see the Nada Halpin show. She has New York by the neck."

When they returned to their room, Margery opened a sewing cabinet and brought out some baby clothes while Gordon tried to read.

"I'm glad they don't use long dresses for babies now," she said. "People are more sensible about children. You ought to read Dr. Holt's book on babies, Gordie." She basted at a hem for a few minutes. "You're not sorry are you, Gordie?"

"Sorry for what?"

"About getting married . . . and the baby."

"I'm tickled to death." What good would it do if he was sorry? You couldn't apologize to a grape arbor, could you? Margery is beginning to grow large with child. She doesn't say so, but she is worried because it will come the

seventh month after marriage. The marriage of Simple
Simon.

"You acted rather strange toward Mr. Christensen."

"How do you mean?"

"Well, when he spoke of that actress, you looked funny
and your voice sounded sort of..."

"Sort of what? What are you getting at?"

"Nothing, only you seemed worried. Now, Gordie, I
know you had girls. Or, I suppose you had girls. I just
want to tell you now that I don't care how many girls you
had. I'm not jealous."

"Then why bring the subject up?"

"Are you going to quarrel with me?"

"Who started it?"

"Let's not quarrel."

"I guess I'm a bit bilious, Margery. Don't pay any attention to me."

"Maybe you should take some calomel."

"Maybe." I had a boyhood of skimmed milk diets. I
shall have a manhood of calomel. I shall have a senility of
repentance and the yellow flowers of rue.... There was a
long, throbbing groan from Mrs. Hamilton's room and
Gordon cupped a palm behind his ear. "Ah, the nightin-
gale!"

"I wish you wouldn't, Gordon!"

III

ONE evening during Margery's fifth month Gordon came
home to find her sobbing and on the floor beside a wicker

bassinet that she had been trimming with pink ribbon. Now what was wrong? Just moody, I guess. Are we steeped for nine months in moods as we crouch in our uteral igloos? Is that where we receive our fundamental fears, our melancholy and our woe?

"Why, what's gone wrong, Margery?"

"It's Mama. She was over to see your grandmother to-day."

"Did Granner say something nasty to her?" I hope to God she did say something. I hope Granner burned old Hamilton loose from her hat pins. I hope she let a buck Belgian hare pursue her all over the lawn.

"They talked about your name."

"My name?" Is Margery going batty, too? A lot of folk think I'm batty; suppose she were batty! Then we'll have to confine our child in a straitjacket instead of pinafores and belly bands. Our child shall be a psychopathic prodigy.

"Mama says your name isn't Dole and that our marriage probably wasn't a legal one."

"She does, does she?" He went to the stairway and shouted: "Mrs. Hamilton!" When his mother-in-law came to them, Gordon fought hard to keep calm. "My name is Gordon Dole," he said, "and it isn't Gordon Dole. It isn't Gordon Christensen, and it's Gordon Warner, but it isn't Gordon Warner.... Figure that riddle out, Mrs. Hamilton, and I'll buy you some stilts for your sleepwalking exercises."

"Gordon!" Margery said. Mrs. Hamilton's slim frame shook and her jaw was relaxed in wonderment.

Mrs. Hamilton finally managed to speak. "Are you legally married or not? I can't sleep until I know."

Gordon couldn't answer for a few moments. I mustn't get Margery upset. I drove a chariot up Lover's lane, but when I took off my rose glasses, I saw that I was whipping a skinny roan mare and the mare was hitched to an ash wagon in an alley. Speak out, Family Tree, and shake your bony branches. Tell how many culprits were throat-tied to thee. I hope you won't miscarry, sweet wife, for I'd like to have a baby of my own.

"Now you listen to me," Gordon said. "I never have gone by any other name than Dole. My mother divorced my father, a man named Leon Warner, and in those days a divorce sounded like an admission of degradation. It was not talked of in our home. My grandmother gave me the name of Dole and my marriage is legal, Mrs. Hamilton. My father was driven from his wife by the stupidity of a mother-in-law. I'll not be driven from mine by stupidity."

Chapter Sixteen

GORDON tried to be good to Margery. He was attentive and he affected to have become reconciled to Mrs. Hamilton. At Christmas time he bought a small tree and told Margery it was for her and "the baby." Next year the baby would be here to see a Christmas tree.

"I never had but one tree, Margery. That was on my first Christmas. Granner told me I saw a gold ball on the top branch and that I reached for it. We never had another tree but I guess I kept on reaching for things—maybe that's why I reached for you."

Gordon stirred within Margery a strong maternalism and she felt that he needed all the love that she could give him. "We'll always have a Christmas tree, Gordie. I love you."

He thought her beautiful when she was in this mood and he wondered why he qualified his reasonings when he asked himself what his attitude toward her was. He could not pin down his feelings, define his emotions or label his mental position regarding her. Whenever he did try to analyze his feeling for her, thoughts of Nada rattled through his mind, making head-noises like pebbles in a dry gourd.

II

GORDON wrote occasional verse for *The Clarion* and Joe Gates said he appreciated these extra efforts to brighten the columns of the paper.

"It's not lucrative, though," Gates said. "I think it's a fine thing to write poetry, but it won't go far toward feeding the young fellow that's coming to your house."

"That doesn't worry me, either, Joe." He found in iambics and trochees a solace and a sweetness that life seemed to deny him. He knew he was no Tennyson, but just the same, he liked to string words together in rhythms and in rhymes. They were symbolic of his theory that life itself was rhythm.

On New Year's Eve, he left the city room, where he had been immersed in cable rewrite and instead of going home to dinner, as was his custom, went to his sports room to write a bit of verse. He was pleasurably busy when the telephone rang. It was Margery calling and she wanted to know why he hadn't started home. Dinner was ready and it would spoil if they waited too long. Hurry up.

"I don't think I'll have dinner, Margery. I'm writing something. Why don't you go ahead and eat without me?"

"Now, Gordie, you've been working too hard. You come right on home. We've got mutton chops. Mother got loin chops especially for you."

Gosh, I wish Margery wouldn't insist, for it's the only time I've got to myself in this factory. I wish I could simply say I'm busy, Margery, and she would say, O.K., Gordie, go ahead and do what you want. But she has mutton chops! I've got poetry. Margery has mutton chops.

"Honest, Margery, I'd rather do something I've begun. You go ahead like a good girl and if I get hungry I'll send out for a sandwich...."

"You'll do nothing of the sort. I don't want you to get another bilious spell. You come on and get something hot in your stomach."

Isn't that a fine argument? "Listen, dear, I'm doing a little verse that I would like to see published in the morning. Won't you please go ahead and eat?"

"Well, just as you say...but Mother got the chops especially and she'll be disappointed. Well, if you don't want to come home, do as you like."

Mutton chops! Mother is disappointed. A man must dash to the barbecue to stuff his gullet full of the braised muscles of animals so that his mother-in-law won't be offended. Mutton, mutton! Who's got the mutton?

Gordon prodded the keys of his typewriter and felt down-hearted and forlorn. Finally he picked up the machine, verse and all, and hurled it out the window to the alley stones.... I'll go out and get rummed to the eyes. I'll slink into Madam Francis' retreat and shake hands with hobgoblins in the drunkard's Hallowe'en. No, I shan't do that, because it isn't Margery's fault that I am what I am. The poor child does what she believes to be right, trying to help me and endeavoring to fit all her life and all her activities about me.... Margery, why did your love fly down to perch on the hay-stuffed shoulder of a scarecrow?

Gordon sat at the table and ate mutton. Go to my head, mutton, and make me a mutton-head. Then Mrs. Hamilton won't be offended. I'd rather be a rum-head than a mutton-head.... Well, you can be both.

III

MARGERY s baby, a boy, was born April 8, 1915. She had a comparatively easy time of it, laboring less than an hour. She was so healthy and strong and motherhood brought to her face an inference of beauty that mystified Gordon and made him admire her and cherish her the more.

The doctor explained to Mrs. Hamilton—who had insisted on a scientific exposition of the case—that it was a seven-months-child. Nothing unusual about this, Mrs. Hamilton.

"But I thought seven-months-babies didn't have fingernails like this one, Doctor. Of course, I know it's all right, because I know my daughter." She laughed mirthlessly.

Margery wanted to name the child Gordon, but he said the boy would have trouble enough as it was without the name, so they compromised on Norman. That had been the name of Margery's father.

Gordon tried to appear matter-of-fact and casual, but in a week he was up to his ears in love with his boy. Margery was elated at this show of affection. Granner heard the news and said that seven-months-babies were remarkably religious and she expressed confidence that a minister at last had descended from her loins. Hiram said the baby would make a man out of Gordon and he brought a freshly-killed pullet to Margery and kissed her reverently on the forehead.

Mrs. Hamilton declared to Granner that it was embarrassing for the child to have come before its time and she did much counting back on her fingers while her night groans moved through Gordon's dreams like dolorous chants in somber chapels.

IV

WORK increased for Gordon in proportion to the growth of the war and he had to help out in the making up of the paper as well as in the writing of it. He rewrote flimsy having to do with Zeppelin attacks off the east coast of England late in April, 1915, and he revamped stories on submarine raids off the Irish coast. He was called on to rewrite an account of the sinking of the Lusitania in May and he wrote stories under Washington datelines regarding the weakening of Wilsonian patience in June.

As he refashioned these stories about far away happenings, he hated war and all that war brought with it. The world at war, he believed, was imbued by a lust similar to that of the Armory crowd the night the Juarez Kid was killed in the fight with Bratton. On a distant to-morrow the world would awaken with a headache and then it would wonder if it hadn't been seduced into killing in the name of democracy.

He was glad when the long day was done and he could sink his typewriter in his desk with a slam. He thought of the typewriter as a disappearing gun. He was glad to get away from the drone of the press, from the smell of paste pots and of ink gutters.

His hours were such that he usually found his household asleep, but sometimes Mrs. Hamilton would be up when he came in and she could be heard, galloping about, taking her nightmare on the domestic bridle path. He avoided her as much as possible and would slip into an alcove, where his boy, Norman, lay, and would listen to the child's breathing. When it was moonlight, Gordon would raise the blind, lean over the baby to look at the button nose and the milk inflated cheeks. Hundreds of thousands of women had gone through terrific, individual battles, to give such boys as this one to war. Well, he hoped his boy never would be given and furthermore, he wouldn't even give himself until he had to do so.

Margery told her girl acquaintances—many of whom admired Gordon but who thought Margery had made a social mistake in marrying him—that Gordon was a perfect husband. He was the best natured fellow, she boasted, when it came to getting up if Norman cried. He never seems to mind it in the least, and he can put on diapers better than I can. Of course he can't feed the baby. Honestly, I think he envies me feeding it at the breast.

The reason Gordon was glad to get up when Norman

stirred or whimpered was that he was lonely. He had so little time with his child that often he was tempted to awaken Norman and to play with him. He liked to spend his days off with the boy and enjoyed bathing him and rubbing talcum powder on the plump little body until Norman was as dry and as smooth as a peach. The child, he admitted, didn't look much like the Doles, but it did have Granner's Irish eyes. Mrs. Hamilton lost few opportunities in announcing that the boy resembled her late husband.

"It's a Hamilton," she would say pointedly. "It looks like it's mother's side of the house."

Gordon fretted unduly over this eternal inference that the child had little of him in it. Mrs. Hamilton implied that it shouldn't have any of Gordon in it. Why did that woman always try to belittle him?

Chapter Seventeen

I

*I*N October of 1916, Gordon was asked to write a series of articles intended to "wake up America."

What a sap the owner of *The Clarion* is getting to be! Imagine a poor, isolated bar-bug like myself sitting five thousand miles away from nowhere, chirping and sawing my hind legs like a starved cricket, and making blustery noises: "Wake! Wake! Now you just wake up at once, America!"

"Can't you get somebody else to shovel out this fertilizer?" he asked Joe Gates.

" 'S'matter, son? Aren't you patriotic?"

"It's crap and it leaves me cold. I don't think anybody could love his country better than I do, but I love it as a land, as a mother. I don't love it as a delirious, drunken father, with its eyes inflamed and its breath stinking with platitudes and slogans that are a creed to-day and to-morrow a heresy. It's sickening and it's tragic."

"Aw, go ahead and blurb. You can sling the words, and we've got to cheer and wave flags in type while Young

America goes to military school." Gates grew serious. "Gordon, hold yourself together and say nothing that will get you in bad. I understand you, but others wouldn't and you can't spit out your young philosophies. I am an old man, and I have every respect for the beliefs and feelings of Youth...but you'd better keep your mouth shut now."

"How long must I keep it shut, Joe?"

Gates patted Gordon's shoulder. "For at least ten years, my boy....Now ramble over the keys like a good kid and bring out the Rise, fellow citizens, stuff. There is no alternative. The man who refuses to wave the Flag until it is shredded and worn is Benedict Arnold reincarnate.... Sorry, son, but that is the temper of the crowd and the crowd supports our newspaper."

O God! Some of the finest men will be killed and their work lost. The bodies don't matter. Even the torn hearts of fathers won't matter. It's the dashed out brains that will matter. Thoughts will be killed. Men's minds will die. For what?

II

In the year 1917, Gordon received another call to join the staff of *The New York Morning Star*. Depletion of newspaper office forces through military service and the departure of writers to become war correspondents caused metropolitan newspaper owners to cast about the country for likely young reporters. John G. Ward, owner of the *The Star,* himself telegraphed an invitation to Gordon. Gordon wavered.

He talked it over at length with Margery, who feared that a New York success might mean that he would be lost to her.

"How do you figure you would lose me if I succeeded?"

"Well, if you make good—and I know you will—you might figure that you could afford to leave me and the baby and go to war."

"I have no intention of volunteering. It is a hard word, but I suppose I am a slacker."

"You're not any such thing!"

"I don't know about that. If I have to go, it will not be as an officer, but as a common soldier."

"Why not an officer?"

"Because I won't lead men to death. I'll follow if it has to be, but I'll not lead."

Mrs. Hamilton had entered during the conversation. "That's a stubborn way to look at it."

"Then don't look at it," Gordon said. "Margery and I are leaving for New York," he added suddenly. "I'm going to seed here and this is the last chance I'll have to go to the big field. I don't feel welcome anyway in your house, Mrs. Hamilton."

"Please, Gordon!" Margery said.

"It's the truth, Margery."

Mrs. Hamilton assumed a hurt air and spoke sadly: "Well, I have tried to give you and your child a home. I did not expect much gratitude though from a common newspaper reporter."

"One of us is very common," Gordon said. "I hope you really know which one it is."

Gordon left to talk over his plan with Granner. He found Blair at the old home and Hiram came in to ask him about the war news. Granner said she had feared all along that Gordon would be taken from her by the war and now she believed it was almost as bad for him to go to New York. What a big bosom you have, Granner! The better to hold a broken heart, my dear.

Gordon asked Blair if he and his wife would move into the Edgeworth Street home to look out for Granner. Hiram half resented this suggestion, inferring that Gordon believed he wasn't capable of taking care of the old woman. Gordon finally explained to Hiram's satisfaction that it would be a fine thing if they lived together and that he would surely send home his share to help keep the household going.

"Well," Hiram said, "I'd like to have Blair, but I hope he won't bring his undertaking business here."

"No," Blair said, "this place isn't showy enough for me, but I would like to set up a laboratory in the attic. I've got a new idea for the movies, a contraption that will direct motion pictures with phonograph records, thus eliminating the cost of directors."

"I hope you don't bring no powder experiments," Hiram said.

It was settled that Blair would move in and Gordon went home to direct Margery to pack up their few belongings. Mrs. Hamilton had told Margery she need expect no financial help from her in this mad change to New York, where her son-in-law was bound to fail. She said that Margery could come home to her when failure dawned on her and when she learned what a mistake she had made in marrying. But, of course, Mrs. Hamilton never again could countenance Gordon in her home.

Margery begged Gordon not to resent her mother's attitude openly and told him she had saved $600. That would be enough to see them through for a while.

III

JOE GATES and Gordon were having a farewell round of drinks at Finner's. The old man was sullen. He loved this boy—he was work of his own hands. But Joe made out that he was cranky, pessimistic and hard-hearted.

"Come on, Joe. Throw off that pose. I know you hate to see me go, but won't you be glad to have me succeed?"

"Well, maybe."

Gordon choked on his rye and coughed. He was glad he had choked, because that would explain the tears that kept coming to his eyes. "Gee, Joe, I'm sick about leaving. I've damned the paper, the owner and you and everything, and I've laughed at the press when they had to use bailing wire to fasten the plates on the old rattletrap. But just the same I love the place.... Joe, why do people who love things leave them?"

"So they can have some regrets to look back on when they're old. When do you leave?"

"I'd like to go to-morrow, if it won't tie up the works."

"That's all right, son, go ahead." Gates ordered another drink. "We'll get on without you ... that is, they will get on."

"What do you mean by 'they'?"

Gates waited until he had had his drink before replying. "I mean this, Gordie, I have resigned from *The Clarion*. I'm through."

Through! Impossible. Joe Gates never would resign, the Press Club oracles had told Gordon again and again. Why, the man was as eternal as Gramper's hills!

"You're not drunk, are you, Joe?"

"I had intended to pass out at my desk, with my shears in my hand and with a parting God damn at somebody that misspelled a name ... but my work is done and I know it. I'm seventy-seven this next spring, Gordie. I'm going to the pasture with the other old fire horses."

"Then come on to New York with me, Joe."

Gates looked at Gordon appraisingly, just as he had looked at him the day he had raised his salary from six dollars to thirty dollars a week, but with more affection this time. "I kind of think you mean that, son." Gordon nodded. "Well, I'll stay here, but I'll be going with you in spirit, if that's anything.... I wasn't going to tell you, Gordie, but do you know why I've been ranting and cussing at you all these years?"

"I think I can guess. You wanted to make something out of me."

"Right. I haven't succeeded very well, have I?"

"No, I guess you haven't, but you're the only one I ever let bawl me out and get away with it."

"Were you always impudent and rebellious, Gordie?"

"Yes, I was. I can't help it."

Gordon ordered drinks. What a great drinking companion old Joe was and how Gordon would miss him, the squeaky-voiced, sarcastic old champion!

"Well, son, it's unconventional advice, coming from an acknowledged disciplinarian, but don't you ever lose your impudence, because there's a great brain behind it.... Son, I've worked hard with you, not only because I like you, but because... because..."

"Because what, you old reprobate?"

Joe Gates stood erect and glared. "Because, sir, I have been trying to make out of you the man I had hoped to be myself!"

Gordon could have cried good and hard now. Damn it, why was he acting so womanishly about this? The newspaper school was a hard one and Joe Gates had been a hard preceptor, and there was no excuse for a man getting weepy this way.

"I wish to God I could be half the man you have been, Joe."

"Well, you're the best job I ever turned out, and I've sent quite a few to the Big Town, and they've all made good, too. My boys know news and they can write in any man's city. Don't you fall down, God damn you!"

Gordon thought that he would write to Joe often, and then realized that people didn't write or keep in touch as they should. They say they are going to write letters, but they don't. When a man gains a pillow of down, he throws away his old pallet of straw. Of all his wealth, a man spends his friendships first. Here, World, don't take my job or my money—let me give you three or four slightly-used friend-ships instead.

"You've paid me the highest compliment I'll ever get," Gordon said.

"You'll get compliments, but don't pay a damned bit of attention to them. Be humble in the face of success, Gordie, but be as proud as Satan himself in time of trou-ble. I was like you and I wanted to live my own life and to write my own way, but I let them make an editor out of me." Joe paused and shuttled the small whisky glass from one pudgy hand to the other. "Your way is the hard way, holding your chin high and aiming at the things that are acceptable to your soul, but in the end you'll respect yourself, even if you're in the gutter."

They left Finner's and walked a few blocks without talking. An old cab man, one of the last horse drivers in Fairmount, a fellow who had taken Joe home for more than thirty years, was following Joe and Gordon with his rattling vehicle, confident of a fare. Finally Joe stopped and the cab came to the curb beside them.

"Damn you!" Joe yelled at the cabby. "Haven't I told you for years not to follow me around the streets? Can't a man have any privacy in this town?"

The cab driver smiled and saluted with his whip. Joe climbed in. "I don't want to say 'Good-by,' Gordie."

"We'll never say 'Good-by,' Joe." Gordon stood there, feeling as though a chariot had come down from the skies to take a great soul from earth. He was still standing there, wondering and sorrowing and fearing, when the high, raspy voice of Joe Gates came to him from the cab which now was half a block away.

"Don't misspell any names in New York, you careless bastard! I won't give you a job if they fire you!"

"Go to hell, you old crab!" Gordon was crying and now he wasn't ashamed of his tears. He waited until the hoof beats of the horses faded and then he went home.

PART TWO

Chapter One

I

GORDON brought his wife and baby to New York City in August of 1917.

Here we come, gallop-a-trot! Here's old Gordon and his troupe.... Were you unafraid, Nada, when you stepped out of your drawing room on the Century? You've got New York by the neck now—Blair said you had—and you can sit beside your silkworm, sipping cocktails. How do you keep New York from getting a fellow by the seat of the pants?

The long train ride had given Gordon another bilious spell. He disliked the train because it was dirty, monotonous and noisy—a jail on wheels. He did much of his undressing in the aisle, despite a look of protest from the professorial appearing old gentleman across the way. Why should I lie on my back to undress, straining my insides just because old Sexless is modest? Perhaps I'm an exhibitionist. Gordon couldn't sleep soundly and the upper berth was hot, the ceiling pressing down on him like the lid of a fireless cooker. Roll and bounce, tumble and fret, chug and clang, sway and slip. What fearful training for the battle with the big bully, Metropolis! I'll get hit in the first round, surely. I'll go down for the full count. One, two, three. Who is the referee that's counting over me? Four. Five. Why, it's Nada, dressed in gray flannel shirt and trousers! Six. Seven. Who's voice is that? It's my second, old Joe Gates. Get up, Gordie! Get up on the nine-count and go in with your chin covered. Eight. Nine. My legs are gone. ... Legs, hell! Your guts are gone. Ochre. Saffron. Canary. Lemon. Parchment. Yolk—don't try to give yourself any of these shades, but just admit you are plain Yellow, the most luminous color of the spectrum. The only color in yours. Ten! Maybe I'm up again and fighting on instinct. I've seen 'em do it. Whole rounds go blank after a slug on the button.... Maybe I'm going in, as Joe said to do.

"Where will we stay when we get there?" Margery asked. "We mustn't get anything expensive. Suppose you ask somebody?"

"I don't know anybody on the train and I hate asking questions. I'm enough of a hick as it is without asking questions."

"I'll look in that book in the corridor. It has hotel ads in it. I hope we have a home of our own soon."

Gordon took Norman to the club car. He could tell by the clutter of the landscape that they were coming near the City, but he looked rather at the Hudson than at the places of human habitation and the river's late summer beauty allowed him to forget his fears for the moment. The child and the man saw boats, large ones, for their first time. Gordon wanted to see the ocean most of all, but he guessed it was quite a way off.

If he had expected to see a skyline that had been shown on postcards and in motion pictures, he was denied. After dinner he sat with Norman on his knee and with Margery on the seat facing them. He had strapped their baggage and it was dusk. He hadn't the slightest idea where they were, but he knew they were due to arrive in an hour. The train whisked past yawning red ovens of factories and he thought the ovens were the inflamed eyes of beasts that were awaiting his coming. Through the hot twilight he saw endless rows of blocky houses and there were lights in the windows. Women and men leaned out the windows on pillows or sat on fire escapes as though watching some morbidly fascinating play.

They entered a tunnel under Park Avenue and after several roaring, burrowing minutes, the air-brakes crunched at steel biscuits and Gordon and his family walked into a mammoth house of marble. Hello, Grand Central Station, my name is Gordon Dole. Meet my wife and my child, marble monster.

"Do you feel any better, Gordon?"

"Margery, I hate to admit it, but I'm scared stiff!"

"Scared of what?"

"I don't know."

II

MARGERY thought they should take a street car from the station—if only she knew which one to take. She had jotted down the name of a hotel in One Hundred and Twenty-fifth street, West, thinking to get off at the One Hundred and Twenty-fifth street station, but there had been a misunderstanding with the porter about it and they had been carried along with the train.

"Your hotel sounds an awful ways off from here, Margery."

"It's advertised at $2.50 a day, and I'm thinking of expenses."

"Let's take a cab."

"If you insist." Margery whispered to Gordon. "I wouldn't give that porter more than a dime."

He was afraid to give the Red Cap less than a quarter. He was in a Big City now and a dime didn't sound like a Big City emolument for porters.

The taxi flag was slapped down. The slender drumsticks of late summer rain began to beat on the roof of the cab. There was a misty veil over all and through the veil Gordon saw the glow of the City, high-hanging and mystic, an ominous halo above the towers, cornices and spires. It is the sacrificial fire burning on the Altar of Mammon.

"For God's sake, Margery, let's ask this driver to take us somewhere closer than the Hundred-and-Something address!"

"I'm afraid the hotels near here will be expensive."

Yah! Yah! Afraid of expenses. Well, I'm afraid of something else and I'd mortgage my loins to get out of this. I must get out. Rather, I must get in. Or, I must get up. No, I must get down....

"Take us to a hotel near here," Gordon said to the driver.

They registered at the Denham in West Forty-eighth Street. Margery maintained they couldn't afford it, but she told Gordon to have his own way about it. She said she'd look for an apartment as soon as she had a breathing spell.

"You'd better get in touch with the newspaper people," Margery said. O Lord! Must I? Wouldn't to-morrow do? Well, I came here at their request and I'd better tell them I'm here, for the chances are they are not clairvoyant.

The size of the New York telephone books added to the weight on Gordon's soul. Finally he made out the five numbers that accompanied the five residences of Mr. John G. Ward, owner of *The New York Morning Star*. Well, howdy-do! Old Five-Star-Hennessy himself. So you have five telephones, Mr. Ward. Have you five senses, too? ... Hello, get me Riverside.... Hello.... Get me Bryant.... Well, then, get me Murray Hill....

Mr. Ward's secretary's secretary answered one of the numbers, and Gordon had to undergo much ritualistic labor to induce the assistant secretary to bother the secretary.... I should have brought a letter from my pastor. I should have approached him with ambassadorial portfolio. ... That you, Mr. Holtman? This is Gordon Dole. I'm reporting to you.

"Reporting to me? About what, Mr.... Mr.... ah...."

"Dole."

"Which Mr. Doyle is this?"

Keep Norman quiet, will you, Margery? Shut that

window. Now what in hell is this? They ask me to come and they don't even know the name.

"I'm the fellow you've been writing to and telegraphing to for the last several years about coming to work for *The Star*.... What's that? Just a minute; there's an elevated train passing, Mr. Holtman.... Yes, it's Gordon Dole. D-o-l-e. Not Mole or Hole or Goal. Just Dole, and I'm here."

"Where?"

"In New York City; at least I think it's New York City. If not I'm sorry." Damn it all! I don't care whether the job's on or off. "I'm the man from Fairmount City."

"Oh, yes. I place you now. Glad to hear from you, Mr. Dole. Yes, I'll see what The Chief says."

The Chief! Am I going to work for an Indian? Maybe Sitting Bull didn't die after all. Ye call me Chief. Maybe it's Spartacus and he thinks I'm a gladiator.

"What shall I do meanwhile, Mr. Harriman?" Ha! I've called him Harriman instead of Holtman. How do you like that, old boy? I'm Doyle and you're Harriman.

"I'll get in touch with you. Where are you staying? Oh, at the Denham. All right. You needn't bother the office until you hear from The Chief through me."

III

GORDON sat in his hotel for three days, waiting for a telephone call from Secretary Holtman, but no word came from him.

"I can't understand the delay," Gordon said to Margery in their room.

"Maybe he got mad because you called him Harriman."

"Well, he called me Doyle."

"You'll hear in time."

"Yes, time. Time! What a knock-kneed, draggy old guy Time is!"

"Most people think of Time as an old man, but I always think of him as a sweet little boy, always growing up and wishing, but never actually getting grown up."

Gordon quit fretting as Margery smoothed his forehead.

"Say, I've got the most goofy thought," he said. "Maybe I shouldn't tell you my goofy thoughts."

"I love your thoughts. Tell me."

"I was wishing for a minute that you were my mother instead of my wife."

"That's not so funny. I often look on you as my boy. Of course, I don't understand why I should, but you really are like a boy to me. I've got two fine boys."

"If I wanted to be downright silly, I'd say I wanted to sit on your lap."

"Well, come ahead. I'd love to have you."

"Honest to God? You wouldn't think I had gone clean off my head, would you?"

"Not at all."

"Aw, I'm too heavy, Margery, and anyway it's crazy."

"I'm waiting."

He sat on her lap and she held him close to her.

"You don't think me crazy, do you, Margery?"

"I wouldn't care if you were. I want to make you happy. I only wish I could give you everything."

"You do."

"Yes, everything I have to give, but somehow I feel that I don't know how to let myself go when you are in my arms as a man and not as a boy."

"Those things pass away, Margery."

"Like Time passes away?"

"Yes, like old man Time passes away."

"But not as Time passes as a little boy?"

"No. Your Little Boy Time never will pass away."

"You will never pass away, Gordon. You are my Little Boy Time."

"Some day I'll be your old man Time."

"We'll see. I'm not afraid."

"You're never afraid, Margery. Do you know why?"

"No."

"Because you're good. Only bad people are afraid."

"Then you shouldn't be afraid, Gordie."

"But I am afraid ... and I'm bad."

"Bad or good, I love you."

"You're a wonderful girl, Margery. I find peace on your breast. Are you my mother?"

"Yes, I'm your mother. It will be our greatest secret."

IV

MARGERY read want-ads and tried to find an apartment while Gordon minded the baby and waited to hear from

Holtman. Gordon finally called Holtman and told him he was going to leave town; that he was tired of waiting; that he believed a joke had been played on him.

"Why, Mr. Dole, I'm sorry you have been inconvenienced. You see The Chief has been busy the last few days at the auction sales. He goes in for art objects and antiques, you know."

He can go in for slate pencils and sponges for all I give a damn. "Well, Mr. Holtman, I'll have to know if I stay in town any longer, because I've got a job waiting for me in Chicago."

"Could you come right over to The Chief's house?"

"I suppose I could. How do I get there?"

Mr. Holtman explained that you took a bus and what number the bus was, but Gordon got two dollars from Margery and took a cab.

He went to The Chief's house prepared to hate him. He didn't see The Chief at once but talked with Mr. Holtman, whom he liked and found very sagacious but kindly. When he told him that he expected a wage of $125 a week, Mr. Holtman almost gagged.

"Why, Mr. Dole, we had counted on giving $60, but your price is a bit prohibitive, if I may say so."

"You may say so, Mr. Holtman, but that's my price."

Mr. Holtman certainly would have to take this matter up with The Chief. The Chief had purchased quite a bit of armor and Thirteenth Century plates yesterday and the mention of such a high salary might heighten his influenza tendencies. Gordon had not known that this demand

would be exorbitant. Why, Harry McGorman had said
that the lowliest reporters in New York drew down a
hundred per. That's why Gordon had made it $125. It
would lift him a rung above the lowliest ones. He didn't
like to be lowly.

"What makes you ask for $125 a week, Mr. Dole?"

"Intuition."

"Will you wait here?" They were in the library. Mr.
Holtman opened huge, hand-carved double doors and was
absent for about two minutes. Gordon would have liked
to handle some of the books on the aged shelves. There
were challenging boxes with labels on them which were
hard to believe. He read such legends as "Original Ms.
Charles Dickens," "Letters Jno. Keats." There was a first
folio Shakespeare, a "Breeches Bible" and first editions of
Goldsmith, Thackeray and Byron. The library ceiling was
beamed and paneled from Twelfth Century church ceil-
ings and there were old choir stalls and aged Spanish
tables with antique brocades and gold candlesticks.... He
probably uses the sarcophagus of Rameses for a bathtub
and swats flies with the court fan of Marie Antoinette....
Mr. Holtman beckoned.

Gordon found Mr. Ward a most likeable person. He
had heard of The Chief's personality—how his men were
spellbound by him—and Gordon, too, was taken with the
charm of the soft-voiced owner of *The Star*. Mr. Ward was
a big, lumbering man, with pale blue eyes and an expression of child-like serenity and an inquisitive, half-humorous
twitch of the long upper lip as he smiled. He shook hands

with Gordon, rising from his chair....Imagine him getting up to shake hands with me. Perhaps he mistakes me for a candidate for Mayor. Well, there's no harm in liking a man, even if he does get into opposition prints as the Devil-on-Wheels, Pro-German and America's-Pain-in-the-Neck.

There was no mention of salary at all, but Mr. Ward chatted readily about western journalism, revealing casually that he knew more about the newspapers of Fairmount City than did the men who owned them. They discussed editors and Mr. Ward laughed when Gordon bluntly said he didn't like them. He liked one of them—in fact, he loved one of them, old Joe Gates—but he hoped he never would be an editor himself. Did Mr. Ward know of Joe Gates?

"Very well." The soft-voiced man smiled benignly and added: "I fired him."

"You what?" Gordon was amazed. Was this a joke? How could anyone have fired a genius, why ...

"Yes, I fired him, but we'll not go into that. As to editors, they are rather disconcerting. I myself prefer reporters and I always think of myself as a reporter."

"Then you don't like editors, either?"

"They're rather necessary under our present plan, but I always feel that a reporter is a promise and an editor is a disappointment....Mr. Dole, I am glad that you are coming with us. The Ward service offers many opportunities and I want to see you happily placed. What do you write best?"

"I can write anything but checks."

"You'll be able to write those soon." Mr. Ward was smiling, but Gordon wasn't so sure of that smile now. He had smiled when he said he had fired Joe Gates. It was the same smile. Maybe he only had one kind of smile. ... Mr. Ward again rose from a chair that had belonged to General George Washington. He held out his hand to Gordon, revealing a cuff link that had been worn by Abraham Lincoln, and they walked together to the feudal door and across a rug on which Napoleon had married Josephine. Mr. Ward waved farewell.

"You'll hear from us when there is something," Mr. Holtman said. "I'm glad you got the job. When I told The Chief how you demanded such a high price right off, he said, 'Hire that man immediately; he sounds as though he will be capable of deviling an editor for me.' Of course," and Mr. Holtman looked worried, "what I tell you is sacredly confidential."

"Absolutely. When shall I report?"

"Don't bother the office at all. Wait until they call you." He smiled understandingly. "You see we do business on a broader scale than others. No hurry. Except when The Chief wants theater tickets or something."

Gordon told the news joyously to Margery, but he still felt afraid of the city and somehow he connected the spirit of the city with the shadowy, half-humorous smile The Chief had displayed in saying that he had fired Joe Gates. There had been something enigmatic in it suggestive of the smile on the terra cotta sepulchral statue of an Etruscan that was in the museum of Fairmount.

Margery was glad a pay check was on the horizon, for they didn't have much left out of her savings. They moved into an apartment on Amsterdam Avenue and One Hundred and Twelfth Street. Flat-wheeled street cars bumped along the tracks fronting their apartment, which was on the fourth floor, and Gordon could see the rough outline of the unfinished Cathedral of St. John the Divine from his windows. At night the rugged outline of the incomplete nave of the Cathedral bulked like a crouching cat. The flying buttresses of rough stone were the feet of the cat.

"There's an awful lot of cockroaches in New York," Margery said. "They say you can't get rid of them; that they come up the dumb-waiter shaft from the kitchens of untidy housekeepers."

"Maybe Norman can tame a big one and ride it instead of a pony.... I wish to God the office would call me. It's the funniest town."

Chapter Two

I

*A*LTHOUGH Margery kept after Gordon to go to Park Row, if only to call on his editors, more than a week went by.

"I was told to wait for a call," he said. "I don't want to bother them." Secretly, however, he suffered the unnameable fear that always was his when he realized he was in New York.

"But maybe you have some pay coming to you."

He looked at her pityingly. "Pay! What would they pay me for when I haven't worked? Say, Margery, they're business men, not easy guys."

He finally did go downtown, however, determined to say something about this delay. Margery told him they had only ten cents on hand and that would be merely enough for subway fare. As he rode the West Side express to Park Place, he watched the faces of those that crowded his car, trying to find out if they, too, feared the City. They didn't seem to be feeling anything at all but wore what appeared to be fatalistic expressions as though the City was Juggernaut and they the ones who were to be rolled upon and mangled.

The offices of *The Star* were disillusionment to Gordon. Warehousey and fœtid. Gloomy and harrowing. Ready to fall apart. The windows were opaque with grime and an elevator that was as impotent as a veteran of the Mexican War rose with groggy lament up a shaft that would have disgraced a coal mine.... Well, they haven't any merchandise to sell. Why should they get out a newspaper in Buckingham Palace, with a guard mount of busbied soldiers in scarlet tunics?

Gordon had had correspondence with Dave Crowder, the sports editor, and he thought he would look him up first. Crowder was glad to meet Gordon and asked him what he was doing in the East. Visiting? No, I'm working on this sheet.... The hell you say? Come meet some of the editors.

"This is Bill Egan, the assistant city editor."

"No, Dole," Egan said, "I haven't heard anything about you coming on the staff. Things sometimes are delayed, you know, but if The Chief put you on, you're on. That's all. I'll speak to Colonel Platt."

"Who's he?"

"Are you kidding, Dole? Why, he's the managing editor. Watterson's pal and the greatest newspaper brains in America to-day. We'll call you when I've talked to the Colonel."

"So they have colonels here, too," Gordon said to Crowder.

"Just Colonel Platt. He's the colonel. My God, what a great man the Colonel is!"

"Made them forget Greeley and Dana, eh?"

Crowder seemed uneasy at Gordon's tone in speaking of such an outstanding figure in American letters—or near-letters. Much incense seemed to be burned to the Colonel.

"How about the city editor? The main one?"

Crowder said they'd go to Mike's and have a drink, and on the way across Chambers Street, Crowder said: "Confidentially, Dole, watch out for Kemp."

"Who's he? The Chief of Police?"

"No, he's the city editor. The Chief put him in a month ago and I think he knows where something is buried. He's mighty independent and mysterious and already he's cut under four experts The Chief brought from California in the Spring."

"They must change editors often?"

"Most of our time is spent in acknowledging introductions to our new bosses. Of course the Colonel is a fixture, but a man with his brains...."

"But Kemp?"

"He'll break your heart, fire you and then desecrate your grave."

"He must be a fine chap, Crowder. I think we'll be great pals. I like the prospect immensely."

"Yes? Well, Kemp exudes poison and the place is so full of politics I wouldn't be surprised to see the next Democratic Convention held in Kemp's office." Crowder peered at Dole over the rim of his Scotch. "If The Chief hired you, you are lucky and unlucky, too."

"So? Let's have another. No, wait...." Gordon was shocked. He suddenly realized he didn't have but a nickel. "Say, Crowder, I'm sorry, but I forgot something important. Do you mind if I run along? We'll have plenty of drinks in a day or two."

"Sure, if you got to go." Crowder looked at Gordon rather speculatively and after Gordon had gone out the door, Crowder said to the bartender: "Say, I think they've hired another nut, only this one looks extra ripe."

Gordon waited for a long time up the street, standing behind a truck and near a chestnut roaster's oven that almost asphyxiated him as he peeped at the saloon door. Finally he saw Crowder coming out and was glad when *The Star's* sports editor hailed a cab and got in. Gordon returned to *The Star* building and asked where the cashier's office was. He was directed to the ninth floor and went to the pay window while a big plug-ugly with a gun strapped to his belt stood near the door. At the window-wicket, Gordon gave his name and a fine-mannered old man looked him over.

"Oh, you're that young fellow from the West?"

"Yes." Well, here's at least one man who has heard of me. Number one. A good-looking old guy at that. The first man in New York to know Gordon Dole without a lot of explanations. Probably the last one, too. "Yes, I just called to introduce myself. Mr. Ward put me to work on *The Star,* I wasn't sure whether he said I'd get checks or be paid here."

"I've got two envelopes for you, Mr. Dole. I wondered why you hadn't come 'round."

"Envelopes?"

"Surely. There's two weeks' pay in them."

Gordon was afraid to breathe. "But I've only been here a week and two days."

"Yes, but your pay began when you started on the train from your home city, Mr. Dole."

"Thanks. Sorry if I troubled you by not coming in sooner, but I was in no particular need of the money." No, not at all! You were just going about with your pants at half mast; just going daffy as hell, that's all. There was $250 in the envelopes.

Gordon took the subway home and kept his right hand inside his trousers pocket, tightly clenched about the bills. No one would steal it from him, you bet.

II

NEXT day Gordon had a call from Egan, the assistant city editor. Come on down, we've got a tip on a big story and it looks as though you're the proper party to handle it.

Gordon found Egan and Kemp, the city editor, "who knew where something was buried," conferring. Kemp was doing most of the talking in an even, colorless voice. He was thin and relaxed and looked more like a race track tout than a newspaper editor. He wore a straw hat, although the City was getting into its fall derbies, and there was a red band on it. He gazed methodically at Gordon, then his colorless voice took on life and he began to speak volubly and his frame lost its relaxed appearance. Evidently he had been resting between duties like a boxer rests between rounds.

"Aren't you from a town called Fairmount?"

"I am."

"Knew pretty nearly everyone out there, didn't you?"

"Hardly that. I knew a lot of people though."

Kemp lighted a cigarette from the coal of one he had been smoking. "Well, we've got a tip—a red hot tip—on a story that you might help out on. You'll have to work quietly on it and do some digging. Two other men haven't been able to get it, but seeing that it involves somebody from your home town, we thought you might land it."

"I'll try. Who is it?"

"Did you know an actress named Nada Halpin?"

Gordon didn't reply at once, because he couldn't. Was she dead? Had she been shot? or had she shot someone? He knew that he was turning pale. Why in hell had he come to New York? His first assignment, too!

"I went to school with her," he said finally.

Kemp was enthusiastic and Egan nodded happily. "That's fine," Kemp said. "It simplifies matters. Miss Halpin, as you may know, is the favorite actress of the moment, and she's getting a divorce." Gordon winced. "I guess you know she's the wife of Hymen A. Grosserly, the multimillionaire silk man?"

"Yes, I know." New York editors were long winded, if Kemp was any criterion. Old Joe wouldn't have dawdled along in this manner. Mr. Ward had fired Joe Gates, but it wasn't because he was an orator, that much was sure. Gates put short, snappy assignments on paper and handed them to you with his scissors. Kemp was Demosthenes and Sherlock Holmes at the same time, but he was confoundedly verbose.

"Good," Kemp said. "Now let's get busy. You don't have to worry about pictures for we've got plenty of poses of that dame." God damn you for calling her "that dame!" I'd like to bust you in the nose for that, but I'd only get locked up on an insanity charge.

"But the story?"

"She doesn't know you re on the paper here, does she?"

Gordon looked at Kemp and Kemp thought him a rather odd-mannered sort; kind of high-and-mighty. Well, we'll take that out of him. We won't have any prima donnas when I get through reshaping the staff.

"No, she doesn't know I'm here." She doesn't know I'm on earth and I wish I didn't know she was on earth. But she is and as long as she is and as long as I am on earth, I'll be calling to her. I can't help it, Margery. I can't help it, my darling Norman. I just can't help it. I can't! So help me, God!

Kemp lighted still another cigarette and puffed hard. "It's a soft spot. You drop in on her between acts and play the home-town visitor stuff. She's leading lady in 'The

Spenders,' The Bradley Theater, West Forty-third Street.
Pump her for all the facts. Sympathy stuff, you know. Then
we'll hop to the story. See you later, Dole. It's a great break
for you and it will make The Chief happy. He doesn't like
Grosserly since he gave that campaign fund to Justice
Swift, the guy that labeled the Chief pro-German."

Kemp wondered why Gordon stood there so stiffly and
so lethargic. Well, if he wanted to be a reporter on *The
Star* he'd have to learn to jump when the whip was
cracked.

"I can see the streamer line now on the street edition,"
Kemp said as though talking to himself. "Eight columns,
ninety-six point Railroad Gothic, with two-column banks.
'SILK BARON RIPS LINING OUT OF NADA'S NEST'.... Hey,
Dole, on your way, boy."

"I'm sorry, Mr. Kemp, seeing this is my first story for
you, but I find it impossible to work on it."

"Impossible! What's impossible?" So he is a prima
donna! I'll break him high and wide right now. "You heard
my orders!"

"I didn't hear a thing."

"You're a good soldier, aren't you? You got newspaper
training, didn't you, even if it was in a hick town?"

"I'm a reporter, but I'm not a rat. I got newspaper
training from a man named Joe Gates. It was a hick town,
I guess, and maybe I'm a hick. I eat cheese, too, but that
doesn't make me a rat."

Kemp shrugged and his voice lapsed again into the
colorless pitch it had had when Gordon first entered his

office. "O.K., Dole. Remember me to the folks back in Fairmount." Gordon went out with Egan.

"Don't worry about it too much," Egan said. "You must have had a good reason for turning down the assignment."

"Who knows?" Be humble in the face of success—that's what Joe Gates had counseled him—but be as proud as Satan in time of trouble. He was as proud as Satan as he saw Kemp go into the Colonel's office. He couldn't help but hear a strange, bass voice: "Well, just fire him. . . . Now what have you got for Page One to-night, Kemp? We're awfully tight with war news."

III

BUT Gordon wasn't fired.

Years later he learned that the Colonel had conferred that evening with Mr. Ward regarding a Five-Cent-Fare editorial, and that Mr. Ward had asked about Gordon. When the Colonel said that he had ordered him fired, the Chief vetoed it.

"Don't you think we should keep that young man with us for a while, Colonel?"

"Yes, I do, Mr. Ward."

Whenever The Chief asked an editor a pointed question, there was only one answer—Yes. It was one of the ways in which The Chief worked his will. No doubt when he fired Joe Gates he had smiled and asked: "Now don't you think you need a rest, Mr. Gates? A long rest? A permanent one?"

Gordon reported at the office daily and was compelled to sit most of the time doing nothing. Occasionally he was asked to do an item or two of rewrite. He felt like a boy with a light case of scarlet fever, quarantined and watching playmates from a window as they romped before his eyes. And he might as well have had scarlet fever or smallpox, for few persons came near him lest they incur the displeasure of the man who "knew where something was buried." Egan was one exception and Crowder was another. They both talked to Gordon and Egan tried to straighten out the situation.

Gordon didn't grumble nor did he confide his troubles in anyone, not even in Margery. He kept waiting for the story concerning Nada to break into print, and it did break. It didn't appear in *The Star*. *The Evening Standard* had it, and that made Egan and the Colonel as mad as unpaid prostitutes.

Egan covertly admired Gordon for his gameness and judged from the few stories that Gordon was asked to do that the young man had ability. One night Gordon was writing a letter to Granner, telling her how wonderful New York was; how he missed her; how glad he was that he could send her $40 a week and how famous he was getting. Egan came to his desk.

"How'd you like to take an airplane ride, Mr. Dole?"

"Swell! Don't send me up with the Colonel, though. He'd shove me overboard."

"Sh!" Egan warned. "The Colonel's O.K.... There's a plane taking off to-morrow from Hazlehurst Field, out by Garden City. It's a Caproni bomber and each paper has been invited to send a representative."

"Count me in, Mr. Egan, and thanks for the chance."

"The paper won't be responsible. You must take the flight at your own risk. It's a trip over New York. Are you on?"

"I'll go out now and get a guide book."

Margery was not at all enthusiastic and said Gordon would be killed sure. You simply mustn't think of it, Gordie.... Well, Margery, I'm going to do it, because it's the only chance I've had in weeks and I am itching to write something.... Well, go ahead, Gordie, and have your own way.

Just think! Maybe I'll ride over Nada's house; over Nada's theater. I must look on the map and find exactly where those places are.

Chapter Three

I

*G*ORDON'S airplane ride above Manhattan Island did more to stabilize his psychology than did any other single happening in his career. His newspaper description of that experience called the attention of his fellows to his talent, but the living of it was what mattered most to him.

He placed plugs of cotton in his ears and drew his helmet over his dark hair and pulled on a sheep-lined jacket. He got into the open cockpit with other news men. An hour later, when the plane returned to the field, he was confidently full of something. He did not know what he had gained, but he knew what it was he had lost. He had lost fear. Fear of the bully, Metropolis.

It was his first time up. So often I've looked at the clouds, he thought, white ones and black ones, thin, stringy ones that run before the high winds. Slow, plumed ones that alter in form; wherein you can see a girl's face change into an old man's face, and then into dancing nymphs, and then into satyrs with pipes swaying, and then into lambs that come in a huddle through the blue pastures of the moon. Now I'm winging into the clouds and perhaps above them. Will I find only emptiness there? I've found emptiness on earth without you, Nada. Forgive me, Norman, if I have found emptiness. You are my flesh, Norman. Nada is my soul.

II

"I'LL hold up my fingers," Captain Milano, the Italian Ace, said. "Each finger will indicate a thousand meters. So!"

The ground men are letting go of the yellow wings. There is a quick movement, as though the plane is about to plunge backward. See, the ground and not the plane is skimming past. See, the ground and not the plane is departing, dropping abruptly, unconcernedly, like Nada dropped Grosserly. Like Nada, the world, went from beneath Grosserly's wing, leaving him there, suspended in emptiness.

We are going into a crisp wind that comes from the west. It may rain to-morrow. To-morrow! Margery said she would miss me if anything.... Milano looks back and grins. Then he holds up one finger. We are climbing steadily in shallow spirals and the greens, parchments and deep orange shades of autumn are getting drab and now they are a gray. My world is leaving an old world. I'd like to fly over your house, old Granner, and drop gold pieces on the shingles. How you would chuckle as you heard the gold disks fall! It's raining yellow gold, Granner would say. Come on out, Blair, Hiram, everybody, and see the yellow gold drop like sweat from the brow of God.

It's getting very cold up here.

Why do you grin, Milano? Do you know that I have secrets? When you hold up two fingers, do you mean two thousand meters? Or are you blessing us with priestly digits? Maybe he'll make the sign of the cross.

Oh, yes, we still can see a world of far horizons, but there's no life there. Circular buildings that were so large on the field are tiny mushrooms now. Gas tanks over there at the City's limit are only drinking cups for dolls. Roadways are baby ribbons and railroad tracks are threads. My foot is asleep and maybe I'm going to sleep all over. Maybe I have died and Milano is Heaven's Eagle, taking my soul to be judged. You can't have my soul! I've given it to Nada. Return your judgment scales to their hiding place, Great Assessor. My soul is not for your balance pans. Nada doesn't know it, but she keeps my soul in her wardrobe closet. Everyone wonders what rare perfume she uses. It's not perfume on Nada's gowns. It's the scent of my soul. It's the essence of my poor, wistful soul.

So that is the sea beneath us. It's not the sea. It is only a boundless pane of frosted glass, such as business men have for partitions between Mr. Joseph's office and Mr. Benjamin's office. It can't be the sea, for there are no waves. No motion. Only a thin, white line against the shore.

But I say it must be the Battery and the harbor. That's the Statue of Liberty, one of the few landmarks I know. It's only a little ornament, a paper weight on an office desk. Now we turn and go uptown. How can I pick out your home on Park Avenue, Nada? I should have flown closer to you, yet it is pleasant to be away from the world. How can I find your theater in West Forty-third street?

Manhattan Island!

So that's you, Metropolis. You're just a little lizard, sleeping in the sun. There's something bigger than you. Aha! I've been afraid of a little lizard!

We go further uptown; that is, if there is any such thing as uptown on a lizard's back. Now we plunge into a cloud and now we sail above it. Below is a carpet of fleece. How like the illusions of a dream. We are out of sight of land. Only an innocent blue, a cold blue, above us and all about us. Only a carpet of billowing samite beneath. Here is isolation. Here is privacy. Here is restoration of one's psyche. Lizard Manhattan, where are you now? Who's afraid of you now? Not I.

Milano gestures that we shall dip nearer to peek at the lizard. It's like going to the zoo. That must be Metropolitan Tower. It can't be. It's smaller than a grandfather's clock. Lower we go. Yes, it is the Tower.

I am among the stars, Nada, and I wish you were here. I would clasp you like the cold sky clasps me. I wish I could hold you like Rodin's Eternal Spring holds the marble woman. You stone and I stone, forever clasped.

We fly low, low. That is Central Park. I'm still too strange to your New York, Nada, to be sure about Park Avenue. We slip away. North, I think it is. How can one be sure what is north when the river they call North River is west and an East River is not always east? They aren't

even on the level with their rivers. How could you expect
Grosserly to be on the level with you? Or myself on the
level with Norman and Margery?

That is a cemetery beneath us. Calvary Cemetery, I
think it is. There's a suggestion for you. There is the end
of all rides. When one ceases to affect one's environment
and when one's environment ceases to affect one, it is
called death. How many Racys lie there? How many
Grampers are there beneath the white, uneven tusks that
are tombstones?

Up we go and back we go. There is Broadway, narrow
and as uneven as a tear in a rag. Kisses I throw you, Nada,
from my couch of cloud-mist. Catch them, for they vanish
so soon. I see steeples of churches. Candle snuffers. Candle
snuffers that smother the light. We are above Long Island
again. We make steep banks, dizzy turns. What is this I
see? The sun is below me, the earth above me. Topsy-
turvy. Everything topsy-turvy! Let it be. I am no longer
afraid of the Town.

Chapter Four

I

*M*ARGERY'S first year in New York was a lonely one and Gordon felt for her keenly; but he didn't see what could be done about it. He seldom reached home before two o'clock in the morning and usually slept until noon. He shaved hurriedly, bolted his breakfast and almost ran to the subway station.

"Why can't they give you your days off as they should? Then we could plan on going somewhere."

"If people would commit murders on schedule, maybe I could get my day off on schedule. You ought to get a maid, Margery, and then you wouldn't be so tied down with the baby."

"We can't have a maid because we've got to watch out for expenses. After you send forty a week home, it doesn't leave us much."

"Lots of people are worse off than we. Anyway, you shouldn't sit here and mope all day."

"There's no place I can go with the baby except to the Drive or the Cathedral grounds. I get mighty tired sitting here alone and looking at that unfinished Cathedral."

"I've got great news for you, Margery. I saw some fellows bringing up another stone for the Cathedral last week. That makes three stones delivered since we moved in. Maybe they're out for a world's record."

"You can joke about it all you want, but it does get monotonous; and when you do get a day off, you say you don't want to go to the theater."

"I'd rather play with the baby."

"With all the great shows of the world here, we haven't even seen one."

"The theater doesn't interest me. I'd rather read or write."

"If you wrote a play, you'd go to see it, wouldn't you?"

"I doubt it. I don't think many others would go, either."

A fight was heard in the court yard and they knew the Superintendent and his wife were having another argument.

Gordon shut the window. "I wish you would move my bed to the front of the house, Margery. I don't get the right kind of sleep. Tomcats and bursting light bulb bombs in early morning; milk bottles, fights, drunks singing, and at dawn the dumbwaiter scraping up and down; then, when I do get to sleep, some damned court singer demonstrating tonsillitis—I tell you, I don't get any rest unless I'm drunk myself."

"I'm sorry I complained about being lonesome, Gordie. Say, do you think we can afford a parlor set? I see lots of ads for second-hand ones."

"Do I ever crab about you spending money?"

"No, Gordie, you never do. Most men are stingy and kick about expenses, but you never do."

"It's hard on a girl that was used to everything to put up with my kind of wages, I guess."

"Nothing is hard if I can have you with me."

On Gordon's next day off, he said he'd take Margery and Norman to a show. She put their son in a collapsible baby cart and against Gordon's advice—he wanted to take a taxicab down to West Ninety-sixth street—they entered the subway. The baby buggy got in everyone's way, clogging the doors and drawing down an epidemic of curses on such goofs as would bring a baby buggy into the subway.

"It is a hell of a nuisance," Gordon said, "and I don't blame them for being sore at that buggy. I think the damned thing was invented by Blair Christensen at that."

When they got to the show house, they were told that children of Norman's age were not admitted, so Gordon and Margery got in a taxi and rode back to their own neighborhood, where they went to a motion picture theater. As they passed a glass wall case, in which a fire ax was racked, Norman spied the implement and yelled for it. The child seemed passionate about hammers and axes. He called a hammer or an ax a "Wah-wah." He began yelling "Wah-wah." You can't have "Wah-wah," Normie. No! No!

Can't have bad "Wah-wah." But Norman wanted "Wah-wah." The picture patrons didn't want Norman. The usher said so.

"You go ahead, Margery, and sit somewhere in the back. I'll take Normie to the Gentlemen's Room and maybe he'll quiet down."

He spent an hour in the toilet with the child, but finally Gordon could stand the ammonia odor no longer. He tried to steal past the fire-fighting tool with his son, but Norman again set up a yowl. This time Gordon was put out of the picture house. He and Margery, with Norman in the collapsible baby cart, went around the corner to their apartment. When they got home, Margery put the baby to bed and then sat and looked through the front window at the stone bulk that was to be a Cathedral. Gordon had several drinks.

As Gordon was sinking into sleep Norman began to cry and to scream "Wah-wah," thus proving some Freudian theory or other. Tenants upstairs began to rap with shoes and metal objects on the steam pipes. A woman across the court shouted for the Doles to shut up that brat. To which Gordon replied loudly that the woman undoubtedly was being kept in sin by a stockbroker who was too stingy to put her up on Park Avenue. Then the Superintendent and his wife resumed their debate.

"To hell with it!" Gordon got up and put on his dressing gown and slippers. Then he drank the rest of his bottle of Scotch.

II

WAR news monopolized most of the newspapers and a fellow didn't have much opportunity to write feature stories or human interest articles. If there was a Liberty Loan Drive or a Red Cross Campaign, you could write your head off; but if you tried to produce something that didn't contain references to "Our Boys" and "Over There" and "Dollar-a-Year Man," you were writing for the wastebasket or the long spike on which second-choice stories were impaled until the paper had been put to bed for the night.

"I wish the Colonel had that spike stuck in him in a fashion dear to Rabelais," Gordon said to Dave Crowder. They were drinking kümmel at Mouquin's. Crowder said it was a hell of a thing to drink kümmel with shad roe, but Gordon said he could drink anything with anything, possibly with the exception of apricot brandy with orange ice.

"I notice you and Kemp are kind of friendly now," Crowder said. "I think I'll switch from kümmel to cognac. Kümmel is likely to make me want a dame too much, and I got to go back to get out a fight extra."

"Kemp is all right. No, I'll stick to kümmel. I'm used to wanting a dame, kümmel or no kümmel. I always want one."

"I thought you were happily married and had a kid?"

"What's that got to do with wanting dames?"

"I thought you were true to your wife."

"I am. What in hell has that got to do with it? You

are married, too, aren't you? But you cheat, don't you?"

"Sure I cheat. You can't be a good sporting editor and not do it. Say, those molls that train with the sports mob would make a preacher lay down his Bible."

"Let's have another drink and quit talking about it." Gordon said he thought Benny Leonard was the nearest thing to Joe Gans that the lightweights had produced but that he had not originated the left-handed parry-and-punch maneuver. He had borrowed it from old Sam Langford.

"You refereed a fight or two for Langford out west, didn't you, Dole?"

"Yes, I was a lousy referee."

"Didn't a man die on you in some fight or other out there?"

"Yes, but let's not talk about that."

"I'd like to have you do some sports for me if Kemp will let you free from the City Department. Do you think it will make us sick if we have some beer on top of the other stuff?"

"If you take beer, it may make you want a dame—a German dame."

"Say, speaking of German dames, did you see that Dutch blonde that called on the Sports Department to-day?"

"I didn't see any blondes."

Crowder got out a small note book and turned pages. "Well, I want you to meet that baby. This is my stud book. Whenever I feel like getting the clinkers out of the grate, I look in this book. Will you come meet her? She's got a friend. You won't be true to the old lady after you've met her pal."

"You're drunk. I don't want to meet anybody. If I got steamed up I'd know what to do about it. Let's knock over another powder and blow back to the office."

"I hate to go back to work, Dole. God, what an awful World Series this is goin' to be. The Red Sox ought to cop. Have another drink?"

"No, I don't want any more. My belly feels like a big caraway seed."

Gordon got home at 4 o'clock in the morning, half-slopped with kümmel. An overdose of kümmel didn't make him want a dame, but he thought he would like to have a few pallbearers. He was having trouble finding the right key as a man came out the door. That saved Gordon the trouble of unlocking the heavy front door to the apartment house. He didn't pay much attention to the man, although he noted that he was a big chap, and middle-aged.

Gordon's apartment house was a walk-up and he had three flights of stairs to climb. When he was woozy it seemed that he lived in the Woolworth Building. As he was weaving past the four doors of apartments on the floor below his floor, he saw one of the doors open slowly, cautiously. A young woman stood there. She smiled at him and he nodded rather sulkily and went up the last set of stairs to his apartment. He poured himself a double Scotch and crawled into bed.

He kept remembering the woman at the door and thought there had been something suggestive in her smile.

He knew vaguely who she was. She was a Miss Eckhert. He had seen her in the ground floor hall a few times and once he had walked behind her up the stairs, looking appraisingly at her legs and her hips, which were rather long and a bit slack. He supposed she was about twenty-three years old and probably had become a blonde by choice.

The first time he had seen Miss Eckhert, she had been getting mail from the battery of hallway boxes. That time he had noticed her hips, long and a bit slack, and after she had gone away he had read her name on the mail box. Eckhert. Florence Eckhert. He had seen her name on the door of the third-floor apartment, too. Eckhert. Hips long, slack.

Gordon got up and poured himself a generous Scotch. The Scotch are generous, he said, as he poured the generous Scotch.

"Do you want something, Gordie?"

"No, I don't want a thing. I'm half-swacked."

Maybe I should go out and stay with a dame, like Crowder does. Maybe it would do me good to wrestle some of the cob-webs out of my system. I think I've been too domestic, like a squire. I'm getting to be a squire with spiders spinning webs over and about my inert loins. Miss Eckhert is not pretty, but she has a tawny, yearning complexion and long, supple hips. He got up again and drank some Scotch.

III

As a reward for three successive news beats, Gordon was raised to one hundred and fifty dollars a week and was on a friendly, though not intimate basis, with Kemp. He bought twenty-five dollars' worth of long-stemmed roses and took them home to Margery. She was pleased, but she warned him against wasting so much money.

"It does me good to make a gesture like that," he said. "That's why I eat in expensive places. My intestines don't give a damn, but my mind reacts pleasantly."

"We can put more money into savings now."

"You'd better get a maid."

"We'll see."

"Kemp has promised me a contract, a two-year contract with a twenty-five dollar increase for the second year."

"That's lovely. Maybe I'll get a maid."

"Dave Crowder says that's high pay for a reporter."

"I don't like that Crowder person."

"You've never seen him."

"Just the same, I don't like him. From remarks you drop, he isn't square with his wife and family. Anyone who is unfaithful to his wife is not worth while."

"It's none of our business."

"I think it is."

"Well, it isn't. I'm going to the Frenchman's to get some ale."

Next day Gordon read over the *City News* telegraphic

printer that Nada Halpin's show was closing. He had been trying for months to get up courage to see her in the play. Now he'd have to wait. Perhaps he'd have to wait for a long time, because Miss Halpin was going to France as an entertainer in convalescent camps.

Crowder stopped at Gordon's desk. "God! I was in good form last night." He held up four fingers.

"Same one?"

"Swellest dame in the world," Crowder chuckled.

"What a liar! Come on out and have a drink."

Gordon thought that a few Martinis would be in order and he had five of them in a row. Then he switched to Scotch while Crowder drank seidels of stout mixed with beer.

"This always brings back my vitality." Crowder seemed to be remembering something important. "My God! I left my box-score book at the dame's house! Imagine going away and leaving my box-score!"

"Your box-score! What the hell are you talking about?"

Gordon asked Kemp if he could go home early and left the office at ten o'clock. He stopped at several places before taking the Interborough and had rum toddies. He reached his apartment house a bit before midnight and as he was letting himself in, Miss Eckhert, loaded with bundles, asked him to keep the door propped open for her.

"I can't get to my key without laying down these packages."

"Let me carry them upstairs for you."

"That's awfully nice. Would you mind?"

"I never mind anything."

"I was to the delicatessen," she said. They were going up the stairs and he let her go first and he looked at her legs as she climbed. He thought her very graceful. "Thanks." She had opened the door. "If you don't think it would be too unconventional, I'll make you a drink and share a sandwich."

"I'm not conventional and I'll have a drink with you."

"In the front room then." She closed the door behind them and after she had turned the bolt she fastened a barlock arrangement that was clumsy and penal looking. It had a brace that extended from doorknob to floor and it took a long time to adjust it. What was she afraid of?

"This must be Houdini's old home," Gordon said.

"I like to feel safe.... What do you want to drink? I'm a wine-head myself, but I have some Scotch."

"I'll try some wine with you. Whatever you want yourself. My drinking tastes are somewhat catholic."

"I have some of the most exquisite claret. It's light and not a bit muddling, but I think I'll open a bottle of Chateau Yquem. It's a bottle that Mr.... a friend gave me. Naturally I couldn't afford it myself, but I'm crazy about Chateau Yquem."

"Better open the claret for I'm no judge of wine."

"No, I feel like a fine golden wine to-night."

"Open anything; only let's not debate about it."

They drank in silence for a while. Miss Eckhert thought the ceiling light too harsh and said that it revealed ugly cracks in the plaster, so she snapped it out and turned on a floor lamp that had a fluted, amber silk shade.

"You didn't want this wine chilled, did you?"

"No, it's all right this way."

"I always decant this sort of wine at room temperature. It is wonderful wine, isn't it?"

"Anything with alcohol in it is good, excepting of course the cheaper brands of shellac."

"I learned to like wine when I was with my people in France." She was sitting beside him on a day bed. "Do you remember that night I stood at my door when you came in?" He nodded. "Weren't you a bit tight that night?"

"I'm a bit tight a lot of nights. I like to get tight, so I go ahead and get that way."

"Well, I had had a caller—the friend that gave me this wine—and I thought it was he coming back. It was you."

"How about opening some claret? Would that be a breach of etiquette, my suggesting claret?"

"Would you rather have something heavier? I have some Italian wine. How about some Chianti?"

"It sours my stomach."

"I'll open some Lacryma Christi."

"You must have bought out a wholesale wine house!"

"No, just presents." She smiled and went for the Lacryma Christi. He wished he hadn't mixed his drinks so wantonly. When Miss Eckhert returned, she poured the wine in fresh glasses and after they had sipped it, she asked: "Do you mind if I slip into my kimono? It would be more comfortable."

"I don't mind anything."

"Nothing at all?"

"Nothing."

The glow of the wine seemed to have cast a thin, shimmering veil over her face, bringing a subdued flush to her tawny skin. Her voice was soft, but her words were direct. "Then why don't you take off your things and be comfortable?"

"I think I'm getting drunk."

"Why don't you take off your things and lie down for a while? It might make you feel better."

"I'm not sick. Anyway, I've got a place to lie down a floor above this."

"Maybe you'd rather lie down here for a while. What?"

"Yes, what. All right. We'll get comfortable."

As Florence's mantel clock struck three, he believed he had lain down long enough. He hadn't the most remote feeling of love toward Florence and told her so. She laughed and said it didn't make any difference. She believed they had found satisfaction in belonging bodily to each other. He said it didn't make any difference to him if it didn't to her. They got up and dressed and had another drink, Gordon taking Scotch whisky.

"I'll have a head on me like a subway trash can in the morning," he said. "Yes, Florence, I'll come to see you often. What's the best time? I work late."

"My friend usually leaves here at midnight. The night you saw me at the door was an exception."

"I don't like the idea of following another fellow."

"You're not jealous already?"

"Not by a good damn, but I don't like the follow up idea."

"I understand. Well, he's only here once a week and if you want to, you can miss that night."

"I'm a cinch to miss that night. How will I know if you are alone?"

"I'll shove an envelope under my door, and extending into the hall whenever it's all right for you to stop in. You rap three times."

"My God, Florence! Everybody, probably including Poe's Raven, raps three times. I'll not rap at all. I'll scratch like an animal ... for that's what I am now."

Gordon went upstairs. He was extremely glad that he was drunk, for otherwise he would be certain to lie awake all morning with remorse. To make sure that he was drunk, he found a bottle and drank two straight Scotch whiskies.

Chapter Five

I

*G*ORDON was sorry that he had been untrue to Margery. He had been true—he computed the time—for four years, lacking about six weeks. Of course, if one regarded his constant agony for Nada as infidelity, then he never had been true to Margery at all. And now he had been unfaithful both to Margery and to Nada, and he was just an animal. Well, who wasn't?

At the end of a two-week period of bodily communion with Florence Eckhert, which had not been interrupted by the weekly call of her friend, he started home from his office. When he got to the third floor of the apartment house, he saw no signal for him. There was no envelope sticking out at the bottom of her door. He was disappointed, but at the same time he was glad not to be a cheat for at least one night.

He never had asked Florence any personal questions. He never had asked any woman personal questions except in the course of his professional duties, when he was compelled to ask such questions. But in his personal relationships, he had no searching inquiries for women. Florence seemed to appreciate that in Gordon.

He wondered if her caller were not the big man who had passed him that night at the door, the night Florence had stood at the entrance of her apartment and had smiled at Gordon? Well, no matter. It wasn't the time now to knock and to thank whoever it was for the fine wine. Thank you, Sir Cuckold, for your wine. Many happy returns.

Margery had been up with Norman off and on since ten o'clock. It was the climate, she said. They'd have to go to the seashore or the Catskills next summer, even though it was expensive. Gordon asked her if there was any beer on ice and she brought him three pint bottles on which a cold dew gathered.

"Is something wrong at the office, Gordie?"

"Why do you say that?"

"You haven't seemed like yourself for a week or so."

"You're imagining that."

"Maybe so. I guess you're working rather hard, though. They shouldn't keep you so late."

"It won't always be this way."

"I hope not. I made you a plate of fudge; if you want some it's in the refrigerator. Good night, Gordie."

"Good night." He opened a second pint of beer. "Say!" he called to her as she was leaving the dining room. "Well?" she asked. He hesitated. "How do you mean I haven't been myself?"

"Oh, nothing in particular. I guess I'm upset over Normie being feverish."

"Should I call a doctor?"

"No."

"Now look here, Margery, there must have been a reason for you saying I haven't been myself."

"Well, then, so long as you make my remark important, I have been wondering what has come over you. I mean you don't seem so keen on the physical side of married life as you always were. Not that it matters to me, but I didn't want you to get tired of me."

"This sounds funny coming from you, Margery."

"I've tried hard to make you happy. I want to do anything you want to do. When you wanted me, I gave me. For two weeks now you haven't seemed to want me. I wonder why? That's all."

"Don't get silly ideas into your head, Margery. I've been hitting the rum so hard I don't want anyone that way right now."

"Perhaps you shouldn't drink so heavily."

"I guess I'll eat some of that fudge, Margery. Do you think it will agree with the beer?"

"It wouldn't with me, but you seem to be different from me in a lot of ways."

"Don't get upset, Margery. I'm sorry I'm so much trouble. Don't worry about me at all."

"I do. I can't help it, because I love you."

"That goes double, Margery. Good night, dear."

Gordon thought he heard voices, angry voices, coming

from somewhere in the apartment house. He put the third bottle of beer back in the ice box and ate a piece of fudge and went to bed.

Later in the morning Gordon was awakened by screams and a disturbance downstairs. The noise awakened Margery and Norman.

"It sounds like it's in the apartment under us," Margery said. "What's wrong with you, Gordie?"

"Why?"

"You look white. Are you ill?"

"I've got a stomachache from that fudge and beer." He was afraid of something. He felt sure it was Florence Eckhert's apartment where the noises came from and he felt he should go there to protect her. The picture of the penal looking door-bar flashed into his mind. It would be a silly thing to rush downstairs and help her, a very compromising thing, but he decided to be silly and compromising. He dressed hurriedly, not waiting to tie his shoe laces.

"Where are you going?"

"I'm a reporter, am I not? It may be a story."

"Shall I go along, too?"

"No, you can't leave Norman. I'll find out the facts."

"Don't butt in if it's just a family quarrel."

As he reached the third floor, he was pushed back by a police officer. Gordon showed his reporter's card, but the officer said it didn't matter; no one could come near the apartment. Gordon saw the open door, the same one at which Florence had stood not long ago, smiling at him in what he had regarded as a suggestive way.

"What is it, officer? A murder?"

"Never you mind, young fellow. My orders is to give out nothing, see?"

Gordon was crazy with apprehension. He hadn't loved the girl. He had found her body good and she had found his body good. The two goods had combined to mean bad, perhaps, but there had been something quaint and honest and pitiful about Florence, whom he had nicknamed "Wine-Head," and she had been almost masculinely frank and unselfish in her brief relation with him.

An ambulance crew had arrived and when Gordon saw them carrying Florence away on a stretcher she was moaning. She had a bandage over her eyes. She was not dead then; only hurt. How badly? Nobody would tell him or permit him to go downstairs. He tried to make out the name of the hospital on the caps of the stretcher-bearers, but the hall light was dim and the men moved rapidly. He ran upstairs, dreading to have to answer Margery's questions, but he had to look out his window. His view of the ambulance was obscured by fire escapes and by the cloudy vagueness of early morning.

As the ambulance began its dash down the middle of the wide avenue, Gordon thought he caught the name "Bellevue," or perhaps it was "Beekman." He couldn't be sure. He asked Margery to wait for a recital of the meager facts he had obtained, or rather had observed, until he could put in calls to all hospitals that began with "B." None of them had had calls from his neighborhood. His teeth were chattering like the bell of the ambulance as it had driven away and Margery asked him why he didn't go to bed and wait until late morning to follow up the "story."

"Your paper has gone to press long ago, hasn't it?"

"Yes, but I might as well find out about it."

"Is it that important a story?"

"No, except it happened in our own house and the office might think it funny if I didn't know about it."

"Oh. But I don't want you to get sick, story or no story."

Gordon called police headquarters and then the station in his precinct. There had been no reports of murder, suicide, accident or other emergency all afternoon, evening or midnight. In vain he argued with the desk sergeant over the telephone and finally called the captain of the precinct. At length the precinct official told him to hang up and that if he was drunk he'd send over to make him quit being such a nuisance.

Gordon never again heard from Little Wine-Head and he developed a fondness for her memory that is not unusual with young men when their casual affairs are interrupted in full flower and by tragic means. He entered one of his ascetic periods and went on the water wagon.

II

On Gordon's next day off he took Margery and Norman to the Bronx Park Zoo and had an all-around busy time of it. They were walking toward the Lion House when from the whole sky there came a piercing, joyous acclaim, wildly sustained. Whistles, seemingly stationed in the trees about them and in the houses where the animals had been lying lazily or pacing their cages aimlessly, broke upon their ears. Gordon stood still for a moment and then he took Margery by the arm:

"Armistice!"

"It's over. Thank God, Gordon."

He told her he must go at once; that he must hurry to the subway to go to his office. It would be a big story, calling for every man on the staff to prepare it.

"Must you go? It's your day off."

"Certainly I must go. It's a story."

Amid the revelry of that False Armistice, Gordon was carried bodily from the water wagon. He stayed away from home—he never could recall just where he had wandered after writing the "crowd" story—until the day after the Real Armistice. He came out of his alcoholic haze early in the morning of November 12 and was in bed with a lady who was a stranger to his more sober self. She was about his age, going on twenty-nine, he conjectured. She was not at all handsome in her relaxed condition, but possibly she would prove good looking after a conference with her powders and tints. He noted that her clothing, which lay haphazard on chairs, was of good quality. The room in which he had awakened was assuredly a hotel room and it was evident that it was in a good hotel, probably an "exclusive" one.

Gordon wondered what name, if any, he had registered under and he would have roused his guest—or perhaps it was his hostess—but he thought of Dave Crowder and of Dave's latest mishap, dressed hurriedly and dashed up Madison Avenue to a physician for a prophylaxis.

When Gordon arrived home, he found Margery looking sad and worried. She said she wanted him to feel free, but that she couldn't help being blue when he hadn't telephoned or sent word he wouldn't be home.

"This happens to be our Fourth Wedding Anniversary!"

Gordon felt cut up about this. Then he shaved, changed his clothing and went to the office, where he learned that everyone except Hobbs, the Sunday editor, had been plastered. Hobbs had ulcers of the stomach, poor fellow!

Even the Colonel had been overserved at his club, but it was put down officially as gout.

III

Late in December Kemp wanted to send Gordon to France to come back with New York doughboys and to write their war history for *The Star*. Gordon sent to Fairmount for a birth certificate so that he could get a passport; but the records had been burned in the city hall fire of 1896. The odd fact regarding his name not being Warner, but Dole, cropped up and after the whole thing was finally cleared, Kemp said it was too late for Gordon to go overseas. The Colonel told Kemp that this fellow Gordon always was having something peculiar happening to him and that he confidently expected Gordon would end in the electric chair.

He was disappointed at not getting the foreign assignment but when he learned that Nada was on her way back to the United States he dismissed the entire matter with the fatalistic resignation that is a characteristic of newspaper folk. They write so constantly about shattered dreams and they suffer so many setbacks themselves that they get to a point—the good ones—where each succeeding disappointment is just another Yesterday that Midnight will abandon and forget.

There followed a winter of demobilization and welcome-home stories and in January, 1919, Gordon was assigned to cover the funeral of Colonel Theodore Roosevelt at Oyster Bay, Long Island. Gordon had a bad cold and wrote his story in longhand for the telegraph wire. Then he ate ham and eggs at Jake's, got mellow on Scotch, lost a week's salary at dice while playing with news photographers and went from Oyster Bay to Mineola, where a rich woman had shot her eccentric husband to death.

The most important domestic development that distinguished this winter at the Dole apartment was the hiring of a colored maid by Margery.

Gordon was away from home much of the time during Spring, going to the Berkshires on an elopement story. When May came, he wrote up a big libel case in Michigan and in June he covered the Yale-Harvard boat race at New London. Then, while he was disgusted by a campaign for Daylight Saving—What will they do with it when they get it?—he received news that overjoyed Margery. He was asked to sit in as play reviewer while Austin Moore, *The Star's* dramatic critic, was in the hospital.

Mr. Moore, in a note to Gordon, explained that he was undergoing a delicate operation, and wrote: "I know you'll do a good job of it. If you help me this once I'll do something nice for you when you have your own prostate gland removed."

"It's about time we saw some shows, Gordie. I don't see why you don't cheer. The maid can look after Normie while we go to the first nights. Just imagine!"

"Yes," Gordon said, "just imagine."

Chapter Six

1

MARGERY, in readying herself for a summer season of theater-going, did it as though she was preparing for Heaven. It was a big moment for her when she could say to the grocer's wife my husband is a dramatic critic. We see all the new shows, and mind you, Mrs. Engleton, we go to the opening nights. Not the next night nor the next.... It must be great to be married to a smart man, Mrs. Dole.... I'll get you some passes, Mrs. Engleton. Say, Mrs. Engleton, that head of lettuce you sent us yesterday was all rusty inside.

Margery made her own gowns. Look, Gordon, I got this taffeta at Lord & Taylor's for next to nothing; just the thing for a party dress or for evening wear.... It looks perfectly swell, Margery.... Do you think so, Gordie? It would have cost us at least two hundred dollars if I had bought it in an exclusive shop.... You're darned clever, Margery.... You must go to a tailor, Gordon, to have a new dinner suit made.... What's wrong with the one I have, Margery? ... Nothing, but in your new position you must look well tailored.

Gordon had a heartache.

He saw in Margery's every move an effort to shield him, to encourage him. He wished he could whip his romantic side into line. He wished he could command the stallions of his desire-coach to stop prancing and fretting and snorting long enough to let Margery get in. He put his arms about her and kissed her forehead; a wistful, penitent kiss that was dry and lipless and starved. She was so happy now. She wouldn't have to sit and look at the unfinished Cathedral that was so silently ugly in the night. Margery wanted to reward him in some way for working up to a position in which she, in a manner of speaking, could participate. She thought she might have another baby for him. His unmistakable love for children—for anybody's children—was something she believed she understood. Sometimes it was hard to understand him in whole or in part, for his moods shifted and swirled about her with bewildering movement, but when she saw him playing with Norman and with Norman's little friends, she thought she saw the real Gordon beneath the headstrong, impulsive, careless and often selfish Gordon. He's only a little boy after all, she said to herself, and she remembered the time he had been so bewildered and frightened at the City and she had held him on her lap in the hotel room. I'll give him another playmate. It will make him happy. What he needs most is a mother and playmates.

Women have flashes of terrific vision unknown to men.

Gordon felt that Margery was being short-changed. She was a beautiful character. Although she was a comparative stranger to passion, giving of herself only because a man wanted her to give, she was nevertheless a refuge. She was a mother. He couldn't forget that when his torso smoldered with desire. He despised himself for posing romance before her and simulating romantic yearning for her. He was a confidence man in his own home; every day and every night selling Margery gold bricks. All gilt outside, and all hard, mocking clay inside. He must work like hell to forget Nada.

II

HE didn't have to go to the office except on Thursdays, when he wrote his column of comment for Sunday's dramatic section. After the shows he would go to the Western Union office in West Forty-first Street and Broadway, where critics wrote their verdicts and filed them to their offices. One Thursday night in August Kemp dropped by Gordon's desk.

"How near you through, Dole?"

"Just two commas and a hiss and I'm done. Why?"

"Let's go out and hoist some fire-water. I'm stale."

Gordon pulled his paper from the typewriter and shouted for a copy boy. "I ought to go home to dress. I've got to be at the New Amsterdam by 8:30 o'clock."

"Why dress? Are you getting tuxedo-conscious?"

"My wife likes me to."

Kemp raised his brows. "You're one of them guys that jumps through for the wife, eh?"

"Yes. If you find me strangled, look for apron strings about my neck."

"Let's go to my Club." Kemp yawned. On the way uptown Kemp said he had dropped quite a bit on Wall Street and that he felt draggy. "What a sucker a wise guy is!"

"The thing for you to do is to open some champagne," Gordon said. "That is, if they have any."

"I didn't know you were a wino. I thought red-eye was your fuel."

"I'm not much for wine." For a moment Gordon thought of Wine-Head and his face was austerely drawn. Then he forgot her and accepted a menu card from a waiter. "No, I don't care for wine especially, but I think it's a good thing to do something expensive and flourishing whenever you feel soppy or low. It fools your gizzard and nowadays the gizzard is master of the mind."

The head steward came and said he could arrange to get a bottle of wine but that he didn't know what brand it might prove to be. "Get one with a flashy label," Kemp said and then looked at Gordon. "I've been following your criticisms closely."

"How do they strike you?"

"I can't hand them much. In a way they are different, but you've got no appreciation of the paper's policy at all."

"I didn't know we had a policy. I thought we had fifty policies, one for each week in the year."

"Look out, Dole. Sooner or later you're going to run in with The Chief, for he has lots of angles."

"Then I'll take up geometry."

"There's the advertising angle."

"Well, give me the angles, Euclid. Here's luck to your next Wall Street raid." Gordon sipped the wine.

"Maybe you're too high-hat to take advice, so why should I waste my breath?"

"I'm not high-hat."

"Well, you're something. What I mean is you go ahead in your articles and say things you shouldn't. For instance, you are too brusque in dealing with the Bossert shows, and you ought to know that any paper that knocks one of their shows is liable to have their advertising go plumb out the window. On the other hand you take a delight in being nice to unknown producers and ham actors and bum authors. I can't get that idea, unless you're grooming yourself to get fired."

"I'm glad you like my articles on the drama."

"My God, but you've got a touchy nature!"

"Let's not quarrel about it, Kemp. It's lots more fun drinking."

A page handed Kemp a call-slip. "Have him come in right away, boy, and I'll sign for him on my way out." He said to Gordon, "Crowder's at the door. It's almost his bedtime. I wonder what his dame will say at him being up as late as seven o'clock?"

Crowder came to the table and said he hoped he wasn't butting in, but he wanted to touch Kemp for a couple of hundred to meet a gambling debt in the morning. He had gone south, he explained, in enthusiasm for a horse named Ecuador. Ecuador had traveled west when he should have run east. Kemp had only a hundred and fifty dollars and Gordon managed the other fifty.

"How you feeling?" Gordon asked.

"Not so good. My Forty-second Street Neuritis is giving me hell." In leaving, Crowder paused to say to Gordon, "I saw your old girl to-day."

"What old girl?"

"I was with the Champ, who has a rapture about her. We went to her house in the Champ's Rolls and the machine was loaded to the noseguard with white orchids for her."

"For whom? Is this a gag?"

"Gag nothing. I'm telling you we called on Nada Halpin and she asked about you."

The snout of the wine bottle trembled against the glass as Gordon poured. "You go to a lot of places, don't you, Crowder?"

Crowder looked at Gordon for a moment. "Sorry if I said anything wrong. I thought it would hand you a laugh if I told you she said to the Champ: 'Did I know him? Well, he once kissed me on the cheek.' I was just kidding, Dole. I was just guessing about the girl stuff when I spoke."

"Your guess is as right as the one you made yesterday on Ecuador."

After Crowder had gone, Kemp puffed his cigarette with short, swift intakes. Gordon wished Kemp wouldn't

look at him so peeringly, so knowingly. He said he would
be late to the theater if he didn't go at once and he got
up from the table.

"Don't let anything bother you, Gordon. Your work is
splendid and you'll go a long way with it. I think I'm beginning to get you."

"Save your imagination for The Chief. You'll need it."

III

THE prospect of having to review a show in which Nada
might appear hung over Gordon like a headsman's ax. He
learned that she had signed with a man named Jedlicka,
who was a patron of art and of artists, but who was a
novice in show business. Broadway gossipers wondered why
she had not signed with one of the many successful theatrical men who had sent agents to Europe to see her at the
convalescent camps. The disappointed producers, with one
or two exceptions, hoped that she would run into a pro-
nounced flop. She was too independent, they said, and no
one could handle her since the death of her old manager,
the patriarchal Willcox Waring. Perhaps a failure would
teach her a lesson.

A new play had been written for her and was now
being rewritten and was to open in Atlantic City. It would
be given its New York première at The Figaro Playhouse
in a fortnight. Press agents revealed that Jedlicka was planning to build a theater for his star next year and was going
to name it for her.

The day before the play opened in New York, Gordon called on Austin Moore at St. Luke's Hospital, which was near his apartment house. He found Moore in a wheel-chair on the hospital lawn.

"I'll never attack another actor," Moore said, "if it is proved to me in affidavit form that he has lost his prostate. The parting between a gentleman and his gland is most touching, most dramatic, most painful."

After visiting for a time, Gordon asked Moore if he felt well enough to do him an important favor.

"What is it, my lad?"

"Cover the opening of the Halpin show for me."

"Would you mind telling me why?"

Gordon liked old Austin Moore. He was a sardonic person in print, but in private life he was generous and agreeable. Well, he would lay the cards on the table.

"It's very confidential," Gordon said.

"I never tell anything but secrets."

"I don't dare confide in myself when I think of it."

"Come on. Come on."

"Well, I'm in love with Nada Halpin. I've been in love with her for years and it's got me so hard that I don't care much what happens."

"So!" Moore stirred in his wheel-chair and then looked at the Cathedral lawn across the street from the hospital. In his searching eyes there was a puzzled light as though he was hearing a long-ago melody, once familiar to him but the name of it now forgotten. "Does she love you?"

"No. I haven't seen her since she left my home town nearly ten years ago."

"Ten years is a long time for love.... I know Miss Halpin. A genius in her way and beautiful. I remember criticizing her severely one time and she sent a messenger to me with a present. It was a demi-tasse cup. There was a note with the little cup which read: 'Here, my clever friend, wear this for a high hat.' Delicious! We became good friends. I used to call on her to hear her sing and I played the piano while she danced. I never shall forget her eyes, tremendously seeing eyes, that could be dreams one moment and then two spots of fire from the bake oven of hell. And her hair, so startlingly blonde, almost white with blondeness, and parted in the middle and drawn tightly, severely back from her intelligent forehead and then ending in classical puffs about her ears. Masculine at the forehead and feminine at the back of the head, truly a paradox, just as she is.... I'm sorry, comrade, sorry there is love that kills. Yet ... I was in love, too. Now ... nothing left ... not even my ... Oh, hell!"

"Will you cover the opening of her show?"

"Listen. I shan't be back in harness for at least two months for one thing. For another, I wouldn't rob you of this chance to fortify your soul. The thing for you to do is to go to that performance, sit there and look at her. Don't look at the woman, at the one you love. Look at the artist. Dissect the play and write it. Observe the actress and write of her. Either you will be cured of your malady or you will proceed from the state you are in to another. How-

ever it may work out, don't cower at the foot of rotted
pedestals.... We may as well meet Life head-on, for side-
stepping won't save us."

"I'll do it.... You know you talk a lot like an old
editor of mine, a man of whom I am very fond."

"It's not Beelzebub by any chance?"

"No. I mean old Joe Gates."

"The hell you say! Why, he and I worked together
nearly forty years ago on the West Coast. So you're one of
his brood?"

"I'm glad you know him. Say, why did Ward fire Joe
Gates?"

Moore laughed. "That's a long story. I must tell you
some time. It had to do with a girl, of course. All real
trouble begins with a girl, but the funny part of it was
that Gates wasn't guilty ... but that story will have to wait,
my boy, because I've got to eat now. It's the only pleasure
we glandless ganders have left to us. Go ahead to that show
and don't crucify your youth."

Chapter Seven

I

GORDON took Margery to The Figaro Playhouse to see Nada Halpin. At first he thought he would go alone, but that wouldn't be the gutty thing to do. No, he would take Margery, and then if he collapsed in the aisle, it wouldn't make any difference. If he were to die there in the seat, clutching a program and toppling against the bare shoulder of a lady in front, it wouldn't make any difference. Nothing made any difference. If Jehovah himself stubbed his toe against the world, his footstool, and knocked it silly—that wouldn't make any difference, either.

He tried to time their arrival so that they would catch the curtain on the rise and the auditorium in darkness, but the curtain didn't go up until nearly nine o'clock. The critics were impatient, for there were other openings that evening. They agreed that Jedlicka might be a godsend to the Metropolitan Museum of Art, but he was clumsy with his theatrical venture.

Margery was thrilled, but Gordon made frequent trips to the smoking-room. He hoped his boiled shirt didn't show wilted spots where he had dribbled water from the paper cup. He hoped no one had seen him put that match in his mouth and try to light it with a cigarette. He hoped Gabriel would appear at this moment to sound his trumpet. The trumpet! How I'd like to hear a trumpet. He went back to his seat beside his wife.

"I want you to write Mrs. Hamilton to-morrow and tell her to pack that old bugle of mine carefully and send it here at once."

"What a funny thing to think of at an opening night!"

"I thought of it, anyway....I want Norman to have it sometime."

"Is that Otto Kahn over there with the beard?"

"No, it's King George."

"Really, who is it, Gordie?"

"Why, it's..."

The curtain rose. This is Waterloo. This is Gethsemane. This is Pentecost and we shall make an offering of the firstfruits of the harvest. This is Calvary, where a skull-shaped rock looks down on Jeremiah's grotto. Can't you see the Damascus Gate of the Holy City? Golgotha and tears. I see it all, because I am one of the thieves—the uglier one on the left of the Christus—and yet the program says we are in West Forty-sixth Street. Maybe it's the Yale Bowl. Maybe it's the Bastille before the Revolution. Did I hear you ring, sir? a stage butler is saying to a fellow who sits at a table reading the *London Times*. What funny papers they have in London. I like to read the distillery ads and the personals....

Gordon fidgeted. Margery looked at the stage, waiting anxiously for the home town girl's entrance. Gordon left his body sitting there like a ventriloquist's doll, while his soul flew away to the spot-light upstairs to play with the rest of the moths that dashed against the hot lenses.

The first act is over.... What did you see, Body? What did you see, Eyes-of-Body, while I was away?...I saw only a woman, Soul. Did you have a good time up there with the moths?...I had a splendid time, Body. I got my ethereal whiskers singed up there, Body.... The woman was tall and white and defiant, Soul, as lambent as moonlight and as independent as the storm, all at one time.... Tell me more. Tell me more and more and more, Body....I'd be glad to oblige, Soul, but I've got to go to the latrine. You know how Bodies are constituted, don't you, Soul?...No, I never can reconcile it, Body....

"I think it's the lousiest show this season," said Christopher of *The Standard*.

"And that takes in more territory than the Louisiana Purchase," said Dorfman of *The Mail*. "Halpin herself isn't enough to carry this bloomer."

"Jedlicka won't build her a new theater when he reads the morning papers," said Rigsby of *The Advertiser*. "He'll crawl on a funeral pyre and let Halpin commit suttee."

Gordon went again to his seat and the first-nighters, many of them leering, trooped in from the lounges and from the street. Some of them didn't return at all but went home or to night clubs for alcoholic research work. Gordon wondered why he should feel guilty about this ostensible failure. He hadn't had anything to do with it but he was downcast and deeply concerned about it. He was greatly annoyed when Margery whispered to him that the Halpin woman wasn't so much; that she didn't see why men went so batty about her. Good looking, true, but who couldn't be, with all those clothes and jewels and six hours a day in the hands of beauty specialists?

Gordon rose to leave shortly before the third act ended. That was the only flaw in Margery's happy hours at openings—this habit of Gordon's of getting up and darting away before plays were over. But he was a critic, wasn't he? And it was worth something to be a critic and to take one's wife to first nights and to have signed pieces in the paper. She guessed she would get up this once and go with Gordon. No, Margery, you'd better stay for the rest of the show. No, Gordie, I'll go to the Western Union with you. I shan't be missing much. Oh, well, come ahead then, but I'm out of sorts to-night.

She sat beside him in an upstairs balcony at the telegraph office while he typed his review.... Say, honey, I wish you wouldn't read over my shoulder as I write. It'll be in the paper to-morrow. I'm sorry, Gordie, I was curious to see how you wrote all those wonderful things. Beg pardon, Margery, I'm just nervous about not getting it done in time for the midnight edition.

II

Kemp called Gordon by telephone at noon next day. He went downtown and Kemp had a copy of *The Star* opened on his desk. The review page was marked in heavy black pencilings and there were scrawly notes on the margins.

"Well, Gordon, The Chief sent me a note directing me to put you back on the City Staff, and I'm tickled stiff. There's a lot of good work for you to do."

"He didn't like my review, did he?" Gordon remembered The Chief's smile and he fancied he had smiled as he wrote the note to Kemp.

"Don't mind The Chief. You know how funny he is on theatricals. He'll forget it.... It was odd, though, you coming out the way you did and not knocking the show, but just glossing it over ... and then writing such a boost for Halpin."

"It was an honest review and the old man can go to hell, because I'm quitting right now."

"You can't quit with your contract, Gordon. You'd be a fool to resign. Between you and me, it wasn't so much the fact that the other papers razzed the show and you didn't, as it was that The Chief remembered Miss Halpin as the wife of Grosserly. He hates everyone connected with Grosserly on account of that pro-German tag they put on him."

"I'm taking a day or two off, Kemp. I've got some drinking to catch up on."

"Take a rest, Gordon, and don't worry."

Margery had a letter from her mother. "I hope she doesn't start until she gets a letter I sent away this morning about your bugle."

"Starts where?"

"She's going to visit us. I hope you don't mind."

"I don't mind."

"I think it will be different with her visiting us instead of us living with her like we did."

"Is she going to live with us?"

"For a little while, if you don't object."

"It's all right with me."

"I'll keep her out of your way as much as possible. I'll take her to the theater. You can get tickets even if I do have to see the shows over again after the opening nights."

"There won't be any more opening nights."

Margery was astonished. She noticed that Gordon looked hollow-eyed and rather thin. "Don't you go and get bilious again.... Why did you say we wouldn't have any more opening nights?"

"I've been taken off dramatics. The owner of the paper didn't like the review this morning."

"Well, don't worry. I wondered myself, though, if you didn't go pretty far in praising that Miss Halpin. Of course I know you did it out of your usual generosity, her having been a schoolmate of yours."

"I'm going to the Frenchman's for some ale." As Gordon walked past the door on the third floor, he thought of poor Wine-Head. He went down the rest of the stairs slowly and then, instead of going to the Frenchman's, he took a cab to a speakeasy in East Fifty-sixth street, where he drank Bacardi cocktails and Scotch whisky until he was madly drunk.

III

GORDON stumbled through the narrow hall of the speak-easy, steadying himself against the wall and colliding with a coat-room girl. As he waited for the proprietor to unlock the area-way gate, a dog rubbed against his calves. He was glad of the dog's company and wished he could take the animal with him. Dogs didn't desert you. Dogs didn't lecture you or quarrel with you. It made no difference to a dog whether a friend was a drunkard, a libertine or a cardinal. He patted the dog's flanks and then held the beast's head in his hands.

Gordon told himself he would drink his head off. Why not? Everything was wrong and mixed up. The sight of Nada had jumbled his senses and the action of his office in removing him from dramatics had been the finishing blow. He would go to another speakeasy and then to another and to another until he was blind. He was indecent and he belonged among indecent people. He would try to find some thoroughly depraved ones. He walked over to Sixth Avenue and then downtown.

If only his right leg wouldn't misbehave; it kept dragging behind his left leg. Lack of synchronism, he said. The frontal part of his skull was numb, like an arm that goes to sleep when blood pressure is low and he was doing his thinking with the back part of his brain. He didn't like the thoughts that came from there and he asked himself why, if the back of his brain were alive, he couldn't balance himself more properly? Balance, he said to himself, is born in the cerebellum, the sack-brain that nestles under the superior or big brain. Ha! I learned that at college. In the hemispheres of the big brain—the cerebrum—is the seat of the mind and the throne of will power. Well, how can I have a mind when there is now no seat left for it to sit on? He began laughing and saying aloud:

"How are you going to sit, Mind, if you have no seat?"

This confused rambling kept him occupied for a time and he thought of his college experiments in dissecting the brains of tumbler pigeons. He decided he had liked the experiments with frogs better than those with the pigeons.

"Frogs and I have the same type of thinking apparatus." He said this to a man who was passing him as he neared Thirty-fourth Street.

"Go to hell, Rummy!" the stranger said.

"It's my next stop."

Gordon thought of a Long Island roadhouse, one of the more frowsy kind, where he had gone two or three times with Dave Crowder. He decided to go there and got into a cab. It was a long ride over Queensboro Bridge, out Queens Boulevard, turning into Hillside Avenue and cutting across to Merrick Road. He went into the roadhouse and riveted his elbows to a bar, planting his feet widely on the bare floor and calling for a drink. The bartender induced him to retire to a small, round table at the rear of the place and asked him to keep quiet.

He could hardly wait between drinks and rubbed his chin with shaky fingers. He hadn't shaved for two days and his beard stubble made a growling sound as he pushed his fingers against the grain. He recalled his youthful ambition to be a doctor of medicine, a surgeon, and then he wondered in an ironical, alcoholic way how his shaky hands would have behaved in an abdominal operation. He began to laugh loudly. Zigzag incision, he said. An incision so zigzag that it chases itself around the belly. Dr. Magellen, the first surgeon to circumnavigate the belly.

"You oughtn't to have no more booze," a waiter said. "You're plenty drunk."

"Got to have more. Dr. Magellen said so."

The proprietor came over. "One more then, and you get out."

It was early morning now and when Gordon resisted the efforts of speakeasy strongarms to eject him, two men took him, one by the feet and the other by the shoulders, and hurled him into the side street. He struck his head against a telegraph pole and lay there as though dead.

As a misty dawn came over the dirty street where Gordon Dole lay, he began to move. He was insensible of the macadam road that couched him on its rough breast and was gripped by a nausea that left him retching and strained. He struggled to his knees, his head down, like a mortally hurt stag. He wanted water, for a fever was withering him and his vitals were stretched in agony, as though they were being wound on the hot drum of a derrick hoist.

Rising from the curb near which he was crouching were three telegraph poles, carrying wires through which the wind of morning hummed. The strange, weird fingering of the wind on this high harp brought imaginings terrible in their vividness. He lifted his head to catch the hymn of the wind, fancying that music, tragic and prophetic, was being sent from the sky. And then, his head still lifted and his throat distended with torment, Gordon saw the three telegraph poles, not as wooden shafts with stiff arms and wires—but as three crosses. He had had a feeling that he was a part of Calvary at the theater the night he saw Nada. Now that feeling came again to him, but this time more horribly real. This *was* Calvary. The central pole—he hardly dared look—bore the body of Christ. A convulsion seized him. He tried to rise to his feet but could not. He crouched there, quivering and gasping. He wanted to shout: "It was I who crucified you!"

Then he looked at the cross at the right hand of the Saviour to see if a thief were gibbeted there, and then his terror knew no limit. For on that cross to the right hand of the Saviour was a woman's body, her garments torn and a bandage over her eyes. It was Little Wine-Head and her cheeks were channeled and her lips distorted.

"Jesus save her," he tried to pray. "For me there can be no salvation—but save her, Jesus, Redeemer!"

There was yet the other cross. Who would be the thief crucified at the left hand of the Saviour? Gordon's eyes were filmed as he stared through the half-dawn at the third cross. The second thief was himself, Gordon Dole, on the cross at the left hand of the Son of God!

Then he saw the head with its crown of thorns turn sadly to the woman. And He smiled on her and the distorted face was suffused with a pale, chaste glow. The bandage dropped from her guiltless eyes and they closed peacefully.

"Jesus, Saviour! Will you turn to me? To me that crucified You?"

But the head of Jesus would not turn his way, and the world went dark and a ringing sound, as of far-off bells, came to his ears...faintly and then no more.

An ambulance stopped beside the unconscious man and matter-of-fact internes rolled him over, while a surgeon ran a thumb under his brow, pressing the super-orbital nerve for reaction. The crew put a stretcher to the road-bed, flipped Gordon over and onto the litter and took him away, away from that avenue of crosses.

He was in the hospital for two weeks and when he went home with Margery he was chastened and full of high resolutions.

Chapter Eight

I

*M*ARGERY was deeply concerned over Gordon's latest spree and she counseled him to quit drinking entirely. She told him she had lied to his office, telling Kemp that he was ill with influenza and that it had been a severe attack. He would die if he didn't quit abusing himself and she pointed out the folly of a presumably bright person handicapping himself with wrong living, which led to wrong thinking.

"I think just the opposite is true, Margery—that wrong thinking leads to wrong living, but I'm not in a position or in a humor to argue. I feel pretty bad about the whole thing, and I'll try to keep decent for your sake."

"I'd rather you'd do it for your own sake."

He wanted to go to the office, but Margery induced him to call Kemp and ask for a week of rest, a week in which to recover entirely from his "influenza." Kemp said he was glad that Gordon was on the mend and that he most certainly could have another week off.

"It's a crazy, weird office," Gordon told Margery, "but

they certainly treat their men fine when they are sick."

It was a quiet, happy week for Margery and she thought Gordon really was beginning to see the error of his ways. They took an excursion to Bear Mountain and visited many places of interest in the city. Mrs. Hamilton wrote that she wouldn't be in New York until the first of the year, and Margery was glad that her mother had postponed her visit.

II

When Gordon returned to the office to resume work, he found a note in his mail box. He trembled after he had opened it, for he saw Nada's signature on it. He could see by the date line that the note had been in his box for about ten days. It read:

"My dear friend Gordon:

"That was a splendid thing you did for us in your review. I'll be free this Sunday afternoon if you would care to call at my home, and I should like very much to thank you in person and to talk over old times."

His first direct word from her in years! She wanted to talk over old times. What old times? The time he had made an ass out of himself in her home or the other time when he had become a fool in declaring his passion for her? The note left him quite blank and stupid and clay-like.

He wondered if she had thought him odd for not having called her or replied to her note. He decided to try her telephone to tell her that he had been ... well, that he had been ill and hadn't received her letter. Yes, he would call. He went to *The Star's* library and looked through the files to see if her show had closed, and he found that it had a few days after the opening. Then he called her home but she wasn't in and he left a message with a maid.

After his dinner hour he was sitting with a pile of miscellaneous rewrite material on the ledge of his desk when he received a telephone call. It was from Miss Halpin's maid, who said she had been instructed to ask Mr. Dole if it would be possible for him to come to her apartment house as soon as he was through work. Yes, he would be there at about 11 o'clock.

III

WHEN Gordon reached Nada's address, he simply didn't know what to think or do. He was still somewhat crushed by the terrible experience he had had at the Long Island roadhouse, and his brave resolutions already were making wry faces at him. It seemed that his soul was a wad in an old-fashioned rifle barrel, the wad being shoved into the muzzle and a merciless ramrod tamping and pressing against the wad, driving a charge of powder into such compactness that the detonation would be terrific. Interspersed in his life's episodes, so grimly real and inescapable, there had been dreams as widely brilliant as the scarves of gypsies and he ached for release. His thoughts became clotted like blood.

Nada occupied the entire top floor of the Park Avenue apartment house. Gordon had been told that she owned it; that it had been part of the divorce settlement by Grosserly. He had expected more lobby display than he found, but there were no brigadier generals of the Bulgarian army on duty downstairs; just a doorman, a man at a switchboard and an elevator man, all dressed severely and simply in tan uniforms. He gave his name and was taken to the tenth floor.

He handed his hat to a colored maid, who showed him into a high-ceiled room in which there were few but handsome pieces of furniture. The sides of the room were paneled with walnut; there were crystal chandeliers, several richly patterned rugs of wine-red and tall casements flanked with delicately traced brocades. There was an antique cabinet about seven feet tall on which rested a marble bust of Bourchelle's Beethoven. He heard the sound of feet, softly treading and the lash of silk and then the woman herself came through a door, the woman he had longed to see, the woman he loved. She was clad in a scarlet evening gown, and the whiteness of her skin and the light amber of her hair, confused his vision for a moment as he rose to meet her.

He had no memory of what their first words were, but retained only the melody that was in her voice and the picture of her as she stood against the background of walnut panels, a splash of wild scarlet, and her enchanting

lips half-parted in a smile. He believed there was an eager
luster in her eyes and her expression stirred within him a
memory of that distant day in high school when they
were in the school play rehearsal and she had tripped and
he had caught her in his arms, sensing the soft paradise
of her bosom.

Gordon's whole being was shaken, as a beach is shaken
when high waves beat down. A wave now was rising in his
soul, and for a split-second it poised there and then fell,
almost bearing him under with emotion. Then he felt her
hand catching his and he became more calm and he promised himself not to falter; not to go to pieces before this
woman who seemed lovelier than ever she had seemed
before.

"It is wonderful to see you, Gordie," she said. She had
said something before that, but it was the first thing he
heard and could remember.

"It has been a long time, hasn't it?"

"Entirely too long."

"It's rather hard to talk," he said. "It's like the time
I rode to your house on my bicycle and had a lot of won-
derful speeches to make to you...but when I saw you,
I couldn't say much of anything. Remember?"

"I remember it, Gordie."

"You were awfully mad at me that day, weren't you?"

"I wasn't a bit mad."

He looked at her wonderingly. "But the day I...the
night I went to the dressing room and...well..."

"Yes, the night you kissed me."

"You were mad then, weren't you?"

"No. Wrong again."

"Not mad?" he wished to God he could think of something new to say, instead of sitting here rambling into the past like an old soldier fighting over a battle. "But I made an awful ass out of myself."

"I didn't think so. It might interest you to know that after you went out of the dressing room, I fainted."

"Don't joke with me, Nada... even about the past."

She had been sitting opposite him but now she came over to him and stood beside him and put her hand on his shoulder. "I'm not joking."

"I never knew you cared, Nada."

"I did care."

"Do you care now?"

She laughed.

"We have such a lot of things to talk over!" She went to the antique cabinet and drew from her bosom a thin rope of pearls to which was attached a gold key. She opened the doors of the cabinet and brought out a thick, leather-bound book. She gave it to Gordon.

He opened the cover. "It's a scrap book." He began to turn page after page. "Why, Nada, these are my newspaper stories, apparently all of them. This is most amazing. Why..."

"That's how I kept in touch with you," she said.

He closed the book and felt himself being drawn into a gulf. But was it a gulf? Perhaps it was a high mountain, from which one might see blue horizons, sunsets and stars long-hidden. He stood beside her, wanting to throw his arms about her, to hold her close, close, forever close to him. But he hesitated yet a time.

"Oh, the hours!" He felt sick and he almost groaned with his longing. "The God damned hours! Won't they ever go? Nada, I've waited and I've paid a bitter price for the waiting and I've done desperate things and I'll have to pay for my desperation. Sometimes I think I am a coin that God and the devil are tossing in a gamble. Heads for God. Tails for the devil. I'm riding on a chain, a chain that clanks. It cuts and bruises me. I've missed you so. You used to seem like a brightly lighted window, through which one peered in passing... and then the shutters were closed and I thought of you here in the warmth of success and fame, and I out in the storm.... I must go, Nada, I can't stand it any longer."

The closeness of her, the perfume of her, the brilliant life of her was maddening. He walked away.

"Open the scrap book again and read what is written on the last page."

He opened it, only half-aware of what he was doing. Then he read: "Call to him who loves you."

He dropped the book and walked swiftly to her and held her in his arms. He burned her lips with his.

"All these years I've loved you, Nada."

"And I you. I tried to chase success, but when it came, I asked who was going to make it up to me if I didn't take my happiness."

"I'm just a puff of wind. I've been like a bat, threshing

about in a dark room, afraid to go into the daylight."

"We'll find daylight together."

He marveled that she seemed so physically frank, so unashamed and so unfaltering. He kissed her half-opened warm lips again and again and felt the breath come from her and it seemed that his body was becoming her body and that he was being summoned to the presence of a sibyl, there to be given an answer.

"The years have taught me that there is no one but you, Gordon. I have waited. Other men were clay beside the memory of you. We women are instruments and men get from us only such harmonies as they are capable of playing. They cannot hammer on us and expect silver bells to drown out the brutal sound of the anvil. Without love day is an agony of hours; music is a clatter; art a nightmare and moonlight but an impotent glare....O Gordon, Gordon, I, too, have been fearfully alone."

"Nada, I want you. I want to take you while you are still young and unwithered." He was in the whirlpool now. "Give me a young, new bosom. You want me....I can feel that you do."

"Let's sit here and talk first."

"I can't wait any longer. We know things without saying them, don't we? Let's belong first and talk afterward."

"We shouldn't rush it."

"Is ten years of waiting rushing it?"

"Don't you think it much better if we take the evening by degrees and not break into it like a thunderstorm?"

Gordon clasped her madly. "No, I don't! I don't think

so! I want to break into Life, into Love, with battleaxes and with rams. Either I must batter against the walls and die, or lift the siege and crawl away, baffled, broken by privations.... Then it will be my soul that dies. For ten years I have been a skeleton on which flesh was hung. A skull in which a rabble of anarchic brain cells have spluttered and surged...."

"Gordon, Gordon! My lover-to-be!"

"Lover-to-be hell! I'm Lover-That-Is! I must be lover now. You are in scarlet. Get out of scarlet. I am in blue. I must get out of blue. There must be no color, no cloth, no light, for we must merge into one self the two half-selves that we are. We must cheat the Fates for they will come soon enough to us, with a summons to leap about in the Dance Macabre, the Dance of Death.... Nada! Nada!... Come to me now."

She went to the high wall and stood there, her ashen blonde hair against the walnut panelings and she let her hand caress the wood of the wall. She cast a glance at the ceiling, on which gold leaf glistened like dragon-scales. Her fingers reached the button controlling the lights. She pressed and said:

"Lover, I'm coming to you in the dark."

The awareness of you in the dark, Nada, the awareness.... There are no hours to cry out against now. I am a drop of quicksilver rising in a tube. I am the first of the centuries and the last of the ghosts. My fingers have a thousand eyes like flies and the fingers multiply a thousandfold what the eye could see. There is a language in touch.

Nada is Astarte of the Phœnicians of Ascalon.... Prodigious flashes sear my hips and there is a stinging where ecstasy beats my back with fluttering wands. Nada is Artemis the Chaste. I am a Visigoth. I am Comus. I am Panurge. I am Orlando. I am Villon. I am as mad as a bee, though I am as sane as a hare. I am milk from the udder of the Hathor Cow of Egypt and I am gall from the bladder of Judas. Oh, the awareness of you, Nada.... A brown priest lies stretched full length in a temple where rise two columns of alabaster. A hungry child charges a porringer with a pewter spoon.... Nada is the sibyl who is giving the answer. Nada is a nautch girl. She is a priestess dancing with the sistrum trembling.... The prophet Ezekiel calls to Jerusalem and Jeremiah laments.... I am town-crier in Babylon, with its fifteen leagues of the voluptuaries.... The stifling, draining awareness of you, Nada.... The darkness cannot see, for the darkness is as blind as the pocket of an alchemist, so the darkness cannot be eye-witness against Love. I cast silver upon the knees of Venus and put a crown of fig leaves about her head. I have drawn away the cincture of cords from the Goddess Mylitta of the Assyrians.... The Pagan in me now is dying, dying.... Give me no inflaming philters, for the echo of castanets and drums dies on the rim of the night ... sinking ... sinking....

"You won't catch cold, will you, Gordon?"

"I hardly think so. I'm sleepy...."

It had been a long pilgrimage from the high school desks of Fairmount City to a sixteenth-century bed in Park Avenue.

IV

As NOON spilled narrowly through the velour pulls of Nada's boudoir casements, Gordon lay wondering. He wished he could compose a Rogue's March with which to drum self-accusation from the regiment of his inhibitions. His early environment had gyved his limbs. Even in moments of exaltation, Gordon could hear the rusty grumbling of chains that Granner had wrested from the sacred forges of her Lord God—each link hammered into a letter, as Blacksmith Granner beat with an iron-shod Bible on a pulpit-anvil of steel—and all the letters of the heavy chain joined to spell: "Thou-Shalt-Not." How rude was the scrunching gambol of the chain as it violated the secrecy of sophisticated linens!

The Thou-Shalt-Not chain on his loins and thighs, Gordon wore on his wrists newer manacles than the cumbrous truss from Granner's smithy. On his wrists, gnawing into his thews, were his marriage vows. Remorse enveloped him like a night sweat. His conscience barked like a bone-raped dog—double remorse it was, an inbred sin-consciousness, while the Thou-Shalt-Not chain clanked dolorously. A provoking terror, while the I-Am-Married manacle snarled with brassy crackle.

Gordon wondered how it was that other men accepted their adulteries so matter-of-factly. Some of them were so robustly braggart in parading their promiscuities, while others were so stoically indifferent. None of his acquaintances seemed to suffer aftermaths of regret.

It was a ghastly thing to be so drivingly polygamous at twilight and so piously penitent at dawn.

Gordon's soul, to be sure, sounded no exultant pæan as he lay in bed at Nada's. The thin slice of noon that entered between the curtains burnished an old crucifix on Nada's wall, and that didn't add to his peace of mind. The roadhouse delirium was too recent to permit him to be at ease in a situation such as this.

Perhaps he should go to Margery, speaking as gently as he could to that gentle and stainless woman. Perhaps he should address her through a mask, telling her that her husband was dead. Lady Margery, your husband, Sir Gordon-the-Spouse, is dead and he left no estate except these personal belongings: a chain of Thou-Shalt-Not, which is being hauled to you by many oxen, straining and bellowing at a great sledge; and manacles of I-Am-Married, which no doubt will bring something in the brass market. Yes, Milady, the man himself yet lives, but the husband in him is no more. Shall you hang out hatchments on the manor gate—armorial bearings of your late husband? His heraldic signs were, as I recall them, a phallus somnolent on a field sere. . . . Alas! They will not give your late husband sepulture in holy ground.

Gordon's stirring about awakened Nada. They had coffee and she asked him what his thoughts had been on opening his eyes. He said:

"Let's not define the flight of a gull in a hurricane."

While they were dressing, Gordon divided himself into historic trinity. In himself he found ancient, medieval and modern eras. Gramper had been the man of the caves and Granner was neolithic and Hiram and Blair were of the kitchen middens of his personal dawn of civilization. Wedlock had brought the Dark Ages, rearing cold and haunting Gothic cloisters in his soul. And now... would Nada prove to be the Renaissance with her da Vinci smile? He waited until he was fully clothed before he permitted himself to think of Racy, his mother, and then he thought of her as the Madonna.

He always was longing for Racy.

"We must work out a plan," Nada said. "Something practical if we can do so, for I must see you occasionally. Otherwise...."

"We'll see each other. I guess it has to be that way now; but let's not enter into any arrangement that will bind us. We must be free or it will kill something."

"Come to me when you can, for I'll be waiting and longing for you."

On his way home Gordon thought of the hypocrisies of life and of his own tremendous shortcomings, his unforgivable sins and his unfairness to such a loving, trusting wife. He rubbed his lips on his handkerchief and inspected the linen to see if any rouge had come off. He wished Nada did not use such persistent perfume. What would he do if Margery ever called on him for explanations? He would deny. No, he would affirm. He would smile. No, he would fume and kick up rugs. He would speak calmly. No, he would roar.

My character is oblique, he said. I am the priest, Laocoön, and I have hurled a spear at the wooden horse of Matrimony. Now snakes will come up from the sea to destroy me and my children.

Chapter Nine

I

*M*ARGERY told Gordon she could not sleep when he stayed away all night and she wished he would let her know when he wasn't coming home. However, she could see he hadn't been drinking again and that was reassuring. She handed him some letters from Fairmount City and as he read them she sat watching him and wishing she could become a part of his life.

Margery, looking at her husband, fancied that he was a door that had no knob. How could she go into his mind with that knobless door there? He read haphazardly aloud ... "Granner is getting feeble but her mind still is clear ... my undertaking business is fine, thanks to my foresight in having a splendid stock of caskets on hand during the flu epidemic." ... Margery wished she were as impulsive as her neighbor, Mrs. Grant, who broke china whenever she wanted to peek into her husband's personality. Perhaps she should kick down that door to Gordon's mind instead of waiting for him to open it.... Gordon said he guessed he would shave.

While Gordon was lathering his face, Margery sat on the edge of the bathtub and Norman played with a toy train in the hall and was singing. Margery said she thought the child was going to have a fine voice. Perhaps he would sing in a boys' choir some day if Gordon didn't object. He said he didn't object to anything.

As he began to scrape his chin with a razor, Margery said she had some news that might or might not please him.

"What is it?"

"I'm that way again."

He stopped shaving and felt rather cheap. "Another baby?"

"Yes. What do you think?"

"I'm tickled to death." What news to give a man who had come from an infidel's bed! If only she was a quarrelsome, nagging, bitter wife, it would be so much easier on him. He could stand up better beneath the weight of his own sins if she, too, were low and vile and without will power. But she was sweet, clean and the embodiment of Mother Earth, and she gave everything and he gave little or nothing.

"I'm glad to do it for you, Gordie. I'd do anything for you—don't you know that?"

"God knows I know it!"

She seemed very happy at the way he took her news.

"Say, Gordie, I found out about that Eckhert woman to-day." Gordon nearly cut his lip. "What about her?" he asked.

"Her folks sent for her clothes and things yesterday. They were stored in the basement. The superintendent's wife told me that the Eckhert woman was kept, Gordon."

"Is that so?"

"Yes. By a big politician, and that's why you couldn't find out about her that night you telephoned hospitals and the police."

"Did you hear what happened to her?"

"Well, it seems she was saying good-by to the man, the politician, and he had a wife and she followed him and waited and when the door was opened she threw acid all over the Eckhert woman. She's totally blind now."

Gordon was finishing his shave in a very clumsy manner and he hastened to hide his expression by applying a wet towel to his face. He held the towel there for many seconds, but left an open place through which he could study Margery. He experienced a sort of horror and for a moment fancied that it had been himself on whom the acid had been hurled. The rawness of his badly shaved skin emphasized the illusion and he pictured Margery as the acid-thrower. Would she do a thing like that? No, she was too firm-minded and too stable. Still, she might do it. . . .

"Don't bother fixing me any dinner, Margery. I think I'll hurry to the office."

On his way downtown the subway train wheels seemed to be shouting over and over at him: "Wine-Head! Wine-Head!"

II

Mrs. Hamilton arrived in New York early in January and when she had a shocking glimpse of Margery's waistline, she knew that the bigness was not caused by gastronomic bloat. Margery attempted to change the subject, telling her mother that Gordon now had a contract that called for two hundred and fifty dollars a week, but Mrs. Hamilton was more interested in waistlines.

"Men have no consideration," Mrs. Hamilton said, "but you can just bet I stopped your father after you were born."

"But, Mother, it was I who wanted to have this baby. I love babies and Gordon loves them more than anything."

"You mean to say it wasn't a slip?"

"No, it was planned."

"Then all I can say is that you're out of your mind!"

Margery told her mother that Gordon had begun a play but Mrs. Hamilton was skeptical and hoped that Norman wouldn't grow up to be a scatter-brain like his father. Anybody that had to stay from home beyond midnight was up to no good. Nothing less than drink and women could keep men from their homes at such ungodly hours.

"Gordon isn't interested in women, and if he drinks, it's because his work is so strenuous. After all, it's his business, Mother, and he has been on the water wagon for quite a while."

"You're too lenient with him. I made your father stop drinking and I kept him away from all temptation by making him go to bed at ten o'clock except on lodge nights."

Gordon gave up his room to his mother-in-law and slept on an overstuffed couch in the sitting-room. Mrs. Hamilton said she had intended to visit only a short while but now that Gordon had got Margery in trouble again she certainly wasn't going to desert her daughter. She would stay to take care of the girl, who no doubt was going to die because of Gordon's lust. Margery begged Gordon to say nothing in reply to Mrs. Hamilton's remarks, and he was glad to make some concession to his wife in the light of his own faults.

On May 15, 1920, Margery had her second baby. It was a girl and they called the child Greta, for that was the name of Margery's aunt. Gordon had wanted to send his wife to the hospital, but Mrs. Hamilton made such a scene when this was suggested that he canceled a reservation he had made at the Woman's Hospital.

Previous to her confinement, Margery had placed Norman in a neighborhood kindergarten class, where a well-poised young woman took the child and some fifteen others to Cathedral Park each morning. There they played games and learned how to curtsy and to bow. This kept the house quiet while Gordon slept, for he worked late and when he got home he sat up trying to write his play.

Gordon had stayed away from Nada's since he learned of his wife's condition, trying to palliate his conscience by saying to himself that it was the decent thing to do. A week after Greta was born, Gordon was sitting at the dining-room table with pages of script before him. Mrs. Hamilton, unable to sleep, came in and sat beside him. He tried to make out that her presence there did not annoy him, but it was no use. He gathered his papers together, placed them in a folder and spread fresh linen on his couch. Mrs. Hamilton looked at him for a while and then said: "I wish you would promise me not to make my girl ever go through this thing again."

He had a desire to begin breaking things. His face was set and he believed that the seething of his intestines would blow out his navel, like a faulty rivet is blown from an overheated boiler. A call from his office interrupted what he later thought might have been a murder. The night editor assigned him to Sing Sing Prison to witness the electrocution of Hardy, the Brooklyn bandit.

"I have to leave right away to be on the ground early to-morrow," he told his mother-in-law. "I don't want to disturb Margery, so you tell her."

He packed a grip and then went to Nada's, where he spent the early morning. He asked Nada if she minded him calling on her at such odd hours and if she was offended by his long silence.

"I want you to come whenever you feel like it. We've both got work to do and we're going to do it, but when you need me, I shall always be waiting for you."

III

GORDON bought Margery a cottage in Queens Manor, twenty minutes by train from the Long Island side of

Pennsylvania Station. They moved into it in October after their apartment lease had expired. Gordon began to build bookshelves and his hammering and sawing at the non-union hours of three and four o'clock in the mornings bothered Mrs. Hamilton no little. She had sold her Fairmount properties and announced she was going to live in the East, staying with Margery until she found herself a suitable home.

"Anybody that works at night like that is crazy," she said.

"Don't you say anything at all about it," Margery told her mother. "It takes his mind off his work to build the shelves, and anyway, he's fixing up a place to write."

Mrs. Hamilton grunted, for she didn't have much faith in Gordon's play-bearing capabilities.

IV

GORDON received word that Granner was dying in the summer of 1921. He sent Margery, Mrs. Hamilton, the children and the maid to the seashore—the Rockaways. Then he wired Blair Christensen to tell no one outside the family that he was coming home, for he wanted to spend his hours with Granner and with memories. Blair met Gordon at Union Station and took him in one of his new funeral limousines to the Edgeworth Street house.

"Don't worry," Blair said, "I'm going to take swell care of Granner when she dies."

"Thanks, Blair. I know you will."

They stopped at the old home and Blair carried Gordon's grips.

"It's my baby," Granner said as Gordon leaned over the bed to kiss her. He held both the brown-spotted hands —shapely hands old Granner had, and always so clean— and kissed them. Her eighty-year-old body seemed dead, but her mind lived on. So strong and agile, her mind, skirting every pitfall that Hunter Death had trenched; skipping over clever snares that Trapper Death had set.

"So you have a little girl, too, Gordie! And does the boy know the Bible stories? You always liked the one about David and Goliath."

Uncle Hiram sat in a corner of the bedroom where Granner lay and he had little to say. Gordon tried to rouse him, but Uncle Hiram was dull—more dead than Granner, Gordon thought. Good old Hiram! The once firm jaw was flaccid and sagging and the eyes were clouded and the hair gray. There was an open hymn book on Hiram's knees. He had been trying to sing as Gordon came through the door and Gordon had heard his voice. Abide With Me, he had been singing to Granner. Fast falls the eventide... the darkness deepens....

V

It was remarkable, Dr. Connors said, how Granner held onto life. She said that Gordie's presence had made her almost well again. She had been afraid they might take her to a hospital, operate on her or put her in the calico uniform of the poorhouse, but now she was not afraid. Gordon wouldn't allow anyone to harm her. Blair told Gordon he had a fine casket ready, a white one—for Granner didn't want to go away in black, but in white, as Racy had gone away.

Gordon's office wired him impatiently, for he had overstayed his leave of absence; but he ignored the telegrams. Blair worried about Gordon and thought he should go outdoors more frequently than he did. When he wasn't with Granner, Gordon would go to the cellar, where William Dole used to sit, and he liked to get out the aged mining tools, now all caked with rust. He handled them reverently. He took one of the wrought-iron candle spikes to the room where he used to sleep on his Cleopatra bed and where he now again read and slept. He put the candleholder in his grip and was careful not to disturb the grimy drippings that encrusted the sconce, for he fancied that Gramper's ghost resided in the old wax.

An unforeseen happening saddened Gordon. Uncle Hiram, who had kept working doggedly at Cousins' store, died at the meat block late in September, but the occurrence was withheld from Granner. The old woman was vaguely aware that something was wrong, but she slept most of the time. Only occasionally did she speak rationally. Once—Hiram had been gone a week—she roused to say to Gordon: "Hiram promised to sing to me to-day. What's keeping him from singing the blessed hymn?"

Gordon asked Blair and Mrs. Christensen to leave the room and then he did something that was hard for him to do. He found the hymn book and began to sing. He had not inherited his mother's voice; rather, his voice was mediocre, as his father's was said to have been. He sat in a corner of the room, the hymn book open, and sang Abide With Me, but he broke down; he couldn't go on with it. The darkness deepens.... He was choked and desolate and alone. He went to the bed and was about to kneel, but he didn't kneel. He just looked for a while and then he drew the cover gently over the still, old face. He went outside, and as he stood in the doorway, Blair knew what had happened.

Gordon started back to New York two days after Granner had been placed beside her husband, her daughter and her son. There was but one vacant place on the tombstone now. Gordon wanted to stoop to kiss the earth above each of the four sleepers, but some people were looking at him.

Chapter Ten

I

GORDON visited Nada with a curious irregularity, sometimes seeing her as frequently as every other night and again not calling on her or communicating with her for a month or more. He was unable to account for this unevenness of attention so he decided not to puzzle himself with analyses; nor did she ever say she thought it odd or perplexing. The nearest Nada came to referring to the time element in their love affair was when she came home from rehearsal one afternoon to find him waiting for her. She threw her arms about him impulsively and said: "I dread growing old. I dread it!"

"You're the last person who should dread age," he said. "You are timeless to me. Indeed, your timelessness startles me, just as your love startles me."

"If only I can live forever in your heart, Gordie, it will make up for old age and everything."

"That's where you will live ... forever."

"But you'll always think of me as young?"

"And radiant and lovely."

"You are young, too."

"But restless and furiously impatient and sad."

"Sad because you love me?"

"Sad about something. I don't know what. You can't explain why buds come and why leaves grow and how leaves dry up and fall and finally how the tree is gnarled, old and then dead."

"Yes, but there are new plantings and new shoots and new trees to take the place of the old ones. Perhaps there will be new lives for us some time, somewhere."

"Maybe it's all one life and we are just phases of it."

"We are big phases though, to ourselves."

"We are in love, anyway, Nada."

"Gloriously in love, Gordon."

"And you don't think it strange that I retreat sometimes from our love, going away and entering long silences and then coming suddenly back to you without warning?"

"No, because the moments that you are here are our moments. They belong to no one else. No, Gordon, I don't think anything strange about it, because your love leads you to do what is natural, and when we meet we resume our talks and our friendship and our love as though it was only yesterday when we parted. And to me it is only yesterday, for the time that passes between your visits simply is blank to me. I live only when we are together."

"It is not a world of shadows when I have you."

"You always have me."

His observation of the love affairs of other men led Gordon to believe that they went to their sweethearts anxiously panting and frequently. Then why did he allow weeks to elapse without going to his beloved? The question kept recurring to him. Certain of his colleagues had left their wives and children even, to facilitate propinquity with their mistresses. Could it be they loved their women more than he did Nada? He couldn't believe it, because she was all of love to him. He knew several men who passed from one emotional storm to another, taking up with a new love as soon as the most recent one had packed her toilet articles, her presents and her night clothing. Gordon wondered why he could not find it within himself to tell Margery the truth and then go at once to Nada, turning on the love lamps and letting them glare until the bulbs burned out.

He even suggested to Nada that it might be the honorable thing if he cut loose from his home ties and admitted his position. She silenced him rather adroitly but finally.

"Gordon, it would be even more cowardly than you think you have been to ease your mind of its guilt by shifting your trouble to others. I have never asked you to leave anyone for me. You have duties and you must go through with them. I think that in your heart you love your wife, and I know you need her."

"But you..."

She laughed. "I live now as I always have lived, in moments. Who am I to covet a lifetime of happiness? Who is anyone, bad or good, so important as to merit year after year of ecstasy?"

"The moments are wonderful, Nada, but I don't like the eternities of remorse that follow them."

"Well, the thing to do is to meet it. If we've got to go to hell, for God's sake, let's go standing up and not be hauled in by the heels, gibbering and weeping."

"Yes, we've got to stand up, even though it's only to fool ourselves."

Nada went to Europe in 1925 and remained there with a theatrical production until autumn of the next year. Gordon felt a provoking emptiness and missed her terribly. When she was in New York, he felt near to her, even though he saw her infrequently, but now that she was abroad, he imagined he never was to see her or hear from her again.

Nevertheless, and in accord with his perverse nature, he became more spirited during this year of wide separation than he had been in some time and Margery noted with pleasure that his old-time athletic vigor had returned. His eye was clear, he still abstained from alcohol and the summer at the seashore seemed to bring him a semblance of peace. They had found a place on Laurel Island, a long and narrow sandbar, that ran parallel to Long Island, with a broad bay to the north and the Atlantic Ocean to the south of them. They built a beach house, half a mile from the bay side of the island and a hundred yards this side of the sea.

On days when there was little surf, Gordon would swim far out and on stormy days he would breast the combers in fighting mood. He was jubilant when the undertow swirled about his lean, brown body. He romped with his son and daughter and the neighbors on Laurel Island said, What a fine home-loving man Mr. Dole is. Always playing with his children; so kind to his wife; not cross and grumpy like some of these pot-bellies who snarl and are stingy. Margery was delighted as she repeated these compliments to Gordon, not realizing that each kind word from her was a stab in the heart. He wondered what the same neighbors would say if they were to have seen him drunk and blowzy in a speakeasy, his eyelids swollen, and Nada, tall and beautiful coming to rescue him from a Manhattan gin pen, taking him away from the rum that made a pudding out of the brain. Away from voices that slid through masks at him ... at them.

As he swam in the open sea Gordon thought the great waters were imbued with a powerful something that reached into the soul of a man. There was a motherhood and a wifehood about the sea that one could feel rather than understand. There was more than just a dipping of a body into the Mother-Wife Sea, more than a mere response of skin to water. He believed that a kinship existed between the ocean spirit and that of man and he wondered if one could not find peace and resignation beside the wide waters that were so challengingly sublime. The sea was a demonstrative wife, a potent mother—yes, and it was a restless, tossing, impulsive mistress in which one could unleash one's nature in a riotous play of instinct. And then again it took you into its great arms so tenderly, so calmly, so forgivingly.... It was a peaceful interlude, that summer on

Laurel Island, and Gordon had finished his play, all but polishing a few scenes. He thought he would submit it to Nada's manager and producer, Jedlicka, as had been suggested by her a few weeks before she had left for Europe.

In the Fall, Gordon was assigned by Kemp to accompany Her Royal Highness, Princess Helen of Balsivaria, on her American tour. He was advised to purchase a high silk hat, a black walking stick, full dress clothes and to charge the equipment to his expense account.

"And learn how to say 'Your Royal Highness,'" Kemp added. "They say she's a pip."

Chapter Eleven

I

HER ROYAL HIGHNESS, the Princess Helen, arrived in the United States in October and brought with her sixty-two trunks and a spaniel. New York bands began a frantic study of the Balsivarian National Anthem, which at first was mistaken by Broadway for a new and weird product of the song shops.

The advent of the Princess precipitated a social war as ambitious Blue Book addicts sought to smother the royal coronet with hospitality. There was a clamorous scramble by socially passionate persons to hitch their private cars to the special train that was to carry Helen across the continent and back.

Gordon was one of five press representatives on the tour and as he lay in his compartment, he wondered if princesses were human. Shortly before midnight, he heard a commotion and removed the screen and leaned out. The train was waiting in the shed of Grand Central Station and was to stay there until morning so that Her Royal Highness could rest after a busy day in the social arena.

He could see a phalanx of silk hats bobbing at the grilled gate and then the Princess came down the ramp. She wore a bulky ermine coat and she had bobbed golden hair with a tiara of platinum and diamonds. She took short steps on a tan carpet that had slender red borders and the toes of her silver brocade slippers were pointed well outward. As Helen passed his window, Gordon saw her dimples, deep ones of large diameter, like the dents that hold the stems of fat apples, and he saw the set smile that framed large, strong teeth.

He wondered if a princess perspired beneath such a surplus of fur; so much fur, an ensemble of a thousand pelts torn from the ribs of little weasels. He could hear the roar of excited social lions—winners of the opening battle for survival. Here, Your Royal Highness...and There, Your Royal Highness.... A tired police officer, flipping his nightstick, stood with his back to Gordon's window, shutting off the view.

Gordon's attempt to sleep was frustrated by the hissing of airbrakes, the clangor of drive wheels and the thrusting of steel rods. The metallic bleating seemed to him like the noises made by his "Thou-Shalt-Not" chain.

II

RAIN spittled the windows of the dining car as the press representatives breakfasted and Gordon watched with interest the actions of self-conscious guests as they took their places at the tables. Many of the society folk on this first day out spoke amiably to anyone who looked alien, for they dared not run a risk of overlooking a possible baron or a confidant of Her Royal Highness.

Indeed, the valet to his Excellency, Professor Georgescu, Minister of Foreign Affairs, received such marked attention during the first twenty-four hours of the tour that he thought America a very mad place. The second day, however, when it was learned that he was just a valet and not a duke, the poor fellow was submerged by a type of snobbery that drowned his soul. Then he knew that America was very, very mad.

At every stop were bands playing the Balsivarian National Anthem, a composition that was to haunt Gordon during the month's tour. The hymn was full of toodle-doos, with a curious fanfare and rat-ta-ta-tas, and a tardy bellow of the bass tuba that crawled up like a brewer's belch.

"What is the low-down on this tour?" one of his fellow reporters, Hal Clarke, asked. "What's she here for?"

"Probably to get Walter Damrosch to rewrite the Balsivarian Anthem."

Gordon worked in his compartment, rewriting parts of his play between stories concerning the tour. He tried to keep his work a secret, but unknown to Gordon, Hal Clarke found a sheet of the script and it suited his mood to sign Gordon's name to it, seal it in an envelope and send it to the Princess. Perhaps a practical joke would relieve the monotony of the trip.

III

NEXT morning and while Gordon was shaving, he received a summons to Princess Helen's car. She had granted no interviews as yet, and he thought it strange that she should call for him. He asked the aide if he must appear in full dress and the aide said it would be an informal call and that Gordon could wear anything he chose except sports togs. He was conducted to her car and found the Princess seated in a deeply tufted chair and smoking a cigarette in a long jade holder. She seemed very young for her forty-odd years.

She talked with Gordon at length, asking him questions concerning American journalism, particularly the tabloids.

Finally she showed him the sheet of script that Clarke had sent and asked him why she had been "honored" by the gift. He was embarrassed and mystified and signed his name beside the Clarke forgery to indicate to her that he had not sent it.

"It's a bit from a play that I have been doing," he said. "I guess it's a joke of some sort. The boys are always playing jokes; it relieves the tedium. I'm very sorry."

"Why sorry?"

"Well, if it annoyed you, and also because I don't like to have my work kicking about."

"I was very much interested in the fragment. What is your play called?"

" 'The Work Bench.' It is about women in general, but

I shan't bore you with a recital of it. You've listened to enough speeches as it is."

She fingered a rope of large pearls. "The language in the fragment is rather challenging. When I read the first line, 'It is the dawn of twilight noon,' I felt curious. Will you tell me a little about the play?"

"It probably will fail, for I have disregarded conventional treatment and have tried only to make it deeply symbolic and beautiful. It is a fantasia, I suppose. The idea back of it is that woman is a Work Bench and that women who are laughed at for talking so much about their physical ills and their baby deliveries should not be laughed at. On this Work Bench are fashioned what are believed to be masterpieces."

Helen was listening intently and studying him as he went on.

"Men who build tall structures or who throw great bridges across wide rivers are not laughed at when they point to their work. Presidents come to dedicate the big bridges and leaders of civic life gather to praise the tall buildings, while the man who has reared them stands there and hears others laud his work and his vision."

He paused, casting her an inquiring glance. She motioned for him to proceed.

"Men laugh at women who gather in groups about baby carriages, the women criticizing and commenting on the quality of the product that has come from the Work Bench. No Presidents arrive to utter smug eulogies, praising Woman, the Architect of Man, and no Chambers of

Commerce pin ribbons of civic pride on the milk-giving bosoms of the child-bearers."

"You love women, don't you, Monsieur?"

"Yes, I love the woman that is in women.... Then, in my play, it is shown that women are tremendously wise in contemplation of their surgical operations. Men think it is small talk in them, narrowness of horizon.... Nothing of the sort, for every surgeon's knife that threatens the body of woman is a direct threat at the Work Bench itself. Woman is the true architect, and Man, so pridefully vain and boastful, is only the contractor, the winner of a bid. Woman must ensphere him, making him her factory manager, lulling him and charming him into certain ecstasies, so that he can work at the Bench without knowledge that it is work—he thinks it is play. Corporations have the same idea, borrowed from Woman, when they lead their employees to believe that the workmen are playing and are happy and blessed in their toil, fortunate in their sweat and their strain."

"And the point of it all is what, Monsieur Dole?"

"The point of it, Princess Helen, is that from the Work Bench of Woman comes Frankenstein—a monster that goes further than all other monsters or golems. He rises to laugh at Woman, his designer; to revile her, to reach into her throat and to bring out her heart. Then, insatiable and brutal, he teaches his brothers a black wizardry, and they crucify the best one among them and later rear churches to His Memory. Then, if that were not enough, they invoke His Name to litter the streets of commerce with hopes and to make the highways of the world run with blood.... The point, Princess, is that Man, fresh from the Work Bench of Woman is a no-good monstrosity!"

"But Woman?" she asked.

"A woman shall be our next Messiah."

"Shall she be crucified, too?"

"She shall be too clever, once she comes.... The beginning of her day is almost here, and as you read in my fragment, she shall come at the Dawn of Twilight Noon. Then there shall be no Time, no Space and no crucifiers, for she shall bear from her Work Bench the long-awaited rhythms that are perfect. She shall know the answers, and through Her, we, too, shall know."

"We'll not be here when She comes, Monsieur."

"No, we're here only now...."

The Princess gave Gordon her hand. "I sense that something in your life has hurt you deeply. I don't know what it is and I wouldn't pry into your secrets. But there is something good and fine in you and I am sorry if the world has hurt you."

He blurted out suddenly: "To hell with the world!"

She studied him a moment. She was not offended. "Well, that's one way of looking at it." Then they both seemed to catch a humorous phase in the exchange of words and laughed heartily. He went to his compartment and sat there, listening to the thrumming of the wheels. Clarke came in.

"What's this about you seeing the Princess?"

"Just a personal chat."

"Didn't you get a story?"

"Not a thing; we're not to quote her, anyway. She's royalty, you know."

"My God! Are we going to have another one of those White House Spokesmen?"

"She's going to see us all to-morrow and we don't have to dress in the monkey suits."

"Thank God for that. I'm going to pour a drink. Want one?" Gordon shook his head. "Well, liquor is a food and I can prove it. I wish there were some good looking gals on this train, because it's my mating season."

Gordon returned to New York in November, made a present of his high silk hat to his delighted porter and stopped at a newsstand to buy papers. On his way home in a cab, he read that Nada Halpin had returned to America and that Jedlicka had completed his theater and had named it for her.

Chapter Twelve

I

THE Nada Halpin Theater on Central Park West was reared in the architectural manner of a mosque and attracted wide attention in the press. Jedlicka, who had inherited fifty millions of dollars from his father, told reporters he didn't care whether the enterprise made a profit or not; that he was more interested in artistic success than in commercial returns. Of course, he added, it would be gratifying if the venture was self-sustaining.

Nada gave a tea in her apartment to which about two hundred friends of Jedlicka and many notables in theatrical fields were invited. Each of the Jedlicka friends had purchased a life membership in the theater, paying $5,000 a seat. Jedlicka's gray mustaches twitched with delight as he described to reporters the unusual features of his theater, the immense stage, the lighting, the studios which were to be given over to worthy but indigent students of stage craft. The policy of the entire enterprise was vested in a board of governors elected from the two hundred life members.

Gordon attended the tea with Austin Moore, who listened to Jedlicka but offered no comment. Jedlicka then explained that he had intended to import a European spectacle for the opening of his theater, but that he finally had decided to produce the play of "this young man," and he pointed to Gordon, who felt out of place and thoroughly self-conscious.

"You and Austin Moore stay after the others have gone," Nada whispered to Gordon, who was planning to slip away from the crowd that murmured so suavely, speaking of this and that play, such and such book, and so and so, the benefactor of here and yonder museum—all names, all materials, all things.

It was after six o'clock when Jedlicka led the retreat of millionaires and art patrons, but the echo of their voices seemed to have remained like birds of prey above a battlefield. One of Nada's servants flung open the casements to drive the flat, stale odor of tobacco from the drawing rooms and Moore and Gordon went with Nada to her music room.

"Play something, Austin," she said. "Something simple and quieting."

As Moore sat at the piano, his slim old body erect and dignified, his eyes undimmed by many years of looking at life and his thick white hair rumpled by the fingers of life, Gordon wondered if Moore didn't know the answer to it all. Gordon and Nada sat, one on either side of the piano bench, while the old critic played German lullabies, sweetly and without effort, understandingly and with great artistry.

What shapely, flexible fingers he had. What a soul he expressed with his fingers.

There was a silence for a time as Moore took his hands from the keyboard. He turned to Nada and said: "Now, you do something for me. Will you sing?"

Nada didn't reply at once, but looked at Gordon and then said rather hesitatingly: "Why, I don't believe so, Austin. I'm really not in the mood for it." Gordon knew what she was thinking; that if she sang it would tear out his heart as it always did when he heard her voice in song. "Suppose I dance instead."

"Great!" He began playing wildly swaying Hungarian melodies and youth seemed to be returning to him as he played, a glow of youth coming to his cheeks and a youthful sparkle taking possession of his eyes. But Nada didn't get up to dance and when Austin Moore stopped playing to look at her, she shook her head.

"I can't sing or dance to-day. I suppose I am thinking of Gordon's play."

"Must we talk shop?" Moore asked. "Remember, this is a sort of day off for the old drama critic, and he'd like to get away from the Work Bench for a few hours."

"Did you intend that as a joke?" Nada asked.

"What?"

"The 'Work Bench' reference."

"Of course not. Why? Oh, that's right. That's the name of our young friend's play. So it is."

"Let's not talk about it at all," Gordon said.

"Why not?" Nada asked.

"I'm fed up on it. Old Jedlicka accepted it so gingerly and raised so much hell about my not consenting to let you play in it, that I've half a mind to ask for it back."

Moore studied Gordon. "It is rather odd that he's opening his theater without the star for whom he named it. Doesn't it strike you that way, Gordon?"

"No, it doesn't. This play is my work and I won't share it with anyone, not even with Nada, for I want to go on my own."

"But if it fails?"

"Then, damn it all, Moore, I want to fail alone and not with her."

"Isn't he the selfish devil?" Moore turned to Nada rather playfully. "Well, I happened to hear Jedlicka talking over the script with one of the members of his so-called board." Moore laughed. "From what I gathered, he was worried about several features of the play."

"What, for instance?"

"I can't quote him verbatim, but his conversation ran something like this: 'That Dole fellow has something here that's decidedly artistic, but he'll have to eliminate certain scenes. For example, that debate between Jesus and the tight rope walker is too grotesque. There's a limit, you know.'"

All three laughed. Moore continued: "He said he was willing to go to tremendous expense in having a huge tank installed at stage level and extending far into the audience, with live fishes and marine flora that could be seen by a special lighting arrangement. He said he didn't mind building replicas of ancient Egyptian barges that would float on these waters and that he'd even redesign the auditorium chandeliers so that trumpeters and choristers could emerge during the course of your play." Moore began to laugh uproariously. "But he said that the debate in which a tight rope walker tried to sell Jesus the secret of true balance was out! He shouted the word 'Out!' like an umpire at the Yankee Stadium. You should have heard him."

"I let Austin read the script, Gordon," Nada said. "I hope you don't mind."

"That's all right! I'm glad you did. But I'm afraid to ask his opinion of it."

"What did you think of it, Austin?" Nada asked.

"It should not be put on at this time."

"What's time got to do with it?" Gordon was half-belligerent.

"You don't want my opinion, do you?"

"Yes, I do. For I know it will be an intelligent one."

"It's very much involved with symbols and there are two or three sermons in it that will mitigate against its success. If people wanted sermons they would crowd the churches. They certainly don't go to a theater to be preached at."

"Then you don't like it at all?"

"On the contrary, I myself like it and I think Einstein and the twelve men who are said to understand his theory might like it, but when you write a play for Broadway, you've got to keep within mental hailing distance of the Forties. What I like or don't like has nothing to do with a play's popularity. I didn't like a play called 'Mrs. O'Brien's Abie' and said so in print. The play ran nearly four years. I like your play, with certain reservations, and I don't believe it has a chance. Am I not the old cynic, though?"

Gordon looked hurt and sad. "No, you're not a cynic. You're damnably honest and decent in your viewpoint."

"Gordon," Moore said, taking him by the hand, "when I read your script, I saw that you yourself have been bobbing about, looking everywhere for certain solutions to this life of ours. Son, it's almost curtain time for this old, doddering critic, and I know only a few answers. But of this I am certain, you can't find them outside yourself. You can't find them in the lives of others, in the deeds of others or in the thoughts of others. The only possible place you'll find them, if ever, is within yourself."

Gordon clasped Moore's hand warmly and then said to Nada: "I wish you would sing, Nada, if you feel like it now."

"I'll sing for you both," she said. She went to Moore and put her arms about him and kissed him. "Oh, Austin, I love Gordon so! What shall we do?"

"I'd give anything if I could tell you, Nada, and if I could tell Gordon, for I love both of you. I can only say that in the eyes of the world you are wrong, and if it is possible for me to do so, I shall find out later on how you stand in the eyes of God....But, alas! We can send no messages back from the place where I soon shall be—if there is a place at all.... Come on, let's play and sing and hope."

II

GORDON was so nervous the evening of his play's première that he couldn't adjust his shirt studs. He finally said he wasn't going to put on evening clothes and then he told Margery to take Mrs. Hamilton to the play; that he wasn't going there at all. Margery was frankly disappointed, but she knew there was no use arguing with him.

He watched the clock closely and when it was time for the rise of the curtain, he went to a front window and raised the blind. Then he got out his old bugle, which he kept in a chifforobe drawer, and when it was time for the trumpeters to come from their chandeliers, he blew long and resounding blasts on it. This awakened Norman and Greta and the maid came from her room to see how drunk Mr. Dole was and if he had fallen and broken his neck. The bugle sounds rallied Gordon, and he wished now that he had gone to the theater just to hear the brave challenges that came from the high-vaulted auditorium. He hastily put on a scarf, a coat and hat and called a taxi. He barely made the 8:50 Long Island train for Pennsylvania Station.

The curtain had risen on the second act when Gordon reached the theater. As he sneaked in and stood at the rear of the huge place, he felt intuitively that his work was a failure and that Austin Moore could not have been wrong in his forecast. He wanted to ask an attendant if there had been any applause at the end of the first act, but instead, he held his body close to the wall. He wanted to go down to Margery's seat to ask her about it, but he just stood there stupidly. Then he saw Nada and Jedlicka in the forefront of the audience and he fancied that Jedlicka looked pained and that Nada seemed disappointed about something. He wanted to run away and to hide forever.

Gordon stood there, and in imagination went to the seats of various persons who sat watching the play. In fancy he sat beside an elderly man who had a goatee that was tilted disdainfully. Drop your chin a trifle, old fellow, and let me point out some of the beauties of this, my play. What! You think it lousy? Say, you, it took me years of toil and of life to create it! Why, you goat-face! To do this I had to be libertine and priest. I was poet and I was ascetic. I was lechery and I was love. I was prophet and I was Baal. Can't you see that each line was lived—not written at all? Now I must speak to that woman who is nibbling a chocolate candy so secretively. Please, my good lady, don't pamper your gut at this time. May I not indicate to you that this play is free from flesh? It is spirit. Yes, it began with the flowing of blood, but I dripped the blood through magic chamois filters. Is it not chastely poignant? Well, go ahead then, and munch your damned head off! But you, Mr. What's-your-name! You with the oxford glasses. Why don't you show more interest in this priceless work? What is it, for God's sweet sake, that you want? I have given you everything. If you are pious-minded, I have provided hassocks for you to kneel upon. I have pressed relics to your thick lips. If you are sentimental, have I not spread about your careless feet the apple blossoms

of Spring? Have I not permitted you to caress limbs with
your eyes? Each of the lines is spoken with sophistication,
yet, if you look and listen, I shall make you encompass
everything within yourself. What! You sneer? Why
you...

Gordon waited no longer but went home like a coward
who has been found out. Margery and Mrs. Hamilton
reached the cottage after midnight and were surprised to
see Gordon sitting in his dressing gown on the porch steps
and looking at the moon through the trees.

"You're bound to catch cold out here," Margery said.
He thought her voice strangely dull and distant. There
was a tone in her voice that indicated she had been terribly
hurt by something, and he thought that the failure of his
play was accountable for it.

"How did it go?" he asked.

"Why...well, I think it will be all right, but why
don't you forget it until to-morrow?"

"I wish I could." He looked at Margery's face as they
went inside the house and he saw in it a strained, almost
coldly resentful expression that he never before had seen
there. My God! Had this play affected her so?

Mrs. Hamilton, too, looked bitter and almost malicious
as she took off her wraps. "Say, Gordon, I sat through the
whole thing, and now I wonder if you'll tell me what it
was about?"

"It's about two sex-starved Armenians, who got lost in
a load of hay, and..."

"Gordon!" Margery almost barked at him. That certainly was unlike her, for she always had been so patient, so gentle with him when he faced perplexing problems, and he was facing one now. "You can be considerate, at least."

"Say, what's wrong with you, Margery? Did the play upset you?"

She didn't answer and he saw that her lips were compressed. Mrs. Hamilton was watching him and he believed there was a look in her rather staring eyes that suggested knowledge of some dark secret.

"Don't you be rattled by any failure," he said to Margery. "We're big enough to stand it."

"I'm not afraid of failure...that kind of failure." There were tears in her eyes now. What could be wrong? Something had happened.

"What in the world is the matter, Margery?"

"I'll tell you what is wrong...." Mrs. Hamilton spoke sharply, but Margery turned quickly on her mother.

"You keep quiet! Nothing is wrong."

In their room Gordon tried to calm Margery and endeavored to find out what, if anything, had happened at the theater to make her act in this unusual manner.

"It's nothing," she said finally. "Only as I sat there, I heard gossip about prominent people and your name came up."

Oh my God! What gossip had she heard?

"People have to talk about something, Margery.

"It's not that, but after we left, mother said that **you** were outgrowing me and that I would be left behind."

"Nonsense. I'm not growing very rapidly for one thing and I simply couldn't leave you behind.... Was there anything bad said about me?"

"Just a lot of loose talk.... I didn't pay much attention, but it bothered mother when they spoke of you as though you were not married and that you were not the marrying kind."

"Well, doesn't that go to show they didn't know what they were talking about?"

"I guess so."

"You guess?"

"O Gordon! I have tried so hard, but maybe you just take me for granted now. If the failure of a play hurts you, just try to imagine what failure of marriage means to a woman."

"But we haven't failed."

"I am afraid I have. Maybe you're not the marrying kind."

"For God's sake, Margery, listen..."

She was more calm now, more her old self, becoming steady, patient and kindly. "I'm so sorry I was fool enough to give 'way to my feelings, Gordon. Please forgive me."

"I knew you'd be sensible, dear. Now go to sleep."

He lay in the dark, recalling Austin Moore's words that the answers to one's life could be found only within oneself. He must quit looking merely at the world about him and he must go inside his soul, not to retreat there, but to see what kinds of old furniture and cast-off bales and boxes were in the attic of his soul.

Surely among all the rubbish in the soul's attic there lay, hidden and dust-covered, a small casket in which was a jewel of understanding—or at the very least, a glass imitation,

Chapter Thirteen

I

*G*ORDON was wearying of newspaper work and often thought of retiring to some small place—perhaps to Laurel Island—where he could work out a moral salvation with his wife and children, hiding from the world of rush and rumble. He was now in his late thirties and he had begun to forget youth. Would he wind up in a cellar, as Gramper had done? Would he sit beneath the floor of his house, listening to the brisk, confident footfalls of a grown-up son going out for a night of fire playing? Or to the clogging of some strange young man who came to dance to the radio with Greta—and if possible to seduce her? Where have I mislaid you, Youth? I would advertise and I would offer huge rewards . . . but no one would bring you back to me.

His contract with the Ward service was about to expire and he felt that his enthusiasm for journalistic work was dimming. "I don't want to sign a new contract," he told Kemp.

"Don't be a fool, Gordon. You're making big money.

What other reporter is pulling down four hundred a week?"

"I've got to quit."

"Why? What else can you do?"

"I don't know. I think I'll write a book. Newspaper work is a young man's game, Kemp."

"My God! You're no Methusaleh."

"I don't want to burn out in this business. They use you until you are all but consumed and then they toss you aside like a handful of wet ashes."

"You've had lots of fun and adventure in this game."

"Heartaches, too."

"Say, Gordon, you've given us more heartaches and headaches than anybody I know. You got away with murder and you know you did. I think you've had it pretty soft, if you should ask me."

"I'll never give you any more headaches. I always said that when I lost my flair for the game, I'd quit in fairness to myself and in fairness to a profession that I love."

"You never got over The Chief throwing you out of dramatics on account of that review, did you?"

"The Chief doesn't worry me, either."

"You ought to be hard-boiled like me, Gordon. Why, only yesterday The Chief gave me hell for trying to identify the Unknown Soldier. If I was sensitive like you, I'd up and quit. But not me—I'm as hard-boiled as a battleship."

"Bugs Baer says you're so tough you'd send your grandma out in the snow to rustle for lovers."

"Did he say that?"

"He certainly did.... Well, what have you got for me to-day?"

"I got something that you'll be able to write swell."

"What is it? Prostitute slays pastor for eating crackers in bed?"

"No. It's the Hazel Eades-Paul Benson story. The Governor has refused to commute their sentences."

"That means they've got to sit in the electric chair."

"Yeah." Kemp did some mental arithmetic and Gordon thought the editor's lips grew moist and eager. "It ought to add twenty thousand to our circulation if we get a good yarn with a lot of guts in it."

"I'm fed up on death houses. The Peters hanging didn't do me any good."

"The chair's not as bad as hanging."

"Well, I'm not keen on seeing a woman bumped off."

Kemp puffed his cigarette avidly. "Oh, hell! She's not a woman. She's a moron. She and Benson used to lie around, soused to the eyes, and they called it love. A couple of rats! Say, the Eades dame is almost as rotten as that play you wrote."

"Lay off my play, will you? Why don't you go to Sing Sing yourself to see them burn the damsel?"

"I wouldn't mind. I thought up a slogan for her when she is bumped off: 'Volts for Women.' Pretty good, hey?"

"It's grand. How much circulation did the paper put on the day they slugged Hazel's husband with the sash-weight?"

"Only thirteen thousand. We were late, damn it, in

getting on the street. Everything went wrong in the stereotyping plant that night. God! but the Colonel was sore!"

"You think this electrocution will give you twenty thousand?"

"Surely, if we can get a quick flash when they fry. You've got to be sober and serious, though."

"You know I've been on the wagon since I had the flu."

"That's right, you have. Well, I want you to put a lot of tear-jerkers in this yarn so that the dirty bastards that read our sheet can realize how sanctified they are in their own moronic holiness.... Well, Gordie, get on the ground early. I've got to toddle along to look over that Ramsey story."

"Haven't you about milked it dry?"

"No, but the boys didn't get enough sex into it this morning to make it interesting. I've told Egan time and time again to keep the customers drooling or there'll be another drop in circulation. Then bingo! The Chief will roll the iron ball and another editor will show up."

"I wonder how our paper gets through the mails."

"Skill in handling the stuff, my boy. Just skill! Pour all the nasty junk into the story and then play it up as a sermon. The wages of sin. Do you want to see a picture of Miss Ramsey in her undies?"

"I'll wait and see it in the paper."

"You can bet your Jesus you'll see it in the paper! It'll add at least ten thousand to the sales."

"I'll give Hazel Eades your regards, Kemp."

"I hope nothing comes up to stop the electrocution. We need all the circulation we can grab. Oh—that reminds me, the Chief wants an editorial against Capital Punishment."

II

GORDON called on Nada and told her he was going to the Eades-Benson electrocution. She sat on Gordon's lap and rested her head against his chest. He kissed her hair and wondered how many others there were than he and Paul Benson who had been greedy in illicit love.

Nada seemed particularly beautiful to-night. She wore a jade negligée that brought out the full quality of her ashen blonde hair. The negligée gave her eyes a deep green value. He told her that her beauty was something from which no one could escape.

"Do you want to escape?"

"Decidedly not."

"Nor do I. If we had married that time long ago, when you visited me in my dressing room out West, what would have happened?"

"God knows. I think it would have been wonderful."

"It would have been, perhaps, but ... would it be wonderful now?"

"Well, we didn't marry and we did go away from each other...."

"You went away from me."

"But I came back to you."

"No, I came back to you.... I'm always coming back to you, Nada."

"Always come back to me."

"Always."

For a while she sat there, the beauty of her in his eyes and the warmth of her in his arms. Then she said: "I don't want you to go up there alone."

"You mean to the prison?"

"Yes. I want to go with you. I want to be with you.... I want..."

"You want what, dearest?"

"I want to see what it does to you."

"How eerily you talk, Nada, darling. You want to see what it does to me? What do you mean?"

"I really don't know what I mean, only I want so much to go with you."

"You can't go to the prison, dear. Only those with special passes can go and I wouldn't for the world..."

"I don't mean to see ... anything ... but to go with you and stay with you before and after it. Mayn't I go?"

He wondered about it and thought that they should not be seen together so much. Already he had heard bits of gossip that had been flung in their direction. Vaguely he felt that Margery's discomfiture the night of his play's opening had had something to do with that sort of gossip. Gordon was feeling more guilty each time he and Nada loved, instead of becoming used to his sin. He had waited for years to become hardened and brazen about it. He couldn't be.

"I don't know where we could stay, Nada. The only hotel that had anything suitable for us burned down recently."

"I know a place." She spoke as though she had been planning such a trip for some time and that it was not just a sudden decision on her part. "The place I know is not in the town. It's at Hawthorne. It's only ten miles from Ossining."

"A hotel?"

"No. Somehow I couldn't let you have me in a hotel. Not that I'm decent, because I'm thoroughly unmoral. But I'd be making a whore out of myself to go to a hotel. I'd feel that way about it. Maybe I am a whore...."

"Shut up!" Gordon put his hand over her mouth. "You needn't make it any tougher than it is."

"Is it so 'tough' then? That's the first time you ever referred to our affair that way."

"Don't let's quarrel."

"If there's any quarreling to be done, you'll do it. I never cross you in anything, do I, Gordie?"

"No, you never do. I guess I'm touchy to-night. Where's this place you spoke of?"

"I'll have to find out about it. I'm sure it will be all right. A girl friend.... Yes, old owl eyes, she's kept!... She has a summer place at Hawthorne, but she's in town now. I think she'll let me open it if I take my own servants."

"What do you think, Nada?"

"I don't do a lot of thinking when I'm with you, lover."

"Let's go there together then. I'll telephone you in the morning to see if you have word from your friend."

III

NADA and Gordon motored to Hawthorne in her town car. Her maid rode with the chauffeur and Nada said the maid could purchase supplies at the village and do the cooking. The chauffeur would care for the heating plant.

"Don't you think it wonderful, Gordie? Our being together on an out-of-town adventure? Just we two away from the whole world?"

"I think it's great."

Nada removed a glove and asked Gordon to take off a glove and she placed her bare hand in his. Their hands were dry and cold. "Well, Gordie, the woman won't have to worry about getting old, will she?"

"You mean the Eades woman?"

"Yes. She's only thirty-some, isn't she?"

"Thirty-four. She doesn't think the State will go through with it."

"It will, though, won't it?"

"It looks that way. She was a damned fool to kill her husband when she and Benson could have run off together."

"Sometimes people don't run off together."

"They want to, but they're afraid of something."

"What is it they fear, Gordie?"

"Scandal, I guess. I really don't know. I've covered a lot of scandals, but I never could figure out the real answers.

People who run off or who live together have lots of handicaps."

"What would happen if you and I ran off and lived together?"

"Don't put crazy notions in my head, Nada.... It would ruin us both."

"Ruin us?"

"Quite."

"We're running off now."

"Yes, but that's just for a night or two."

"I love to-night, Gordon."

"I love you."

"We can forget everything to-night, can't we?"

"I hope so, Nada. I'm sorry I was cross when you spoke about my having you in a hotel."

"You could have me anywhere, any place. I love you that much, Gordon. My lifetime belongs to you, whether you take a moment, a year, or all of it. I am yours."

Nada kissed him, kissed him rather forebodingly, he thought. He had a feeling that something ominous hung darkly above them, mocking them and baiting God himself. Look, God! See what you let Yourself in for when You equipped these fools with procreative implements.

IV

THERE was a studio building on the estate where Nada took Gordon and it had a large fireplace in it. He found some kindling and back logs and they sat on a divan after he had made the fire, their arms about each other and their faces to the flames that were reflected by the patina of the furniture.

"I tell you what, Gordie. Let's stay here to-night instead of moving into that big house. It will be more private, more romantic. I'm so tired of big houses and luxurious appointments. Sometimes I wish we were in the woods with just a tent and each other.... Are you cold, dearest?"

"Just a bit nervous." He was shivering. "After I leave you to-morrow, it will be four o'clock the next morning before I come back from the prison."

"Hush. That's to-morrow night. This is to-night—our night, and there can be no other night while we have this one. Let to-morrow take care of to-morrow. Now we are here, alone and in love. That's all that counts with me."

"Then let's think only of to-night."

"Are you hungry? We'll have something to eat right here."

"I'm only hungry for you, Nada...as usual."

For a long time after their dinner Nada sat on a rug at Gordon's feet and he played with her hair. How young she kept—this Nada person! She was talented. She was wealthy. She was followed everywhere by powerful men. He wondered what she saw in him to love so madly. Why did she keep herself for him?

"What is it you see in me to love?" he asked her suddenly.

Nada raised her face. "Many, many things, lover. For one thing, you can be primitive without becoming gross. I love the mad storms that sweep through your soul. It's late, Gordie. I'll try to show you why I love you ... but in your arms."

The love madness tore at his vitals. He forgot everything else—there wasn't anything else. There was only Nada. That's all there ever had been ... this way. Let a man and a woman go to the electric chair on account of their desires. It was worth it. What else had the world to offer? How dizzily spins the pebble that is called World—a finite body hurled into the infinite. The pebble whizzes through the universe and occasionally it catches a ray of light.

"Let's sleep here on the rug and watch the embers die, Gordon, my lover." The crackling of the logs had ceased and only a faint, amber light fought the shadows.

"Each time with you seems like a new time, Nada."

"It is forever new, darling. We make it so."

"Other women's caresses become mellow and time worn."

"I never denied you the right to have other women, did I?"

"You were safe. You knew there couldn't be another woman."

"All I ever demanded was the right to own the moments when you and I were together. What you did yesterday or what you do to-morrow is of no importance. Am I not unfeminine, Gordon?"

"You're more than human, Nada. You never could have a rival in any man's life. No one knows how to love as you do. You make a divine art out of the thing that others bungle and mishandle—or begrudge. Your responses are as fresh as springtime."

"You are the sun, Gordon. You are the sun, my lover. Each time you run your fingers through my hair and touch my skin, it is as though you were draping my body with garlands of pristine blossoms. Come to me, dearest ... I am answering all your questions now...."

Once again I am lost in you, Nada. What if I am to be excommunicated to-morrow? Console me. Console me with nocturnes.... When first I sought you, did you see me in your crystal? Did you see me as I was wandering, blind-folded through the rain? Did you see my hands searching the great, wet air? See, Nada, even now there are callouses on my palms where I gripped nothingness so tightly that the unyielding nothingness made welts.... Cry out in vain, unwelcome Ezekiel! Tell me that I have set up the sign of my lechery at the head of each crossroad. How can I attend your minatory words now? To-morrow! To-morrow I'll confer with you. Plenty of time then for your threats. I'll meet you in the Death House to-morrow at midnight. So long, Ezekiel, you Peeping Tom! ...

"Nada! Nada! Say again that you love me. Say it quickly, for to-morrow is almost here...."

"Now do you know? Have I not answered you, lover? Have I not told you everything?"

"I must build up the fire. I can't sleep."

"We'll sit together.... Gordon, I am afraid."

"Why, Nada?"

"Stay close to me. Something keeps saying that our day is done; that love will pass away. I'm so afraid."

"Put your head on my heart and let my heartbeats sing you to sleep. Dream and forget. . . . I love you."

Chapter Fourteen

I

DEATH HOUSE days are long to all save them that are to die. The watchers find it tedious to wait for a man and a woman to come from their steel cages to sit in the electric chair; but the condemned ones say that the hours roar like rockets, hurtling with hissing rapidity through the air. These mortals, once heedless of whole years, now cling with miserly grasp to little minutes. They call on Jesus Christ the Redeemer to have mercy on their souls.

The prison gates are closed to all after 8 o'clock, but a telephone wire is kept open between the warden's office and the Governor's mansion at Albany. It is the only thread that has not yet been cut between life and death for the man and the woman. The witnesses are here and the doctors are here. The gargoyle-faced executioner, who has eaten a thick steak and two portions of strawberry ice cream, is here. The warden is here. He shrinks from sending the man and the woman to their deaths, but his duty is clear under the law. Everyone is here except the chief guest of the evening—Death. Between the hours of 11 o'clock and midnight, he will ride down to visit for a little while inside the walls of the prison. He will collect a debt and then he will hasten away, without so much as a Thank you, my good friends, I'll call on all of you some day. Can you not hear him laugh?

The reporters lounge about a reception room for a while, watching prison guards moving mechanically. Now and then one can hear the bang of steel gates and the rattle of large keys, and there is a permeating smell of disinfectant. It is a building of drafts and stony echoes.

As a trusty comes from the warden's office, a guard jokes with the newspaper boys. "There goes one grand little forger. He'd be glad to give you a signature of George Washington or of any other notables."

The journalists confer with prison officers, with clergymen, with anyone who can give them bits of news from the death cells. Hazel's mother has said good-by. Her twelve-year-old daughter did not come. She thinks that mother is away from home on a long journey. Paul's wife has sent a note and he is crying over it while a barber shaves him. To-morrow Paul's three boys will be beneficiaries of his life insurance.

Two homes are wailing. My daughter, says one home. My husband, says the other. Later one home will say, My Mother, and the other home will say, My Father. The State says, Our Duty. Holy, holy, holy. Keep your bedsteads holy. I install famine in your loins, the Power says to Gordon, but when you sate your hunger, I place death upon your brow. Mortify the flesh! Shun the very appearance of evil! Verily, Love is a pestilence. To know Love is to partake of poisonous fruit.... Woman is a sacred vessel.

"Hazel is praying in her cell," a clergyman announces to the reporters.

"Don't you believe it," a guard whispers to Gordon. "She's fighting like a hell cat and they may have to dope her."

"Benson is speechless," another minister confides, "but let us rejoice that he is dying in Christ Jesus."

The voice of an irreverent reporter is heard. "I thought he was dying in the electric chair." The clergyman is aghast and there are many laughs. The executioner comes in and the press men encompass him, milking him for news. He refuses to talk, but veteran reporters know how to make people talk.

"We hear that your method makes them suffer to beat hell."

The executioner wheels on them. He is angry. Aha! He'll talk. "That's not so! Who said my method makes them suffer?"

"A fellow who works for the Westinghouse people."

"He's talking through his hat. They don't feel any pain at all. It paralyzes their brains and stops their hearts." On and on he talks, in vindication of his system. He uses one rising and falling current instead of three distinct shocks as employed by his predecessor. It makes good copy and gentlemen sipping their morning coffee will read it and ladies who insist on fidelity in wedlock will shudder piously. The executioner goes to the Death House to make a last minute check of his circuits and his instruments.

A matron comes from Hazel Eades' cell and after much cajoling she is induced to reveal the contents of Hazel's last note:

"I have sinned. I am paying dearly for it. Paul and I sinned together, and I guess we're going together, God knows where. All I want the world to know is that I am not the woman they said I was. Mother, it is all so unfair. Why should I be done away with? Don't worry, mother darling, I love you. I have asked God's forgiveness. Now I ask yours. Good night, dear, and may God bless you all."

It is ten o'clock. Attorneys for the condemned have seen their clients for a last time and now they leave the prison with the manner of candidates for election who have conceded defeat. Their names will not appear in newspaper headlines until another time, another trial, and perhaps another electrocution.

The newspaper men are called to the Warden's office. He says he will answer any reasonable questions. What did Hazel and Paul have for their last meal? What a mockery the last meal is! They could have had "anything they wanted to eat." For what? The Warden says that Hazel didn't have a "last meal" at all but that Paul had a vegetable plate and coffee.

"Have they been dressed yet?"

"Yes, they have been prepared for the chair."

"What will Hazel wear?"

"A smock, like stenographers have. A brown one."

The reporters scribble notes. "Will she wear stockings?"

"Yes."

"Silk?"

"Cotton."

"Rolled down?"

"One of them—the right one is rolled down."

"Is she calm, frightened or fighting mad? We've heard conflicting reports."

"I don't care to discuss that."

"Will she be given dope?"

"We never administer narcotics."

"Will her head be shaved for the electrode?"

"Only a small place, the size of a silver dollar. You'd hardly notice it."

"How do you feel about executing sentence on a woman?"

"My views on capital punishment in general are well known. I oppose it, but I have my duty to do as warden."

"Don't ask him that. Don't embarrass the warden, fellows."

"Is there anything else?"

"Did Paul's wife become reconciled to him? Did she visit him to-day?"

"Ask me something else."

"Our papers would like to know."

"Ask me something else."

"Is Benson going to take his medicine like a man?"

"I believe he will. He has been a model prisoner."

"Was she a model prisoner?"

"I do not care to say. She's a woman."

"We heard that she thought she could run the prison to suit herself; that she raised hell."

"I have no comment to make on that. Is that all?"

A few more questions. It is eleven o'clock and the warden's face is grave and pale. He was a good soldier in the World War and he is a good soldier now. He gives final instructions:

"Your papers must think you are capable reporters or you wouldn't have been chosen to be here. I do not pretend to instruct you as to your stories, but I merely ask you not to misstate things. Write what you see, but only what you really see.... We are ready, gentlemen. Be as quiet as possible and do not leave the death chamber until you are told to do so."

Twenty reporters of metropolitan newspapers and four visiting medical men, one of whom is an alienist, begin the march from the Warden's office to the Death House. They move across frozen ground and the crunching of their shoes brings gritty echoes from the prison walls. The outline of the turreted walls is inharmonious. A mist drifts on the wind that skims the ice-floes of the nearby Hudson and it veils the wall lights and hovers wanly above the barracks of society's outcasts.

It is not Gordon's first journey to this Death House, yet he would like to pass it as you wish to pass, without speaking, a man you do not like. It is a dumpy structure, with smooth walls. Gordon holds back until others have preceded him. They file singly past a guard, who looks keenly at each man as he collects the special permit slips. It is not politeness that holds Gordon back, for he wishes he could retreat now; he wishes he had not taken the assignment. He is thinking back to the Peters' hanging in Connecticut. Peters' death undid Gordon. He again sees the new, yellow rope gripping Peters' neck and he again calls to mind the swift movement of feet as Peters died six feet off the floor. The feet had fluttered like the wings of a butterfly and the slim fingers had moved like those of a pianist as Death made love to him.... Gordon finally goes inside, where the lights are garish as he leaves the night mist.

There are no windows in the four walls, but there is a skylight and the room is a high one. There are two doors, through one of which the condemned are to come. There is a sign that reads "Silence." Some of the men press forward to gain seats in the first of five rows of benches. Gordon takes a seat in the third row, wishing it had been in the last row. The seats are of quartered oak and they resemble church pews in an "Amen corner."

Twelve feet to the front of the first bench and a bit to the right is the Chair. It holds the center of the stage, dominating the scene with its ugliness. It is solidly fashioned, squatty, yet spidery with its black straps and strong buckles. It has two widely separated arms and they appear to be opened more widely to-night than ever, expressing a grisly welcome. I must be gallant to-night, the Chair says. I am to be given a bride. What would you do, Gordon, if I were to take Nada, your mistress, from you? The Chair is bolted to the concrete floor. There is a black rubber mat under it, the mat extending about two feet in front of the Chair.

The executioner stands in a sort of alcove to the right of the Chair. He is hanging a football helmet on a curling wire that comes from a conduit beside the Chair. Inside the helmet, which is rubber lined, is a screen of copper wire. To that screen a sponge is affixed. The sponge is wetted with a salt solution. What passes through the mind of the lean executioner? His face is immovable and set, but his eyes are bright as he examines the instrument board.

The steam pipes cackle. The only other sound in the room is a subdued cough. All eyes are watching the sturdy door of golden oak. The arms of the Chair seem to be opening still more widely. The bridegroom is eager for his bride.

II

THE door opens. No hands are seen opening it. It is 11:30 o'clock. Who will be the first to go? Benson or the woman? There is a voice, like the voice of a frightened child:

"Father, forgive them, for they know not what they do."

A priest, crucifix uplifted, is at the door. Close after him, shrunken, stumbling, comes a woman. In one hand is a wooden cross. With the other she seems to be fending off Fate.

"Jesus, have mercy."

The priest in black cassock presses the crucifix to her

lips. The lips are bloodless and taut. Her eyes are wet. Two plump matrons support the woman by the elbows. So small and wispy she is. How lost she is among big men in uniform who now take charge of her. She has had an eager, vibrant body in hours of lust. That body now is flaccid and spent as she advances to give it to Death. She has gray felt slippers. She seems inches shorter than she did in the smart, high-heeled pumps she wore at her trial. The stalwart guards accentuate her smallness. She used to wear silks. Now she is haggish, unkempt and slatternly in her wrinkled smock of brown cotton.

"Blessed are the pure in heart."

They seat her in the chair. It begins to embrace her obscenely, lewdly. She has ashen hair—almost white in the play of the harsh light. Nada has ashen hair.... O God!

The leather helmet is placed over the pale hair. The eyes are covered by a visor of leather. As the blindfold is being drawn over those eyes, there is a terrible light in them. They look accusingly at the destroyers of her body.

"Father, forgive them," say her lips.

"Rape me with your white hot blasts, you cruel sons of bitches!" say her eyes.

Matrons and the Principal Keeper stand before her. They try to shield her limbs. The keeper shifts. How slovenly is the sprawl of this once vain woman! Her short, cotton dress is above her knees. Blue bloomers of cheap material are beneath the skirt. One tawdry, ill-fitting stocking is drawn to the thigh. The other is rolled to her ankle. The black fist of an electrode clasps her calf.

"Jesus, have mercy!"

Stringy bunches of hair protrude from the helmet. The Queen of Lust! This is her coronation. Cackling steam pipes for ceremonial trumpets. Men kneeling at leg buckles for courtiers. Nada, how would you look with the State's sable millinery on your head?...Drops of water trickle across her mouth. Are they tears? Or the drippings from the helmet sponge? The priest drones the litany in practiced syllables. The responses grow more feeble.

"Father, forgive...know not...do...."

Black leather bands corset her. Her breast is flabby and wasted. This smallish hag cannot be the woman that sang and danced in yesterday's bacchanal. Her breath comes in gasps. Her wrists and legs are buckled to the chair. The State's physician waits. The lean executioner half crouches at his lever. Big men work earnestly. They truss Hazel swiftly. Only a minute has passed since she entered the white walled chamber. It seems a long time. The voice quavers. It is a whisper.

"Father, forgive..."

The voice is cut short.

Zzzzzzzzzzz...Psssssssssssssssssst!

The holy litany is snuffed out. The hiss of a serpent. The body now is beyond priestly ministration. Hazel's feet are at the abyss. Her face is blanched. The insidious buzz sweeps into the veins and the body goes forward. It strains the straps. The parts that one can see turn a brick red. The current has struck with devastating power. The form is outthrust, like a tightly strung bow. The chin is high.

Only the hands seem to have escaped. The cross in one. The other rests palm upward. Forefinger and thumb together, as one might hold a pinch of snuff. The leg electrode splutters. Smoke comes from the calf. Wisps of smoke stray from the ears, like incense from a pagan image. The Warden faces the wall. His arms are folded across his chest. The Priest has turned away. The gargoyle-faced executioner shuts off the current that has sounded like the noise made by an electric refrigerator. Slowly, after a half minute of the death dealing stream, the arms, right leg, throat and jaws—which are the parts you may see—bleach.

The State's Doctor steps forward. His stethoscope sways from his ears. He explores the now bared bosom for heart beats. He is a customs inspector. He must make sure that Hazel Eades smuggles not a single faint tick of the heart across the border of mortality. As the Doctor listens, the hand that was held palm upward turns in its strap. The movement of the hand fascinates those who sit numb and horrified. The finger and thumb that have been pointing upward point downward. The finger and thumb are not held together now. Life is a pinch of snuff. Hazel Eades has let the snuff drop.

"I pronounce this woman dead."

III

Two guards don white coats. They wheel an ambulatory stretcher to the chair. The stretcher has a white porcelain top. The men look like internes. They jockey the vehicle to the feet of the killed woman. Now everyone may see the repellent work of the chair. An attendant wraps a towel about the legs. The towel slips. There is a greenish, purple blister. It is almost as large as an egg plant. What a fiendish garter they gave her as a token of her love!

The men lift the leather hood. The side of the head is scalded and scarred. The white coated men hoist the body. Gordon turns away in horror from the gaping grimace. What a sorry gift the State has made to Eternity! Gordon is very ill at the stomach. He recalls Granner holding rabbits by the hind legs and dealing death with an old hammer handle.

The body is wheeled to the autopsy room. There is a mopping up period of about three minutes. The executioner's work of the night is only half completed. He gives his mechanism a hasty check. A viol player tuning up between movements of a symphony. He kneels above a galvanized pail. He holds the leather crown in one hand. With the other he dabs new salt water on the sponge. The Queen of Lust is dead. Long live the King.... But not for long.

Gordon rises to leave. He is almost to the door. He is frantic to go into the night. The guard there puts a hand on his shoulder. The guard backs him to his seat. So high strung is Gordon that he fancies the guard is backing him into the electric chair. His note paper falls to the concrete floor. He buries his face in his hands. A reporter friend whispers: "Steady, Gordon. It will be over soon."

It has taken the State six minutes to truss and kill its woman victim. Now the guards are again at their stations. Again the door opens from the Death House aisle. That aisle which is a one way street to Nevermore. Gordon cannot look. He wishes he had not looked at the woman. He hears a chaplain. It is not the voice of the priest this time.

"Blessed are the pure in heart."

There are no responses.

Gordon was told that Benson's lips moved. No words got past his teeth. Gordon was told that Benson died courageously. Gordon heard that Benson's eyes roved the place; that it was written in his face that he was wondering if the woman had been there before him or if she was yet to die. The reporters told Gordon that a religious ecstasy upheld the man to the moment of dissolution.

"For God so loved the world...."

"I pronounce this man dead."

IV

GORDON sat there dazedly until a reporter tapped him on the shoulder. Then he rallied to a professional pose and joined other newspaper men in their dash to motor cars that awaited them in the prison areaway. The automobiles took the press representatives through a large crowd of morbid folk that stood at the prison gates. They went to a telegraphic headquarters that had been established in a nearby speakeasy.

It was hard for Gordon to write his article. The air

in the cramped barroom was stuffy with tobacco smoke. The telegraph instruments chirped like crickets and the typewriter keys hammered in machine gun tempo. It was like the basement of the bells, long, long ago. The noises knocked chunks from Gordon's brain; the acrid smoke inflamed his eyes and his throat was as dry as a brick kiln. He was dead tired as he wrote the final paragraph and he didn't wait for "good night" from his office. He packed his typewriter in its case and started to leave. His telegraph operator stopped him and pointed to a paragraph in Gordon's copy.

"Here's a funny line that I don't understand." Gordon looked at the man absently. "You've written here.... Wait until I can find it. Oh, yes. Here." He indicated with a pencil. " 'Her mother will claim the body of Nada Halpin!' ... How come, Nada Halpin?"

Gordon was sure that he had gone completely crazy. He seized the operator's pencil, almost wrenching it from the man. He corrected the line to read: "the body of Hazel Eades." He didn't try to explain the mistake. How could he? He went into the early morning with terror in his soul.

V

Nada's chauffeur was waiting across the street from the speakeasy. Gordon got into the car. He kept his eyes closed until the automobile stopped before the door of the studio. Nada came to the door as the car skidded on the gravel driveway and Gordon went to her, haggard and worn.

"You're tired, lover. I'll have some coffee made right away. Here, sit by the fireplace."

He slumped to the divan and Nada stirred up the fire. He hadn't said a word. She watched him narrowly. His head was bowed. He didn't look her in the face. She knelt and loosened the ties of his shoes and then she drew them off his feet. Still he didn't speak. Still he didn't look at her. She was heartbroken and frightened.

"I'll get your bed ready," she said. "You need rest. I had no idea it would be so terrible on you."

He raised his hand. "No. Never mind the bed. Never mind coffee. Never mind anything." His tone was strange, hoarsely thick and final. Nada had risen. She stood against the firelight. He lifted his head slowly and she saw deep lines in his cheeks, channels of suffering.

"Please, dearest Gordie! Lie down and I'll hold you until you sleep."

"No!" His tone was more than final this time. Why was he so surly? What had she done? Perhaps he was ill. Then he said: "As soon as you can get your things ready, we're going to the city. We shan't stay here to-night. Do you understand me?"

"Whatever you say." She had an odd sensation as Gordon spoke. It was so unlike him to be gruff with her. He had no doubt been witness to a grueling spectacle. Still, he should not treat her like that. No other man would dare. For a moment she was sorry she was a slave to his love. She had made few demands on him. Why should she be subjected to this indignity? No, she didn't understand him. No, she didn't understand why she allowed him to be cruelly, brutally domineering.... Yes, she did. She understood it all. I love him! I love him! I'd love him even though he beat me and trampled upon me. I love him!

She called her maid, who was roused from sleep with difficulty. Nada gave instructions to the chauffeur. An hour later they started for New York. Gordon did not speak the whole way. Nada couldn't explain her feeling, but she kept fearing that she and Gordon might never meet to love again. Something had happened. What? She could not tell. She said nothing about her presentiment.

She sat in the motor car, holding one of his hands to her cheek. She wept.

~~~~~~~~~~~~~~~~~~~~~~~~~~~~~~~~~~~

PART THREE

~~~~~~~~~~~~~~~~~~~~~~~~~~~~~~~~~~~

Chapter One

I

WINDS a thousand miles long swept across the dunes of Laurel Island. The nights were blackly deep and Winter had lain down on the tawny sand to die. The shutters of deserted beach houses banged in the wind like shields on which heavy lances fall. The hardy natives of the long and narrow isle sat at their mist-wetted windows, listening to the organ tones of the sea. They drank wine made from the blood of wild plums and rested beside driftwood fires, watching the pale flame that licked the timber stumps of forgotten ships. The blaze of the brine-soaked wood was pungent with sea salt.

The Islanders waited confidently for Winter to die. His grip was breaking and only a death rattle was left in the throat of the high gale. Soon Spring would come and the horizon would throw off its mourning cloak of storm-clouds; and after Spring, Summer would appear, dancing across the sea, with rose dawns in its fragrant hair. The sadistic beating of Winter's iron-hard fist would cease. Blood would rise like sap. Cottagers would come down from the anæmic city and the laughter of children would sound all day beside the sea and in the sand patches bordering the cement walks of the village.... In Winter the natives sit beside their driftwood fires and drink wine made from the blood of wild plums.

Illness had left Gordon's face gray and as he got off the train he staggered beneath the weight of his rucksack. He took a taxicab to the ferry, which operated only one day each week in the off-season. He looked forward with an anxious craving to the eight-mile trip across the bay from the Long Island shore. It would be an hour on the water, an hour in which to place Yesterday a bit further behind him. He had the taxi driver stop at a store while he ordered supplies and then they went to the dock where the gray ferryboat bobbed on drab water, its nose dipping in seaweed and in rime.

The only other passenger was Kirby, the carpenter, who was glad enough to find a listener for his gossip. What had brought Mr. Dole to Laurel Island as early as March? Gordon explained that he was writing a book and that he wanted solitude.

"That's all we have," Kirby said. "There's enough solitude to drive you crazy. Isn't Mrs. Dole coming?"

Even on this almost deserted sand-bar Gossip flourished. The boat swung into the channel and Gordon opened his rucksack to find his pipe tobacco. While he was feeling about in the rucksack, Kirby noticed the brass bell of a bugle protruding and Gordon saw Kirby's mystified expression. He hastily tucked the bugle—his boyhood trumpet—out of sight. If I want to bring my trumpet with me, whose business is it? If it were a bottle of whisky, the gossiping Kirby wouldn't think it odd; but it is a bugle and it makes the poor sap gawk and ask himself riddles. Who can know what a mighty symbol my bugle is?

Gordon wanted to smoke and think, but Kirby insisted on telling the news. The plumber's boy, Ike Holmes, had got a girl in trouble and Ike's old man had hit him with a blow-torch. Mrs. Anselm, the retired school-teacher, was coming to Laurel again this summer and had instructed Kirby to glass-in her front porch. Mr. Larkspur, the great inventor, would be down after his wife had got her divorce, in pursuit of which she was now in Paris....

Gordon was gazing at the low shore line toward which they were bearing. Beyond that island lay the open sea. How glad he would be to walk to his beach house, leaving his rucksack there and going immediately down to the sea. No telephones to bother him. No drunken acquaintances hammering with gin bottles at his door. No Mrs. Hamilton to harry his nights with her sleep walking groans or to embitter his days with her strangely knowing, mocking eyes, in which lay an accusation....And no Nada now. Where was she? Did she think it strange that he had not tried to get in touch with her since....If only he could erase that scene from his mind! Forgive them, Father.... Blessed are the pure in heart....

"You need to get tanned up, Mr. Dole, for you're a bit peaked.... The lighthouse keeper's wife had another baby, but I guess you knew about that. It happened at the end of last summer."

Yes, Gordon remembered. Women of the various Laurel Island settlements had sent baby things to the lighthouse. Blankets, dresses, caps, hoods and bootees. Mrs. Hamilton had sent some literature on birth control.

"They say that the lighthouse keeper's wife formerly played a piano in a cabaret." Kirby certainly knew more weird gossip—perhaps he was a Broadwayite at heart.

"I suppose she just couldn't stay away from the bright lights." Ho! H'm! A honeymoon in a lighthouse—that must have been exciting. Honeymoon in a tall, cylindrical, phallic lighthouse. Beacons and babies. Let there be light. And there was light.... Too damned much light. Gordon could see the lighthouse plainly now, rising from a runty hill. In the thin twilight mist the shore looked like an old man lying on his back and smoking the lighthouse for a cigar, the flare of the beacon becoming the glowing coal of a cigar.

After the boat was made fast in Laurel Basin, Kirby helped Gordon with his things, shouldering a large supply box while Gordon carried the rucksack and a portable typewriter. They walked half a mile to Gordon's cottage and as the thunder of the surf grew in volume, he felt as though he were beginning to live all over again. The solace that one found in the sea was incomprehensible; it was so vast, so enfolding and it beckoned to one with white-plumed tides and caressed one without reserve.

Sometimes it embraced you madly like a mistress and then stroked your flanks with soft, moist palms.

"I'll take the shutters down for you," Kirby said. "I think I told you about the Larkspurs getting a divorce, or did I mention it?"

"Yes, you told me all about it."

"Could I get you a drink of gin?"

"I'm on the wagon. So long, Kirby."

After he had got rid of his things he buttoned his windbreaker closely about his throat and chest and took a barrow to the end of the walk. Then he went from a platform that faced the sea, descending several wooden steps, and began to gather driftwood while the March wind beat against him, rousing something in his soul. An outbound freighter lay low in the water to the southeast and the tide was ripping in. Where was the freighter going? Where was Gordon going? He returned to his cottage and made a fire and cooked beans and brewed a pot of tea.

As the fire died down Gordon slept and dreamed he was a boy again. Racy kissed him on the lips and he was happy.

II

GORDON left Laurel Island for a few days in May to attend the celebration of his daughter's eighth birthday. He had improved vastly in health and told Margery he was taking the first part of his novel to a publisher in New York.

After a day of wandering about the city, he was eager to go back to the solitude of Laurel Island and he now

could understand why old men sat in cellars or lived in
mountain wildernesses. He put his manuscript in the hands
of a literary agent and decided to visit New York as
little as possible. The City had been kind to him, but its
embrace was too heavy. He felt that the only way to meet
the blare of the metropolis was to plunge into it heedlessly,
recklessly, squandering health and character, and he didn't
elect to play that game to the end. Perhaps they who surged
along Broadway were chasing happiness, but all he wanted
now was peace and clarification of soul.

He was having a glass of milk and a sandwich at his
club when old Austin Moore came in and Gordon missed
two trains for Queens Manor to talk with his friend. Moore
complained that the movies were making his old age
miserable.

"They are an abomination," he said. "Art is being
dragged to the devil. And the modern writers! Son, it will
be a long time before Hollywood is Stratford-on-Avon."

"I must be getting old myself, Austin. I'm growing
blind to progress."

"Progress hell! They don't want real writers or real
actors any more. Anyone that can wiggle his ears harder
than another gets a big contract for the movies. Now it's
the talkies and if you have a lisp or a stutter, you're an
artist.... Of course you know that Nada has gone to
Hollywood?"

Gordon coughed nervously. "I haven't seen any newspapers since I went to Laurel Island, Austin. What about
her?"

"She had a quarrel with Jedlicka and he sold his theater to the motion picture people."

"And she's...."

"Gone into the talkies. I tried to dissuade her, but she said she was through with the stage forever. Gordon, I think you have broken her heart."

"My God, Austin! Please...."

"I understand, Gordon. I'm sorry. I'm just a garrulous old man."

Gordon went home. Only a few days ago he had walked beside the sea and had thought that the swish of the waves sounded like the lash of Nada's skirts. She was going into the talkies! Talkie. Speakie. Squealie. Squawkie. Voices that come from overcoat pockets; from the shoes of the man who sits next you in the Broadway Palace-of-Courtesy. Nada has gone. Day has gone. Youth has gone. No more morning cigarettes in bed at Nada's and coffee in a cup as small as a watch fob. But watch fobs are out of style, Gordon. Yes, and so is Gordon.

Chapter Two

I

*I*T was raining when Margery and Gordon reached Laurel Island late in May and the wind was from the south. Gordon wanted to leave her at the basin while he went for oilskins, but she laughed and said she liked the rain. She was healthy and strong and he liked to see her cheeks catch the rain. On the way to their cottage, and while they discussed the coming of the children with Mrs. Hamilton in June, they passed Kirby. He was dressed in a rubber coat and hip boots and was carrying a creel and some tackle.

"To-morrow'll be a great day for flounders," Kirby said. "The Larkspur divorce is expected to be granted by the end of the summer."

Margery cooked supper and Gordon built a fire to take the dampness out of the house. There was a heavy ground mist and it grew quite dark outside as Margery and Gordon sat beside the fireplace and played cards.

"I wish you wouldn't let Kirby do any work on the house this season, Margery."

"Why, dear?"

"He's such a damned gossip and his wife's worse. One of the things I want to get away from most is gossip."

For a moment there was a pained expression on Margery's brow. "I hope the babies will be all right."

"They'll be all right."

"It's the first time I ever left them and I feel lost."

"They're lucky to have such a fine mother."

"And father, too."

"I can't say much for their father."

"Well, I can." She shuffled the cards. "Do you realize this is the first time in nearly fourteen years that we have been absolutely alone with each other?"

"I hadn't thought of it that way."

"I'm glad to be alone with you, Gordie. I often wonder if we wouldn't have..." she checked herself.

"If we wouldn't have what?"

"Oh, nothing.... Let's tell fortunes with the cards."

"Never mind the fortunes but tell me what you were going to."

"I was going to say we never had any real privacy and I wonder if a couple can find true happiness without it?"

"We've done pretty well."

"I'm not complaining, but I'm selfish enough to want all the happiness possible."

"You're not selfish. I think you're a wonderful girl."

"I'm just a woman, I guess."

"But a hell of a fine woman. I'm going to try to make

up to you all that I've denied you.... If only I could become reconciled to life itself!"

"I've tried to be patient. I've tried to think that some day you'd come back to me."

What did she mean exactly by the words "come back to me"? He got up to throw fresh wood on the fire and then stood beside her chair and put his hand on her shoulder. "I guess I've been pretty wild and bad."

"Not bad. Just wild. You see you never really grew up, but I loved you enough to stand almost anything." She was crying softly. "I'd love you even though you loved some one else. Because ... because...."

"Because what, Margery?"

"Because I care so much. Sometimes I think that I care for you in the same way I do for the babies. You see I was taught to be indifferent to physical love, and I know now that I couldn't come to you as a wife should. I tried to make up in other ways, but now that I think I know a few things, it is too late."

"Don't say it is too late. You're a grand girl and it's all going to be different."

"You won't leave me, will you?"

"Nonsense. What makes you say that?"

"Nothing, only you heard what Kirby said about the Larkspurs, and it makes me feel sad whenever I hear of such things."

"Larkspur didn't have such a fine wife as I've got and they didn't have any children."

"No. All they had was money."

Gordon was uneasy about the words "come back to me," but he didn't dare probe deeply. Instead he attempted to joke. He laughed. "Yes, Larkspur made his money by inventing a lock for pay toilets. That's a great background for his social ambitions! I always had a yen to write a news story about a safe-cracker breaking into a pay toilet. Imagine a lead such as: 'President Adolph Larkspur yesterday led a posse in person in an attempt to capture the daring Pay Toilet Bandit. A cordon of police was thrown about the wash-room of the Hyde Hotel, but all that the clever rogue left as a clue was a pants button. Detectives said it looked like an inside job.'"

It was getting late and the south wind had blown away the mist. There was a moon and Margery and Gordon put on their sweaters and walked to the sea. He thought Margery's profile alluring in the moonlight and wondered if he hadn't been overlooking the beauty of her character, beauty that showed through her eyes.

"Do you remember that time in the cafeteria when you asked me if I liked babies?" she asked.

He smiled. "Yes, and then you asked me if I liked horses."

"Then you do remember! What did I say?"

"You said that when you were married you would have at least three babies."

"Well, we have only two."

"You're not hinting, are you?"

"Perhaps."

"You mean you would go through it again?"

"I'd love to ... for you."

When they returned to the cottage, Gordon asked her if he should build up the fire. "No," she said. "It's going to be warm enough."

He placed a fire screen in front of the embers. He was thinking things over. Then he took Margery in his arms. "How'd you like to sleep downstairs to-night on the couch?"

"You mean together?"

"Yes."

"I'd love to, if you want me to."

"You're a grand person, Margery. I guess I've been a lot of trouble to you."

"It was worth it."

II

MRS. HAMILTON and the two children came to Laurel Island the latter part of June. Margery was happy to see her children but she half regretted that the weeks of pleasant association with Gordon were done. It had been such a peaceful interlude. He had worked mornings on his novel and had spent the afternoons in the water. The sea was not yet warm and the surf held a stinging, lashing whip that stirred winter's lethargy from the blood. Margery and Gordon spent their evenings beside the fire and then they slept together on the couch ... but now they would have to move upstairs to separate beds, for Mrs. Hamilton would be there.... Well, Privacy, if you really must be going.

...Come again some time when you can stay longer.

Gordon carried Greta on his back from the basin and Norman, who was going on fourteen, walked beside his father. The boy seemed crestfallen and Gordon wondered what had gone wrong. He questioned Norman but got nowhere with his inquiries and thought his son was making ready for manhood and was likely to be morose. Still, the child's mood worried the father. The boy was growing tall and athletic. He was healthy and intelligent and he shouldn't be melancholy. Gordon stayed awake for a long time that night and then it dawned on him. Mrs. Hamilton had said or done something to fill the boy's mind with terror. What could it have been? What else could it have been but something to do with sex?

In the morning Gordon told Mrs. Hamilton he wanted to speak to her—alone. They went to the sea and walked beside the ebbing tide and then Gordon accused her bluntly of frightening Norman about sex matters.

"I believe I was justified under the conditions."

"You needn't have scared him to death. He wasn't guilty of any crime."

"I call it a crime! When any boy takes a girl's clothes off and parades naked with her, it's a crime. He did a lewd thing and I told him where it would lead him."

"He was terribly hurt."

Evidently Mrs. Hamilton misunderstood. "He didn't hurt himself at all. He was just bluffing."

My God! She had driven his boy to that, had she? To attempt suicide! He wished he could take a brick and dash out the brains of every sex-starved lunatic in the world. He wished he could bash in their skulls.

"You've done a desperate thing, Mrs. Hamilton."

She broke loose from the restraint Margery had placed upon her for the last months. "That's all the thanks I get for working my fingernails off caring for your children! Cleaning them and waiting on them. Washing clouts for them, watching over them and guarding their morals."

"It might have cost my boy his life. I can't forgive that."

"You can't forgive! You who have been a drunkard, a spendthrift ... and even worse. You can't forgive! Why, your goings-on are common talk everywhere. It would kill my girl if she knew what people say about you. Better she had been in her grave...."

"Shut your mouth before I shut it for you!" He had lost the peace he had thought was his. For a few brief weeks he and Margery had achieved something. They had gained respite, but now it seemed the erratic pilgrimage was to be taken up again. The interlude they had had was all a lie and a jest. He listened to the moaning of the sea and it seemed to be calling him away ... away from his errors and away from a stupid and hypercritical world that magnified the errors into unforgivable sins. That world grew articulate in the throat of this old woman.... "Don't you ever speak to me again!"

"Only for my girl do I keep my peace. It would kill her completely...."

"If you speak to me again I'll choke you."

Gordon walked hurriedly to the cottage and looked for Norman at the sand fort that the boy and his playmates had built last summer. But the shack was empty and the logs that had been placed on ramparts of sand to simulate cannon were unmanned. There was no brave flag at the homely staff and the wind had riffled the sand, covering over small footprints where desperate battles had been waged....O God! O God! Suppose he had died and suppose I had come on this reminder of his play!

He found Norman in an upstairs room. The boy was sitting on a bed, his head down and his boot kicking the edge of a reed rug. Gordon placed his arms about his son and kissed him.

"Well, fellow, it's great to have you here. Let's take our baseball things down to the beach and have a catch."

They had a long talk that afternoon with baseball and skin swims in between and Gordon complimented the boy on his speed with the baseball. "You sink them in fast, son, but you have to learn control first. Without it a pitcher might as well leave his arm in the clubhouse....It's the same with Life, Norman. Life is a baseball that God puts in your hand. Most of us try to be speedy with it right off. We want to throw the baseball with all our mights, but the fellow that comes through is the one who first learns to control the baseball that is called Life."

"Did you learn control first?"

"No, I didn't. I hadn't anyone to tell me what to do and I threw the baseball hard. It made me unhappy."

"I've been unhappy, too."

Gordon slapped his son's back affectionately. "Well, fellow, would you be any happier if I told you that anything you have done up to now is O.K. with me? That you are not going to hell for a mistake? That I did exactly the same things that you have done when I was a boy?— Don't you worry about it, son."

Norman looked at his father thoughtfully. "Then you know what I did, don't you?"

Gordon laughed. "Sure I do and I understand it, too. Say, don't let anyone ever frighten you into believing you are going to be struck dead for wondering about girls. The only thing is you've got to be patient. Whenever you are tempted to do something that is annoying to the rest of society, remember the control idea. When you're in doubt, come to me and we'll talk it over, man to man. Is it a bargain?"

"It sure is, Dad. You're the swellest guy in the whole world. You know just how a fellow feels."

"That's because I'm a fellow. And I'm going to make you a present of that bugle of mine. Whenever you get dumpy and blue, take it out and blow a good, whacking snort on it and you'll feel better."

"Gee, that's swell to have your bugle! Thanks."

Chapter Three

I

GORDON worked in a room above the living room, staying there as much as possible to avoid Mrs. Hamilton. After finishing his day's task, he would go far down the beach to swim and then lie in the sun, closing his eyes and looking inward. He saw strange images as he peered into his soul's looking-glass. I am a stallion, spurred by whims, goaded by passions, ridden by fancies, foundered by regrets. He tried to formulate a philosophy, but the nearest he could come to one was "What-of-It?"

Toward the latter part of August, many cottagers had departed from the Island and Gordon regretted that he, too, was going to leave soon after Labor Day. The children had to be returned to school. Neighbors were hustling about, boarding up their houses and herding together their brown-bodied children. The boys and girls had to go back to their educational galley seats. Education is such a help to girls who don't choose to push baby carriages. It is such a boon to boys who are compelled to grow up to be commercial throat-slitters.

A few days before the time of their departure, Norman was very sad. "I've lost our trumpet," he told his father. "It's the worst thing that ever happened to me."

"We'll look for it, son. Where did you have it last?"

"I laid it down by the Larkspur house, meaning to pick it up when I came out of the water. It was careless of me to do that."

"We'll probably find it."

"I hope so, Dad, for I know you liked it a lot."

"I liked what it meant to me, son. It was a symbol."

They searched all day but failed to find it and Gordon felt as though he had been shorn of a mighty talisman. He was careful not to let his son note his concern. Gramper had given that trumpet to him. He had hugged it tightly in his mountain cabin as Racy lay in her last illness. He had blown it innumerable times to frighten away doubts that besieged his soul. The notes he had sounded on his scarred old bugle had more than compensated for the callous reception of his work the night his play had failed. He always shuddered when he heard the words: "The trumpet shall sound no more."

Mr. Larkspur, the pay toilet magnate, came to the beach the day Norman lost the trumpet. He had been in Europe, buying Van Dycks and making sure that his wife would get that divorce. Mr. Larkspur arrived with his yacht and a large party, all of which was duly reported by the gossiping Kirby. Mrs. Hamilton, who kept in constant touch with Mrs. Kirby, reported to Margery that the Larkspur party included several show girls and that there would be a drunken celebration of the Paris decree. The Larkspur party had cocktails and a beefsteak fry on the beach and as the evening advanced the merriment grew.

"I think I heard somebody blowing a bugle at the Larkspurs'," Norman said at the dinner table. "I didn't want to appear fresh and butt into their house to find out about it."

"We'll go there after dinner, son."

The Larkspur bungalow faced the sea from a high dune. Gordon and Norman went to it and knocked. Mr. Larkspur's physical trainer, an ex-pugilist, opened the door.

"Did anyone here find a trumpet? A bugle? It belongs to my son."

"What in hell would we do with a bugle?"

"I don't know. I merely asked if you had found one."

"We ain't found none. Is there goin' to be another war?"

"Sorry I troubled you."

"No trouble. Want a drink?"

"No."

"Want a blonde?"

"Come on, Norman." He told his son to go home to bed. "I'm going for a walk beside the sea." Gordon went down the steps to the beach and stood for a long time, wondering if peace and understanding ever would come to him in this life. Then he gave up thinking and went home. The blinds had been drawn at his windows, but he could see a shadow that he believed to be that of Mrs. Hamilton against the front blind. To avoid meeting her, he started around the back walk, and as he was passing the side window, which was half open, he heard Mrs. Hamilton talking excitedly to Margery. She was very angry about something. He didn't want to eavesdrop, and he would have hastened past the window, but he heard his name mentioned. He stood there, making up his mind whether to go in and tell her in front of Margery just what he thought of her; what he always had thought of her.

II

MARGERY had not told Gordon that she was pregnant again, but he had sensed it and only last Sunday when they were swimming he had noticed that she was rather full about the waist. Now, as he stood on the walk, listening to Mrs. Hamilton's tirade, he knew that his mother-in-law had found out about it.

"I tell you," Gordon overheard, "you're a fool to get that way again. I've held my peace, ever since the night of the opening of his no-good play, the night when you heard those people say that he was a wild one and a bad one."

"I won't stand for you saying things!"

"Yes, you will, because it's the last time I'll be here to say them. You yourself heard them tell how he was running around with that actress."

"Mother!"

"Well, didn't you hear it?"

"Yes, but . . ."

Gordon was frozen to the walk. He could not have

moved away if he had tried. He would not interfere now. No. He had been trying to come to some conclusion about this thing, planning to tell Margery everything and then at the last moment backing down.

"Well, my blind daughter, I've heard the whole story from Mrs. Kirby. And now everybody on the beach will know it. They'll know that he's been lying around with bad women for years."

"Stop! You shan't say another word.... Now you listen to me. If he did do the things you say, the things those people said at the theater, then it's your fault."

"Are you insane?"

"No, mother, I've suddenly become sane. It was you and your damnable, cold and selfish teaching that a woman must fight off a man, that she must never let herself be loved as God intended that she should be loved, that made me unfit to be a wife."

"Margery!"

"Yes, and that's how many a woman loses her husband, but by God I've fought for mine and I'll continue to fight for him. He did wrong, perhaps, but he did it because he needed something I couldn't give him."

"You're crazy! I taught you to respect yourself, and what that man wants is a common, filthy whore. I'm leaving your house for good."

"Then for God's sake leave! It's the only thing that can save us."

"You'll regret this day, mark my word!"

Gordon couldn't go in now. He went for a walk and

didn't return until late. He found Margery in the living room, seated at her desk.

"I'm getting our bills straightened out," she said. "You were gone a long time."

"Where's Mrs. Hamilton?" He would say some things to her now, no matter what the consequences.

"She's spending the night at Mrs. Kirby's."

Gordon went upstairs and Margery stayed at her desk.

III

He undressed but tossed restlessly in his bed, waiting for Margery to come upstairs, but she still sat at her desk. He felt he must reach a decision soon...to-night. How could it be done? Would he feel better or worse after he had recited the facts to his wife? Facts which she probably knew more fully than she had indicated in the scene with her mother. He couldn't feel worse than he did. He let his mind grope hazily, as though waiting for an inspiration, just as a hungry man goes along the street with his eyes fixed on the walk half-expecting to find a coin there. He thought of discrepancies in the Four Gospels....Go into some dark cell, Gordon. A loaf of black bread on a rough wooden table. A crock of water. An ikon on a stone wall. ...I must fast, for now I am food with a voice. When I eat, the food becomes me. I become food. An automaton of cooked wheat, cheeses, sauces, roasts and lettuces....Mrs. Hamilton is pure. She sings hymns to sacrosanct pelvic regions. She chants the womanly recessional: "Lest We

Beget." ... Jesus is the Light of the World, the Redeemer. Without sin how can he redeem? The pure ones, to meet this issue, declaim that man was conceived in sin. Behold, I was shapen in iniquity; and in sin did my mother conceive me—David said so.... We are the clay, and Thou our Potter; and we all are the work of Thy Hand—Isaiah said so.... If we are made thus and so, how can we unmake? ...

He rose and put on an old tan bathing robe. He'd go down to the sea, his sea, for a while, and perhaps in the moonless night he could review his life, reason things out and then come back.

He had been amazed at Margery's words to her mother. He had felt shame-faced and broken. The goodness, the breadth, the courage of this wife was unbelievable. What a dog he had been! He couldn't quite believe that she had forgiven him. What she had done was to explain him to herself in the best way she was capable. She was benevolent, that was it. Her benevolence showed through her every act, her every gesture. It had been benevolence that had led her to give herself that night in the grape arbor—certainly it had not been passion, and it never had been passion with her. What had he given in return? Only a roof and a bit of bread. He had provided nothing spiritually. Perhaps his failure to give something of himself to the woman who had every right to expect that gift accounted for their unhappiness and his guilty unrest.... He believed now that it wasn't so much his sins that terrified him as the fact he had been found out. Found out! Hazel Eades and Paul

Benson had been found out. That was the gravest sin in this civilization.

Even if she accorded him full forgiveness, it would leave a raw memory, for she had known what he had done and she always would know it. All the time she had known. He felt certain that she had known. Well, he had done everything to proclaim his love affair except posting bills about it in Times Square. He might have realized that he couldn't get away with it forever.

Gordon kissed his son and his daughter as they slept. They would be the real sufferers in this domestic mess. He should have thought of that before. The party at the Lark-spur bungalow was getting noisier than ever and the singing and laughter came harshly through the south window of Gordon's room. He bumped into his typewriter table in the darkness, cursed some and then went downstairs, slowly and almost numbly. Margery was sitting with her back to him. She was going over the accounts of trades-people.

"I'm going to take a skin swim, Margery."

She didn't turn about. "Be careful. It's a dark night and the sea has been rough all day."

He wanted to kiss her and he stood for a long time, hesitating. Why didn't she turn to face him? How could she after what she knew? Not a word more did she have for him. She had told him to be careful. Did she really care if waves bore him away? He half hoped she would say something about the scene with her mother. Not a word from her. Should he delve into the reason for Mrs. Hamilton going away for the night? Was she coming back? Still not a word from either of them. Perhaps, after all, it was just as well that Mrs. Hamilton had blurted out the accusations. I couldn't have gone on this way much longer. What does Nada think of my long silence? Shall we ever meet again? You dog! So you think of Nada even when you are crying out within yourself that you want to save your home!...Margery's turned back seems symbolic. She knows. I know. The knowledge we both have is a terrible bar between us. She has said that there is a great door and that I must open that door before she can see inside me. The door now seems locked beyond the power of anyone to open it. The key has been lost.

He had to go into the open air, for all the mistakes of his life seemed to be trooping through the secret passageways of his soul. They were mobilizing for a public display and they would be secrets only a little while longer. Retribution. Be sure your sin will find you out—that's what Granner used to say in the feather bed.

Gordon opened the front door and went into the night. Except for the revelry at the Larkspur place, all was quiet and black.

Chapter Four

*W*HEN the blanket of midnight covers the sea, there is a shuddering. How cold and reaching is the sea! Mother-Wife sea, shuddering sea that clasps the naked body of man, drawing him into her with incestuous lust. The blanket of midnight covers both sea and man. The south wind murmurs its canticles across the dunes where the coarse beach grasses give thatch to the cricket. One blazing scar of lightning, like the trial thrust of an archangel's sword; and distant thunder, rising from the belly of eternity. Then all is dark again. All is quiet. All is rhythm.

Gordon left his beach house at midnight. There were no stars, no moon, no understanding. Gordon's tan bathing robe hung from his shoulders like a panther skin on a priest of Osiris. The lamp light against the window blind of Gordon's house seemed as hard, as unyielding as bronze. Margery sat the other side of that shield of hard light. She was writing checks ... to the hardware man, who had sold them copper screens at the beginning of the season; to the butcher, to the baker. Margery had said they must not leave the beach for their winter home with a trail of unpaid bills behind them, following them, mocking them. The darkness seeped into Gordon's soul, entering through cracks of his character. He became dark inside, only he was blacker inside than anything that is called black.

There was a sloping concrete walk beneath Gordon's bare feet as he began his journey. The narrow, cold road connected bay and sea. He would have to walk a hundred yards. For many years he had been crawling on bruised knees, but in a few minutes he would be at the sea, the great baptismal font. There his soul must find a verdict. Acquittal or condemnation. His mind must find release.

When I came here in early Spring, he said within himself, I was drawn and tired and sad. I said I would seek sanctuary here. The blistering lights of the City blinded me...the sea would bring me peace. The sea! My wife, my mother, sea....Go into her.

Past the night-swallowed houses Gordon stalked, as lonely as a hearse with no mourners following. His feet were peppered by sand that eddied across the concrete walk and the wind rumpled his hair. Where had the moon gone? Was the moon as pure as poets sang? Or, did the moon steal away on dark nights to cohabit with Mars?

The voice of the sea grew louder, more challengingly confident. The revel at the Larkspur house was wildly noisy. A welter of recollections surged through his brain. His boyhood, the dreary Sundays and the play repressions. Racy who did not dare kiss him openly. Cousins' store and the wine bottling. The harlots, Trixie naked. High school, Elizabeth Wells and the day he began carnal activities in the upstairs hall of her home. Nada and the school play

and the party after the track meet. College, Portia Mann
and the futile pilgrimage to the hillside and the chaste return to his fraternity house. Why had Racy been taken
away so soon? The basement of the bells and another
memory of Nada, the time he went to her dressing room,
mad with his boyish love of her. Nada had been.... What,
indeed, had she been? She had been everything. What had
Margery been? She, too, had been everything. How could
one reconcile man's mad urges with God's immutable laws?
He must find an answer. To-night. Now. Either that or
madness. For years he had looked for love, as he defined
love. Now he would risk everything that was left for peace.
He must find salvation or die. He must sweep his soul
clean.

Gordon passed a small, dumpy cottage. Pallid Mrs.
Huntington had lived there until the last week with her
daughter, who had a club foot. Mrs. Huntington's husband
had been dead for eight years, but she wouldn't marry
again. She kept getting more and more dried up, starving
emotionally. How did women manage to do that? How
could they resist desire? Were they so different from men?
Women could stay pure, fulfilling their obligations—no
matter what they were—without a murmur. Even in love-
less marriages they knew how to banish lust.... Mothers
should reveal this great secret to their sons. When strongly
sexed men fought against desire, it made them sick, melancholy, fanatical. In every man's soul, Casanova sat with St.
Anthony. They took turns in directing the behavior of the
helpless body.

A pine tree bough brushed Gordon's cheek and he
knew he was passing the cottage of Mrs. Anselm, the retired teacher. He remembered that she had given him a
flower, an unusually large nasturtium, a few weeks ago. She
had told him how kind he was; what a beautiful character
he was, so quiet-mannered and understanding of elderly
women. She knew he would write beautiful books and was
eager to read the one he was finishing. God help her if she
did! And now he was passing the Kirby home. Mrs. Hamilton was spending the night there. Was she dreaming of
monsters that sought to seize her senile body to wrench her
thighs apart?

Frogs were singing to Gordon. Nada, where are you
now? Frogs and locusts and crickets sang in the beach
grass. Nada, is Love kneeling beside Youth's deathbed?
Was it a magnificat or a dirge? Gordon was all but beaten
under by the anthem as he shuffled toward the platform
from which steps led to the sea. Now he paused beside the
brightly lighted house of Mr. Larkspur, the genius of the
pay toilet.

Gordon, flexing his legs in descent, knew he never
should have tried to write books or plays. To be happy, he
thought, one never should dabble in books or plays, for it
was not a time for creation. Materialism, as interpreted by
and in the machine, was the creed for the era. The Four
Gospels: Money, Mills, Motors and Morons—soon a new
Jesus would appear, a steam shovel in one hand and a
bank in the other. The old Jesus was worn out. He
preached love and charity to all. Yes, soft toned ministers

still spoke of Him. The spires of many churches rose half way up the flanks of the City's structures; but if those spires were trained toward Heaven, each and every one of them should have on it a sign: "Pardon me for pointing."

Creative art was not the thing, Gordon said, as he left the patch of light made by the Larkspur door lamps. One should invent pay toilet accessories. Mr. Larkspur had an airplane, three imported motor cars, a yacht, many servants and a new blonde every six months. To-night he had a divorce. Hooray! They were singing praises to the Goddess Adultery as bottles were being emptied. Libations to the Goddess. And why not? Mr. Larkspur was rich. Why shouldn't he go to bed with lovely ladies from revues and smart shops?

Poor Gordon! A writer of books and of a play that had failed. Gordon had had blondes, true; and brunettes and others of moot complexion, but he never had them on a six-months' basis. He was not as honorable as Mr. Larkspur. He did not give a fur coat to a winter blonde or a limousine and chauffeur to a pale summer mate. Roses grew from manure. The lotus had its feet in the mud. Fur coats, limousines and square cut emeralds came from the pay toilet. Gordon had given only his body, and in having given that he had lost his immortal soul.

Gordon strode through the cold sand.... Look out, Gordon, for broken glass and rusty nails in the driftwood! He heard the full crescendo of the sea. His sea. Beside it he had sat and had wondered about sin and redemption. Amid the desolate booming of his sea, he again heard the lash of the rip tide, that sounded so much like Nada's silks. Then the falling of the high waves. It was a majestic tambourine, quivering. Bells in a frame of midnight ebony, pulsating against the gut of cosmos. What hand shakes the tambourine, Gordon?

Gordon says that Yesterday is a widow with weeds of satin, weeds of linen, weeds of sackcloth and of brown burlap. Gordon says To-day is a harlot, her lips passionately parted—lips that draw in kisses and breathe out annihilation. Gordon says To-morrow is a virgin, never known and never clasped—a virgin sleeping on the hidden hemisphere of the moon.... Where is that fugitive, infidel moon tonight? If Mars were to see To-morrow, the Virgin, he would violate her with heavy blows and whiskered, comet-tail kisses. If only the moon again could be lifted like a monstrance before his eyes!

He now let his feet and ankles meet the slavering puddles that washed toward him beneath the major beats of the waves. Wet feet and dry mouth. Lapping tongue of shallow wetness and behind it the swirling tide.

The sea is gaping wide for you, Gordon. There she lies, the great Mother-Wife, tossing frenziedly beneath the limitless black blanket of midnight. You cannot see her? But can you not hear? You must go into her, Gordon, all naked and brown.

Gordon stood as though beside a mighty nuptial couch and thought of his father, kneeling before a rock virgin. Where was his father? A sojourner somewhere, lost and wandering. What was the use of it all? What was the answer? Austin Moore had said that the answer lay within self and not outside self. Come, Self, be my oracle and give me your answer.

Again and again he lived his life in retrospect. Granner in the rabbit hutches. Margery in the grape arbor. Little Wine-Head in the stretcher. Nada in an ancient bed. Hazel Eades in the electric chair.... Far down the beach he saw the bright eye of a wood fire, where sparks rose and flurried like shooting stars. Did the sparks know the ways of the wind? Did they find peace and calm after the soul of the flame was dead? To his right, he saw the sweeping finger of Shoal Lighthouse, the finger writing widely on the inscrutable page of midnight. It moved boldly and mercilessly: "You are not the marrying kind. You are not fit for love."

Why had Margery kept her back turned to him? God! It was too late. Margery was lost to him, too. He suddenly knew that it was the greatest of all his losses since Racy had gone away. He tried to suppress sobs that juggled with his breath. Then he sobbed aloud. Only the loudly calling sea could hear. It was as though some fever had reached a crisis.

Gordon stood there, the water now up to his hocks, the shocking water making his loins writhe. For one instant there came to him a desire to swim far out and never come back. That would be a way of escape. Just lie in the trough of the sea. Then the mysterious awakening.... Where?

Roll in, sea tide! Roll, pitch, toss and reach. Little, mortal women have rolled and tossed, burning for Gordon.

Why should you not fret, greater and more capable courtesan, threshing about in the night with your wet, salty thighs? He's thinking of coming into you. If he comes, he'll forever be true. What? He is too proud! He says he is the grandson of a man named William Dole, who beat fearlessly at rock doors. He says he is the nephew of a man named Hiram, who sewed up wounds in his own belly. He says he is the father of two children and of one not yet born. He says to hell with cowardice....

Gordon heard above the roar of the tide a trumpet blast.

T H E   E N D